A Murder For Brother Hermitage

A Murder For Brother Hermitage

Interminable

Chronicles of Brother Hermitage

by

Howard of Warwick

From the Scriptorium of
The Funny Book Company

The Funny Book Company

Published by The Funny Book Company
Crown House 27 Old Gloucester Street
London WC1N 3AX
www.funnybookcompany.com

Cover design by Double Dagger.

ISBN: 978-1-913383-27-5

Also by Howard of Warwick.

The First Chronicles of Brother Hermitage
The Heretics of De'Ath
The Garderobe of Death
The Tapestry of Death

Continuing Chronicles of Brother Hermitage
Hermitage, Wat and Some Murder or Other
Hermitage, Wat and Some Druids
Hermitage, Wat and Some Nuns

Yet More Chronicles of Brother Hermitage
The Case of the Clerical Cadaver
The Case of the Curious Corpse
The Case of the Cantankerous Carcass

Interminable Chronicles of Brother Hermitage
A Murder for Mistress Cwen
A Murder for Master Wat
A Murder for Brother Hermitage

The Umpteenth Chronicles of Brother Hermitage
The Bayeux Embroidery
The Chester Chasuble
The Hermes Parchment

The Superfluous Chronicles of Brother Hermitage
The 1066 from Normandy
The 1066 to Hastings
The 1066 via Derby

The Unnecessary Chronicles of Brother Hermitage
The King's Investigator
The King's Investigator Part II

The Meandering Chronicles of Brother Hermitage
A Mayhem of Murderous Monks
A Murder of Convenience
Murder Most Murderous

Brother Hermitage Diversions
Brother Hermitage in Shorts (Free!)
Brother Hermitage's Christmas Gift

Audio
Hermitage and the Hostelry

Howard of Warwick's Middle Ages crisis: History-ish.
The Domesday Book (No, Not That One.)
The Domesday Book (Still Not That One.)
The Magna Carta (Or Is It?)

Explore the whole sorry business and join the mailing list at www.*Howardofwarwick.com*

Another funny book from The Funny Book Company
Greedy by Ainsworth Pennington

A Murder For Brother Hermitage

Caput I: Death Of A Monk

The monastery cloister collected darkness as if hoarding it for a time when it was going to come in useful. The middle of this heavily clouded night had plenty of darkness to go round and so the cloister piled it up in corners where it got quite deep.

There was a full moon up there somewhere, but it clearly wanted nothing to do with the goings-on in this cloister, on this night.

In one pool, of the particularly deep and dark variety, a monk quivered. This monk generally liked cloisters and monasteries, even though they weren't the friendliest of places. A cloister at night could be marvellous, free, as it should be, from any other monks; or priors, abbots, priests, novices and anyone else who had business being there. He tended to get on well with the buildings, not so much with the people.

It was unfair to tarnish everyone, and he was always scrupulous in his fairness. He had to admit that the abbot had welcomed him. Abbot Abbo had invited him to visit, for goodness sake. It would be a bit much for the abbot to encourage a visit and then be all difficult about it.

But Abbo had other duties, he couldn't spend all his time with his visitor; or any of his time, it seemed. The invitation in the first place, and the subsequent distance the man kept, led the monk to the conclusion that it was unlikely to be the abbot who was stalking him around the cloister in the middle of the night.

He tried to tell himself that the suggestion of stalking was completely unjustified. It was pure coincidence that someone else had entered the cloister at this late hour. Someone who hadn't announced themselves, or come over to say good evening, and who seemed to be making great efforts not to be spotted.

If it was the case that some other Brother wanted to make use of the place, he only had to say so. The monk in the dark would go happily back to his cell and leave the new arrival to get up to whatever he wanted in the dark of the cloister. There might even be several of them. The monk had suspicions about what some brothers got up to in the dark of cloisters. Well, he knew it was suspicious, as it generally involved a lot of noise and a refusal to discuss the matter. What it actually was, he had not a clue. He didn't want to ask, and further suspected that he didn't want to know.

Whoever the new arrival was, he was subtle and discreet. The monk had been whiling away these quiet hours considering how many bones the prophet Ezekiel had actually seen in Chapter thirty-seven, verses one to four. Obviously, the valley in question was full of bones, and they were dry bones at that. But how big was the valley? It was the sort of topic that might make a fascinating conclave. All he had to do was find some other brothers who were as interested in resolving the question. He gave up that idea straight away.

It was then that he had noticed the first movement.

To begin with, he thought that it might be some animal of the night, scampering about the place, looking for something to eat. A simple mouse, scratching at a door or doing battle with a particularly large and obstreperous beetle. But then the noise came from another part of the cloister altogether. This would have to be a mouse with remarkably long legs; or one that had just been carried away by a giant, scuttling beetle. He told himself to calm down, as he started to worry about the beetle coming back for him.

A flicker of darkness against a background of greater darkness had convinced him that he was not the only person in the cloister this night. But that was no problem; he would simply sit still and quiet and let this new companion go about his business. As soon as the business developed into anything unnecessary, he would make his excuses. Except, of course, as soon as he had sat still for a moment he realised that he should have made himself known straight away. It was too late now to stand up and apologise for being there.

When no one else arrived to join the other presence, the monk thought that it was simply another contemplative brother who sought the peace of the cloister. He quickly concluded that this was nonsense. He'd only been here a few days but already knew that any contemplative and peaceful brothers would have been driven out of this place years ago. No, this was a monk up to something. And monks up to something were best avoided.

Doing his own version of subtle and discreet, the monk had left his seat and moved down the cloister, towards the exit and his cell. He knew he was being ridiculous, but he felt it was too awkward to make noise and pretend he hadn't noticed anyone. He felt, rather than saw the motion that cut off his escape and forced him to retreat to the pool of darkness in which he had begun his quivering.

The next rational thought was that this brother probably wanted nothing to do with him. The poor fellow doubtless thought he would have the cloister to himself and was now just as awkwardly trying to find a way out of the situation without being noticed. The silly pair could end up spending hours carefully navigating their way around one another. No, this situation simply needed him to speak up. He could pretend that he had been buried so deep in Ezekiel's bones that he hadn't noticed the other arrive.

Rational thought put carefully to one side, he cowered and did some more quivering. Soon, he became resigned to spending the entire night in his deep, dark pool while the other got on with whatever he wanted.

Ah, blessed relief, the new arrival cleared his throat. Well, that was fine then. The universal expression of embarrassed discomfort had been made and both men could now cough and bluster their way out of this place, and then spend the next day pretending that they'd never met, or ever been in a cloister at all.

But the cough was followed, and the monk wished that the deep of his dark pool would swallow him completely.

'I know you're there,' the coughing voice said with great confidence.

The monk would have stood and announced himself at this point if there hadn't been something off-putting about the voice. The words were spoken by one who had found just what he was looking for and could now get on with exactly what he'd been planning to do all along.

Whatever that plan was, it wasn't a good one; the monk was sure of that. At least the cough and the words had not been right in his ear, which would have scared the habit off the monk. It sounded as if they were away, across the cloister, but as he was crouched down with his head on his knees, it was hard to judge.

'It's no good hiding in the dark,' the voice went on.

Well, the monk would have to disagree with that proposition. Hiding in the dark seemed to be an excellent response to this situation. He had no experience of encounters with monks who were looking for you in dark cloisters but felt that one who said it was no good hiding in the dark, probably meant that it was no good for you.

'You're wanted,' the voice now explained.

Ah, that could be quite reasonable. Perhaps the abbot wanted to consult him on something at this late hour and had sent a messenger.

The urge to respond was overwhelming, but a nagging doubt controlled the urge and told it to wait a moment.

'Wanted? You're supposed to say. Wanted by whom?' The voice even changed its pitch as it took on both sides of the conversation. The monk in the dark was sure that his voice wasn't quite so high and feeble sounding.

'Wanted by whom? I say. Then you say, yes, wanted by whom? And I say, no one. You're wanted by no one, and that's why I'm here. Ha ha.'

This nonsense annoyed the monk more than anything. Being pursued by a brain-addled brother in the middle of the night really was too much. But then brain-addled monks were seldom dangerous; apart from the dangerous ones. He swallowed.

'Come on, come on,' the voice now urged. 'There are only so many corners in a cloister you know.'

The monk did know, there were four. He was hiding in one of them, so that left three. And the cloister was a simple square. If this strange brother-in-the-dark really did try to find him, they could just end up going round and round until dawn. Unless the follower could run faster than the monk, which was a strong possibility.

'Oh, enough of this,' the voice in the dark called out, impatiently. 'Where are you?'

The monk now heard quiet footsteps moving across the

flagstones. As best he could tell, they were some way away, probably on the other side of the cloister courtyard. It was hard to tell as the steps were careful and cautious and the walls of the place disturbed the passage of the sound.

There was one quality to the paces that did get the monk's attention and bothered his curiosity. This feature also gave him the courage to stand from his crouched position and take his own step, back towards the exit.

'Ah, there you are,' his follower called.

With his ears now elevated above the floor, the monk was gratified to confirm that the voice was on the opposite side of the cloister.

The monk took his own careful steps towards the way out. The steps on the far side followed, caution abandoned.

If the monk hadn't been willing to speak up at first, the steps following him demanded that he say something, natural human sympathy getting in the way of common sense. 'Are you all right?' he asked, gently.

'What do you mean by that?' the voice snapped.

'Oh, nothing, nothing,' the monk replied, embarrassed. 'It's just that, well, I mean, I noticed your, erm, steps were, ah. Never mind. It's nothing.'

'You mean my limp?' The voice was all demanding anger now. 'Have you got something to say about my limp?'

'Oh, no, no. Nothing at all. Not a thing. Just that I noticed, that's all.' The monk used these moments to take quick steps forward, hoping to find the way out quite quickly.

'I've got a limp, all right.' The voice was clearly quite used to addressing this topic. 'Do you know how I got this limp?'

Well, of course the monk didn't know how the man had got his limp. He didn't even know who the fellow was, and until he'd heard the paces had no idea that his gait was uneven. As he gave it some thought, he couldn't even recall any other brother in the monastery who had a limp. From the tone of the question, he knew that he was going to be told how the fellow got his limp, whether he wanted to know or not.

'The Battle of Hastings,' the voice said, with some pride.

'Battle of Hastings?' the monk couldn't help asking.

'When we fought off the Norman invaders.' It sounded as if the pursuer had stopped for a moment of happy reminiscence.

'Is that what they're calling it? I thought it wasn't actually at Hastings.' The monk didn't like to mention that fighting off the Normans had been spectacularly unsuccessful, in that the Normans were not, in fact, off.

The voice was heavy and insistent. 'The Battle of Hastings,' it stated, for the record.

'Ah.' The monk didn't want to engage in a debate on the nomenclature of battles; it really wasn't his area. What he really wanted was to leave, but it was so dark he was having trouble working out where he was. Being pursued in the dark by a limping, brain-addled monk didn't help his concentration.

'Took a wound defending the country, I did. Defending it from the scourge of the Normans.'

'Very good.' The monk tried to sound supportive and impressed at the same time.

'Except they tricked us,' the voice complained.

'Did they?' The monk turned his head and called over his shoulder, hoping to sound as if he wasn't moving as quickly as he could.

'We won,' the voice declared.

There was no way the monk was going to stop to

contradict this blatant error. He'd let the man discuss the matter with King William or one of the Norman overlords. He was sure they'd sort it out in no time at all.

'The king withdrew from the field of victory and then the Normans said that they'd won.'

The monk felt that some reply on this point was expected. 'Outrageous,' he said.

'And what with the king being wounded and all, there wasn't anyone to stop them.'

The monk didn't like to point out that this sounded very much like a Norman victory.

'And that's where I took my wound.'

In the pause that followed, the monk could sense that his hunter was standing nodding to himself as he recalled the happy moment of getting his leg sliced by some sword or arrow.

'I bet you haven't got a wound,' the voice accused. 'Well, have you?'

'Erm,' the monk sounded as if he was thinking about this for a moment, while in fact, he was desperately looking for the door that he knew was here somewhere. 'I don't think so.'

'No, I don't think so either. Bloody monks.'

'Are you not a monk then?' This statement worried the monk more than the fact that someone was chasing him around a dark cloister.

'Me, ha!' The voice seemed to find this idea quite funny. 'They wouldn't have me.'

Now, the monk knew he was in trouble. Anyone so depraved, dangerous or insane that even the lowliest monastery wouldn't have him should be avoided at all times; let alone in a dark cloister.

He knew that most monasteries were quite selective about

who they took. Moneyed younger sons of the nobility were best, but after that, it would need to be people prepared to work and follow their devotions. But there were lots of monasteries in the land. Moneyed sons of the nobility were in pretty short supply and the establishments lower down the order could get desperate and would take anyone capable of digging vegetables.

And then there were the truly Christian places that took the sick and the feeble.

Of course, this fellow had only said that the monasteries wouldn't have him. Perhaps he'd never asked. In which case, what was he doing in one at this time of night?

'Can't fight for the king anymore, monasteries won't have me; now I do favours for people if you know what I mean.'

The monk did know what doing a favour meant. He couldn't immediately reconcile this with the current situation.

'Someone's got a problem they need sorting out, they come to me. And pay me well.' The voice sounded quite proud of this, the contradiction of payment for favours seeming to have passed him by.

'Well done,' the monk replied, thinking that supporting this man in his efforts to improve his lot might be best in these circumstances.

'And you're the problem I'm sorting out today.'

'Me?' The monk was truly puzzled. He'd never been a problem to anyone, let alone strangers in cloisters at night.

'Made a lot of enemies, you have.'

The monk paused and gave this some serious thought. He couldn't immediately think of any.

'And they want you gone.'

'I shall go then,' the monk responded promptly, thinking

that he would be quite happy to leave.

'Not that sort of gone. Properly gone. For good, gone.'

'Good gone?' the monk was getting lost.

'Absolutely. Glad you understand.'

The monk didn't understand immediately but soon did. 'Good God. You mean…,'

'That's it,' the voice sounded content that they both understood the situation now.

'You can't be serious.'

'I can,' the voice sounded offended at the implication of levity.

The monk really couldn't believe what he was hearing. There had to be some argument to make this whole situation go away. 'But the limp?'

'What about the limp?' The voice was angry once more.

'Oh, er, nothing really. It's just that, well, I don't have a limp, and you do.'

'Meaning?'

'Meaning that you find moving about much more of a trial than I do. Due to your courageous action, of course.'

'Your point being?'

'Well, not wanting to offend, but I can move quicker than you, I suspect. And we are in a dark cloister, which just goes round in a square.'

The expression "round in a square" would have fascinated him for days in other circumstances. He had rather more practical matters to trouble him at present.

'So?'

'So, if I move around the square you will have to come after me, but I will always be ahead.' The monk couldn't believe that he was inviting this limping, brain-addled killer to chase him around the cloister. 'And with your unfortunate injury, it is unlikely that you'll catch me.'

'Ah, I see.' The voice was content that he understood the proposal.

'Well, that's good.'

'Yes, I see your error.'

'Error?' The monk couldn't see an error, but he felt that a significant one was about to be explained.

'Yes, error. You're forgetting about the crossbow.'

'Crossbow?' The monk managed to squeak and swallow at the same time. He was in no mood to point out that he could hardly forget something he'd never been told about in the first place.

'Of course. You're quite right, there's no point a fellow with a leg that barely works trying to chase people. That would be ridiculous. No, a man in my position would have to organise a pretty fundamental advantage over their opponent.'

The monk was now very worried that the conclusion about brain-addlement may have been presumptuous.

'And in my case, it's a crossbow. Very handy Norman invention, I think. Have you ever seen one?'

'Just the once,' the monk managed to say.

'Nice, aren't they? But what with it being very dark and all, you're probably not going to get the chance to look at another one now.'

'But it is very dark,' the monk pointed out, deciding that crouching down again would be a good idea now. 'To shoot someone in the dark would be a very difficult task.'

'I agree,' the voice concurred. 'That's why I get paid so much.'

The monk heard a click.

Caput II The Dear Departed

The brain-addled, limping killer, who was most certainly not brain-addled, but was definitely a killer, now had all the after-business to sort out. It was all very well doing the deed in the first place, but the true professional made sure that everything was finished off properly.

He never enjoyed the clearing up as much as he did making the mess in the first place, but it had to be done.

The first task was to check that the most fundamental bit of finishing off had been completed satisfactorily. He limped over to the site of the latest notch on his crossbow to check that everything was in order.

The body of the monk lay where it had fallen, and it was now a body. There was nothing worse than walking away from a job only to find the job recovered and walking around a week later. Word spread, and that sort of thing did real damage to a reputation and the prospect of future work.

Once confident that no further action by way of encouragement towards death was required, he retrieved his crossbow bolt. These things were expensive and there was no point wasting one. Sometimes it was important to leave a calling card, but in those instances, he added the cost of the bolt to his bill.

Content that everything was in order, he tucked the bolt away and slung the crossbow over his shoulder. Despite what he had said, the thing was a bloody nuisance. It was heavy, took a lot of strength to prime, and however he carried it, it dug into him mercilessly. A longbow would be much easier to carry about, but his wounded arm made the use of one impossible. He hadn't mentioned the wounded arm to the monk, he never liked to make people feel too bad about their killer being in worse condition than they were. Although the appearance of infirmity had been a real boon on more than one occasion.

Even those who knew they were under threat tended to turn their back on a man with a limp and a bad arm. Big mistake; the back was such a big target.

Despite its size, the crossbow was easier to hide than a full longbow. With a voluminous cloak, just the sort of thing a wounded old soldier would wear, he could smuggle the thing about quite effectively. There was no chance of secreting a six-and-a-half-foot longbow anywhere.

Even though it was dark, even though the monk had been alone, the man knew that he had to leave this place quietly and quickly. There was no telling if some other monk would be wandering around the place, poking his nose into murders that were none of his business. He knew from experience that you could never trust a monk to have any common sense at all.

Checking that he had everything, he shuffled off through the darkness and out of the exit to the cloister. He stepped over the monk, firmly believing that treading on the person you've just killed was simply rude.

He would have liked to hide the body, just to give him some more time to get away, but his instructions had been clear. This particular monk needed to be found where he fell, it was a message of some sort. Or a sign. Something like that. Once the actual deed was agreed, he seldom concerned himself with the peculiar requirements of his employers.

And this lot wanted him to come back and report in person. Apparently, they wouldn't be satisfied just hearing rumour that this monk was no more. They wanted the tale straight from the only participant left alive. That was another pain, but another addition to the bill.

Outside the cloister, the monastery was quiet and peaceful, and the killer smiled as he thought that his exit would be as easy as his entrance. Honestly, did these monks know nothing about keeping potential murderers at bay? Not even a lock on the door, or an armed guard in sight. It was no wonder the job had been easy. These people deserved all they got.

And he tried to avoid the word murder wherever possible, it seemed rather tawdry, somehow. Everyone was going to die; that was for certain. All he did was arrange for it to happen a bit earlier than expected. Death Arranger was a much more accurate description of his trade, and it gave some customers a bit of solace. They hadn't had their nearest and dearest murdered, they'd just arranged for their death to be brought forward. It could be seen as a bit of a kindness when you thought about it.

And he'd just come across a marvellous new word from the east, apparently. Very civilised people, those easterners. If anyone was going to think about things carefully and explain the very deepest motivations of human nature, it would be someone from the east. And then, when they'd thought about it long enough, they'd come up a word to go with it. Assassination sounded so much more like a craft than murder. He was an assassin, although his customers seemed more concerned with the outcome than the name for the process.

He did wonder, momentarily, if monks probably weren't supposed to be subject to assassination in the dark, but it was only for a moment; everyone was at risk of assassination in the dark, if only they knew it.

Relaxing his guard, he strode, as best he could, across the

ground towards the main gate of this place. Once through that, he would be away and clear.

He almost tripped over his own crossbow when a loud bell started tolling somewhere high in the darkness. Had someone found the body so quickly and rung the alarm? He spotted a favourable accumulation of murk against a wall and quickly climbed in. He peered about, very cautiously, to see which direction the inevitable trouble was going to come from.

Even though there was no immediate movement, it was too risky to try and get away. People were bound to be on the move, that bell was enough to wake the dead. Although not the dead he provided, they were always properly gone.

He didn't dare risk going round some corner, only to find a monk coming in the other direction. True, his crossbow needed priming again, but he had several knives about him, each of them quite capable of dealing with an unarmed monk.

Unfortunately, his instructions had been clear on that as well. All they wanted was this one particular monk. A trail of dead brothers littering the place would not be tolerated.

The bell continued to toll as the first door into the building opened and a monk emerged, followed by several others. They didn't look to be in any hurry at all. In fact, they wandered out yawning and stretching their arms, most of them only looking half awake.

The killer knew that it was important to know where his enemy was at all times and so, once the last monk had passed by, he emerged from his shadows and crept along behind.

Of course, being a master of his art, he had scouted out the plan of this place as soon as he had got in, and he quickly determined where this line of monks was going. To chapel. At this time of night? What on earth were they going there for? Was it their place of refuge if ever a killer got loose in the place? If the bell rings, we're under attack and so make for the chapel?

Even more bizarre than showing little interest in getting to the chapel quickly, this bunch now started singing. It wasn't a jolly song, or something lamenting the fact they'd been dragged out of bed, it was a chant of some sort. They all seemed to know the words, which were in Latin, and they groaned them out as they paced slowly along. The killer knew what Latin sounded like, as someone had used it that time he'd been excommunicated.

Good God, he had it. These monks were going to church. In the middle of the night. Voluntarily.

He had thought that once his killing days were over, once he really was no longer capable of surprising people in the most fatal manner, he would retire to a monastery. He knew that he had led, and was leading, a very bad life indeed, but there was always time to repent. A year or two in a monastery should do the trick.

But if you had to get up to go to church in the middle of the night, he'd look for an alternative route to salvation. Perhaps he could become a priest?

He stopped his following and shrank back as he reminded himself that the route from here to the chapel was through the cloister. As the result of his night's work would still be lying in the middle of the floor, it was more than likely that a bunch of monks in the dark would trip over him.

And they did. At first, there was the sound of confusion as the monks at the back of the line wanted to know why those at the front had stopped. Then the ones at the back joined the ones at the front and they all tried to find out what the problem was, none of them carrying torches, or anything

16

helpful.

One of their number clearly knelt to examine the obstruction, as he announced loudly that there was an idle monk lying sleeping on the cloister floor.

One of the others suggested that kicking said monk would be a sure way to rouse him and remind him of his duties.

The sound of a monk kicking a dead monk was followed by several more kicks until one of them suggested that the one on the floor might be sick and that kicking him probably wasn't helping.

As is usual in groups like this, one of them eventually took charge and bundled the rest out of the way. After some shuffling and hissed whispers, this one announced that the monk on the floor was, in fact, dead.

'Probably old Brother Hegnal,' someone from the back called out. 'He's about due.'

'Do you mind?' a voice replied, 'I'm right here.'

'I can't see who it is, it's too dark. Go to chapel and fetch the abbot.'

The killer took this as his opportunity to depart. If these monks all had to go to chapel when it was pitch dark, so much the better for him. He moved away and headed for the main gate.

'Who's there?' one of the monks called out.

The killer ducked low, cursing his stupidity in thinking that he wouldn't be noticed.

'Brother Nult, do you have your sling with you? The one for the rats?'

'Of course,' what must be Brother Nult replied.

'Someone is making for the gate. I have a horrible feeling some great wrong has been done here.'

The killer had no idea what was going on until quite a large piece of rock flew by him at speed. He ducked as far as his leg would allow and moved on, quietly cursing the outrageous behaviour of monks, who really shouldn't be throwing rocks at people. What was the world coming to?

'Go to the gate, Brother,' the lead monk now instructed. 'If anyone tries to leave, use your great strength to wrestle them to the ground.'

It was irrelevant if that was a real threat, or just something intended to alarm, the effect was the same; the killer stopped ducking and rose up to move as fast as he could.

He found the gate and was hauling on the metal ring to pull it open when he felt, rather than heard the presence of a monk join him. It must be a pretty big monk to have such an impact in the dark, and it prompted the killer to pull harder. The gate moved but its hinges shrieked their complaint at a complete lack of oil or fat for as long as they could remember.

The large monk in the dark took a step forward to where he thought the door opener would be.

'Got you,' he cried.

But he hadn't. He hadn't allowed for the fact that the figure escaping had one bad leg, and so had to lean much farther to his right than anyone else would. Instead, the monk grabbed at the side of the door and neatly smacked it as hard as he could with his forehead.

'Ow,' he said, as he sat down.

The killer limped over his attacker and out into the wider darkness of the night.

...

As morning hurried the gloom of night away to the west, the killer entered a town and walked up the main street with a clear destination in mind.

His escape from the monastery had been a close thing, but not so close as to give him any lingering concerns. He had known that he would get away, and he was quite pleased that he hadn't had to stab anyone to do it. Not that he minded stabbing people, but his instructions had been not to do so. And he hadn't. He could happily report that he had injured no one else in the completion of his mission. If a big monk had walked into a door, that was hardly his fault.

Obviously, he'd killed someone, but then that was what he'd been asked to do. And that could hardly be counted as an injury, anyway. You recovered from injuries.

He would also be able to report, truthfully, that no one had spotted him. It had been as dark as the place behind your eyes, so of course, they hadn't spotted him. No one had seen his face, or even his shape and so would have no way of finding out who he was.

It was less true that he had gone unnoticed, but then the dead monk now had a hole where a crossbow bolt had gone, and that sort of thing tended to get noticed. And it didn't happen without someone else being involved; someone with a crossbow at that.

To his own mind, the night had gone very well. It hadn't been perfect, but he now knew that monks went to church at night. He'd be ready next time. As far as his employers were concerned, his performance had been immaculate.

Finding the building on the edge of the town that he was looking for, the killer took a quick glance around to check that he wasn't observed. True dawn was still some moments away, and the people of this place were making the most of the last dregs of nighttime. No point seeking out the toils of day until they came knocking.

The killer left the main highway and ducked down the side of a tall, imposing building. At its back corner a wooden door was set into its side, the sort of door that probably looked ancient and mysterious the moment it was put in. It appeared never to have been opened, and years of grime and dirt had blurred it into the surrounding walls.

With yet another not-suspicious-at-all glance around, the killer knocked a very particular knock on the door. After a wait, which seemed to be expected, a differently patterned knock came from the inside. With a slight sigh of irritation, the killer knocked the appropriate response. At this, there was the clunk of a bolt being withdrawn, followed by another, after which the door creaked, and a crack appeared.

'Yes?' A voice croaked, the sort of croak the owner of a voice uses when they don't want to be recognised.

'It's me,' the killer said, impatient to be let in.

'Me?' the croak asked.

'Yes, you know. The one who has just done a particular job for you, and could do another one right now if he's not let in.'

The croak coughed and pulled the door further.

'Thank you.' The killer shuffled forward and into the dark chamber behind the door.

'Are they here?'

'They are always here,' the croaking one said, mysteriously, beckoning that the killer should follow.

'Glad they've nothing better to do.'

The croaking lead stepped on into the darkness, a long cloak flowing around the floor. A cowl covered the head, but largely to keep the cold out, rather than for any official function. It was impossible to tell from the outside whether this man was old or young. It could even be a woman if she was good at croaking. The steps the figure took were slow and purposeful as if some awful fate awaited them in this grim place.

'If we could get on then?' the killer urged.

'Other people to kill?' the croak had diminished now, and the voice was definitely male.

'There are always other people to kill,' the killer replied, with a purposeful glance at his guide.

Through winding and decrepit corridors they walked, the drag of the killer's limp adding a tone of impending doom to their passage.

Eventually, they came to a short flight of steps, topped by a large door, banded with iron, and firmly shut.

'Wait here,' the guide said, the croak having completely gone, or been forgotten. 'I'll see if they're ready for you.'

'How many people have they got out there, killing monks?' The killer snorted, as the door was pushed open and the cloaked figure slipped through to the other side.

The killer spent several moments looking around at his dour surroundings, followed by some blowing of his cheeks. He then took to smacking his lips, sighing and eventually looking for somewhere to sit. Concluding that it was the floor or nothing, he was almost surprised when the door opened and the cloaked one indicated that he could enter.

The chamber was just the same as it had been when he had been given his instructions, but there were a lot more people in it now. And they were still as truly bizarre as the first time he had met them.

Where his guide wore a cowl to cover his features, this roomful wore hoods. Real hoods with eye holes cut out. He'd been asked to kill by some odd people in the past, but never a band like this.

The one who had handed over the first portion of the

payment along with details of the target sat behind a long table. The killer could tell it was the same man as the nasty eyes glared from the holes in the hood as if they'd burned their way through.

On either side of him, a bizarre collection of individuals sat. It was all very well people wearing hoods to cover their faces but keeping their normal dress on at the same time rather ruined the effect.

Some were wearing priestly garb of their title, or position, while others were in everyday clothes. There was even one dressed in a very peculiar and specific manner. Surely his sort wasn't part of this gathering.

'The conclave is assembled,' the leader announced, implying that this urgent meeting was the killer's fault somehow.

'Conclave?' He'd never heard that they had a title.

'The conclave for the removal of the aberration.'

'Aberration?' The killer was thinking that this was all getting terribly complicated, all of a sudden. Either that or incredibly pretentious. Or both.

'The aberration is removed?' the one behind the desk demanded.

The killer just stood and looked blank.

'The monk,' the man sighed. 'You've killed the monk we asked?'

'Oh, right, yes,' the killer nodded. 'Quite dead, just as ordered.'

'How do we know?' another voice down the table asked.

The killer would have spun on the spot if his leg allowed. He stared at this hooded figure, trying to discern what sort of face lay behind it. The clothes were a giveaway; he hadn't been expecting a nun. He knew nuns could be pretty nasty but assassinating monks? Seemed a bit much. Still, not his business to enquire too far. He always found out things he really didn't want to know when he enquired too far.

As he cast a glance around the table he considered the very disparate group and it did raise questions in his mind. He knew very well what to do with questions. Ignore them, they only caused trouble.

He reached into his cloak and pulled out the crossbow bolt. He stepped forward and laid it on the table.

'What's this?'

'Crossbow bolt from a dead monk.'

The man behind the table sniffed. 'This could be from any monk. How do we know it's ours?'

The killer shrugged. 'You'll have to take my word for it. He was where you told me he'd be. He was with the abbot you mentioned. He looked like you said and before I struck I tested his nerve.'

'And?'

'He didn't have any.'

Sighs wandered the length of the table.

'He's gone.' The leader smiled grimly and with horrible satisfaction. 'He has finally gone. The world is rid of that troublesome monk, and we can go about our business unhindered.'

'Praise God,' one voice cried out.

The leader of the conclave leaned forward and planted a heavy bag of coin on the table. The killer stepped forward to lay a hand upon it. As he did so, the leader's hand landed on his.

'This is a great deal of money. A very great deal for one monk.'

'The price was agreed.' The killer was on the alert for any

cheating. Cheats he killed for free.

'It was. But if by chance we find out later that the one monk is still alive.' The man pierced the killer with his own sharp edge. 'We'll come looking for you.'

'More than welcome.' The killer smiled and pocketed the money. 'I haven't been in the business this long not to recognise a dead monk when I see one.'

Caput III The Departed was Dear.

'This is awful.' Abbot Abbo stood in the chapel, his head bowed. His prior, Thulred stood beside him, and on the table before the altar, the body of the monk lay with all due dignity. 'Awful,' he repeated. 'And I am to blame.' The old abbot's frame, usually upright and robust, despite his age, seemed to have shrunk and sagged under the weight of this event.

There was no doubt that it was a truly shocking occurrence. Monks died in monasteries, of course, they did; that was where they lived their lives and those lives were bound to come to an end sooner or later.

It was also true that monks came to those ends by a variety of means, but these were usually natural. Old age, disease, mishap on a rickety ladder, eating the medicinal mushrooms, that sort of thing. It was not entirely unheard of for a monk to be done to death, usually through dispute with one of his fellows that got out of hand. That could be dealt with. The miscreant would normally find himself moved to some other house of devotion. A house that concentrated less on devotion and more on penance. The monastery of De'Ath's Dingle was a favourite.

For a stranger to enter a monastery and murder a monk was beyond imagination. Well, there was the renowned case of Brother Slimney, of course, but then he had gone into the local town one night and behaved in such a manner that he probably deserved what he got. But this was nothing like that.

The young brother lying before them was innocuous in the extreme. In fact, Thulred suspected that most of the other brothers didn't even know the man was here, such was his humble demeanour.

'No, Father.' The prior tried to comfort his leader. 'You played no part. Some devil-driven monster came to our community and did this.'

Abbo shook his head. 'But if I hadn't invited the dear fellow to visit me here, he'd still be alive.'

'It could be that whoever had been in the cloister would have fallen to the same end. And if not the cloister, the killer may have prowled on until he found someone. The devil wanted his work done tonight, and it was done.'

Abbo stepped forward and laid his hand on the deceased's forehead. 'I have let you down, old friend. Brought you to your doom and let you down. I was not even there to offer unction in extremis at your final moment.'

Thulred had no more words but gently shook his head at his abbot's distress.

'Nothing was stolen,' the abbot confirmed.

'Nothing, Father. We are not a rich house, but even our one silver chalice was untouched.'

'Just confirms my suspicion. Our brother here was the target,' Abbo sighed. 'There was no other. This devil, for you are right there, came seeking just one person, and he found him.

'How can you know that?'

'Because our brother was special. Unique.'

'We are all unique.'

'This brother had made enemies, young though he was. He did not choose his path, but such was his loyalty and sense of duty that he followed it. It was a path no other trod, and he was despised for it. It is no surprise that those who carried hatred for him have taken this step.'

'Shooting a monk in the cloister?' Thulred couldn't help

the incredulity coming out in his voice.

'You don't know what he has done,' Abbo said. 'Now is not the time, but it will come out.' He cast his eyes to the body. 'It must come out.'

'You start to worry me, Father.'

'And so I should. The very greatest in the land will need to know about this. Those who have carried out this deed need not think that they will go unpunished.'

Now Thulred considered the body before him and shook his head, more in puzzlement than anything else. 'We are a humble establishment, Father. We are not at the centre of the world or even the centre of the church. Or anywhere near it, come to that. This brother came without ceremony. Is he someone's son?'

'Doubtless, he is someone's son, but that is not the reason for my concern. It is not his birth, but his actions thereafter that have given him significance. A significance he never sought, never wanted, but never shirked.'

Thulred had nothing more to say and it was clear that Abbo was not going to go any further with his explanation.

'Word must be sent,' the abbot announced.

'Of course, Father. I shall find a suitable messenger.'

Abbot Abbo held up a hand. 'No. This is word I must deliver myself.'

'You, Father?' Thulred knew that curiosity was a sin and not something any monk should indulge in, but it was starting to make his feet itch.

'There can be no other. This whole sorry situation is my responsibility and so delivering word of it falls to me as well.'

'Delivering where, Father?'

Abbot Abbo took a great sigh and told Thulred where he was going.

'Really? Well, Derby's not that far away, half a day's journey. Allow me to select a robust brother to accompany you. Perhaps Brother Nult? His sling and his staff may be of use on the road. As well as his club and that knife he thinks no one knows about.' Thulred found himself changing the subject. 'I do wonder about Brother Nult's past, sometimes. I wouldn't be at all surprised if someone turned up looking for him one day.'

The abbot's hand of pause was up once more. 'I must go alone.'

'Alone? Father, that is rash indeed. We have already seen that there is a killer on the loose. One who is prepared to shoot an innocent monk in the dark. Alone on the road, your habit may not protect you.'

'I am not concerned. As I said, the brother here was the target, there was no other. I strongly suspect that the killer will be long gone by now. Reporting back to his masters, no doubt.'

Thulred held his own hands out now, this time in protest. 'A dead brother, killers in cloisters, masters behind it all. These seem to be matters beyond us. Should we not simply send to the bishop for aid?'

'All in due course. First, word must be taken to Derby, and I must take it alone.'

Thulred was clearly not prepared to just accept this. 'Why, father? Why alone? Surely there is no harm in Nult accompanying you.'

Abbot Abbo breathed deeply and turned to face Thulred. 'I go to Derby, that is true. But I go to a particular place in Derby. A place I would not inflict on another brother. Of all of them, I think Nult would be the most at risk.'

'I've been to Derby, Father,' Thulred said, with some

irritation now. 'I can't think of anywhere there that would give rise to such concern.'

The abbot looked around the chapel to confirm that they were alone. He beckoned Thulred to draw near.

'I will tell you, Thulred.'

This really was significant, the abbot using the prior's name.

'But you must tell no one. I command this as your abbot. It is unfair that I keep this from you and leave you to fret. It is not through deceit or lack of trust, but rather through a wish to protect you. If you would know, I will tell you.'

'Please, Father,' Thulred asked.

Abbo leant forward and whispered the name of his destination in the prior's ear.

The prior stepped back. 'Good God! Really?'

'I have been there before.'

'Oh, yes?' Now Thulred's tone was full of suspicion and quite a bit of surprise. He'd never thought that the abbot was that way inclined.

'Not for that,' Abbo snapped at him. 'I had cause to go there once under a somewhat similar set of circumstances.'

That didn't help Thulred's suspicions at all. 'Another dead monk in a cloister?'

'Not exactly.'

Thulred was now feeling positively alarmed, and it obviously showed.

'Don't worry. I cannot explain all now. I will, I promise, but I must make this journey first. It will give me time to think.'

The prior blew out heavily. 'I thought a dead monk was bad enough on his own. At least let Nult accompany you part of the way. He can rest in Derby while you go, erm, there.'

'Very well.' Abbo conceded. He laid a hand on his prior's shoulder. 'When I come back all will be revealed, I swear this to you.'

Knowing where his abbot was going, Thulred wasn't quite sure what sort of revelation he needed to prepare for.

. . .

Striding away from his monastery, Abbot Abbo was quite confident that he could look after himself on the road, after all, he had travelled alone before without mishap. There was some comfort in the presence of Nult, though. These were troublesome times and Thulred was right, the habit was no protection anymore. Robbers and thieves seemed to have grown in confidence with the arrival of the Normans. Perhaps they thought that the chaos in the land and the fact that armed men walked about causing havoc was licence for them to do just the same.

Nult was certainly capable of seeing off any attack, but when there was no attack he had to be restrained from starting one himself. Any passing stranger, from a young man on his way to the fields to an old woman with an arm full of kindling, prompted the impetuous monk to reach for one of his weapons so that he could deal with the potential danger by hitting it.

At least he took the authority of his abbot seriously. A sharp word, which Abbo was quite capable of delivering, brought Nult back to order.

Thereafter, people passing on the road gave the abbot an acknowledging bow until Nult growled at them and they moved on.

One pair of very rough-looking fellows did appear to be

appraising the abbot and his companion as they drew near. They even engaged in a quiet, but purposeful looking conversation while they were still some way off. It looked as if they were planning something and were just waiting for their moment. Such signs were obvious to anyone and told of robbers who really weren't approaching their calling with any guile.

As they got within striking distance, one of them threw his eyes wide as he seemed to recognise Nult. He nudged his companion hard in the ribs and whispered hurriedly. They quickly decided that they had business away from the path and went off to examine some trees.

Nult simply grunted and shook his head in what looked like disappointment at such pathetic behaviour.

After that, the monks were given a wide berth. It was almost as if word had spread up and down the road that these two were to be left alone.

The enclosing wood, which had been their companion for most of the journey, started to thin, and fields of crops or grazing animals became more common. The occasional hovel lurched into the side of the road and shepherds with their flocks stared with naked interest at a pair of monks walking the path. Anything was better than looking at sheep all day.

The ever protective Nult was casting an aggressive and warning glare at a passing dog when they arrived at the edge of Derby.

'Now, Brother.' The abbot stopped and addressed Nult directly. It was important to see his eyes when you were talking to him, to make sure that the words were getting in. 'I must go a short distance to deliver my news. You cannot accompany me.'

Nult looked ready to get very angry at this.

The abbot reached into his habit. 'Here is a coin. Go to the tavern and wait for me there.'

Nult looked at the coin with awe, as if expecting it to do something remarkable.

Abbo held it out between his thumb and finger. He nodded encouragement that Nult could really take it. When nothing happened, he took Nult's hand and pressed the coin into his palm. 'Buy some food and drink,' he instructed. 'And pay for it properly; don't just take it. And don't bother any of the people you meet. In fact,' he put on his instructive face. 'Give me your knife.'

'Knife? What knife?'

'The knife we all know you've got. I'm not leaving you alone with the innocent people of Derby with a knife in your habit.' Abbo held out his hand.

With a reluctant sigh, Nult delved about inside his clothing and produced a small but well-cared-for knife. He handed it over.

'I shan't be long, and I don't want to come back and find the place in disarray. Clear?'

'Yes, Father,' Nult mumbled.

'Good.' The abbot pointed a final, warning finger, before walking off and leaving Nult to find the tavern on his own. With any luck that would take some time, leaving less for any disputes to arise.

With a final great sigh, Abbot Abbo carried on through the town and took the familiar path to his final, unique destination.

The place was just as he recalled it from his previous visit; unnecessarily lavish, inappropriately comfortable and flagrantly ostentatious. As he walked up the path to the main door he saw another figure coming out. This was not someone he recognised and was probably just some man of the town.

The man of the town looked at the abbot with blank curiosity. 'Hello, Father,' he said. 'Need any help?'

'No, no, my son. I am quite content.'

'You, er,' the man nodded back towards the house. 'Found the place you're looking for?'

'I have.'

'You do know who lives here then?'

'I do.'

'Right.' The man paused. 'And you're sure this is the place you want? The house of Wat the Weaver?'

'Exactly.'

'Wat the Weaver who makes all those tapestries that show, well, everything really, if you know what I mean.' The man winked at the abbot.

'I do know what you mean. And I know that those very particular works are no longer produced. Wat the Weaver has been directed to more wholesome trade.'

'Of course, of course,' the man agreed, rather too quickly. 'Nothing like that here anymore. No point visiting for that sort of thing.' The man smiled. 'Disgusting,' he added, as an afterthought.

'I bring sorrowing news,' Abbo said, quite pointedly. 'That is the purpose of my visit, although I know why most people come here.' He gave the man a very knowing and rather accusatory look.

'Ah, yes, there you are then. But it's just as you say; nothing like that available anymore.' The man hurried away, grasping his jerkin tight as if stopping something that he was hiding in there falling out.

Shaking his head in sad disappointment, Abbo arrived at

the door and, with a final pause for thought, raised his arm and knocked.

After a few moments, the door opened and an elfin-like woman stood on the threshold. She was young and as slight as a mild breeze. Short hair framed a face only just veiling a smile that could charm the creatures of the forest.

When she saw that there was a monk at the door, the smile was replaced by a scowl that would have the creatures of the forest climbing over one another to get away. The breeze became a gale driven by an inner ferocity that clearly went very deep indeed.

'Mistress Cwen,' Abbo bowed his head.

'Abbot Abbo?' Cwen relaxed as she recognised the abbot from their previous meeting.

'It is.'

'What brings you to Wat's workshop? In broad daylight?'

Abbo's face was as grim as his words. 'I bring sad news.'

Cwen's face lost all expression, both friendly and fierce. 'Sad news?' she asked, quietly.

'The saddest. The most burdensome.'

Cwen's mouth fell open. 'It's not about..,?'

'It is.' The abbot let go a breath. 'There is no easy way to say this, so I must just let the words do what they must. There has been a death.'

'Death?' Cwen's breath was short.

'A murder. At the monastery.'

Cwen now stared at the abbot, as if not believing those words would make them retreat.

'Not...?'

'Yes. I fear so. That is the purpose of my visit.' Abbo took a breath. 'Brother Hermitage,' he said solemnly.

Cwen shook her head very slowly as she took this in.

'Hermitage,' she shrieked out a wail that could pierce armour.

She spun slowly on her heels and repeated her awful call into the depths of the house. 'Hermitage,' she cried, plaintively. 'It's for you.'

Caput IV A Heretic for Death?

Brother Hermitage, alerted by Cwen's shout, like a moth alerted by the arrival of a whole colony of bats, jumped from his cot, where he had been working steadily through the alphabetisation of the post-Exodus prophets; C would have to wait for another day.

This first shout of his name had been sufficient. That probably meant that he had done something wrong. Or had broken something that he was now being summoned to clear up. Although he was slightly older than Cwen and had all the authority of the monk's habit, while she was a weaver, against all the rules of the guild, he still knew which one of them was in charge.

The subsequent call that something was for him sent a shiver down his back. There was only ever one reason people came looking for Brother Hermitage at the house of Wat the Weaver: murder.

He had been considering recently that his unwanted title "The King's Investigator" should really mean that he had a staff of investigators working for him. He was sure that anyone else called a king's anything, wouldn't have to do all the work himself. He was positive that the king's armourer would have a whole workshop full of armourers who bashed the stuff out. Similarly, the king's cook may cook for the king, but he wouldn't have to do the washing up as well.

He supposed he should be grateful that he didn't have to attend upon the king all the time. He wasn't required to be at court just waiting for the next suspicious death to turn up. But hiding in Wat's workshop hadn't turned out to be much good either. People knew where he was and brought their murders to him.

The last couple of occasions had been murders a bit closer to home though: Cwen's family and then Wat's weaving guild.[1] That only seemed to be worse, somehow. Not only were reports of murders being brought to his door, the actual things themselves were turning up.

Still, he knew there was no point loitering when Cwen had called. He certainly didn't want to make her come and get him.

Wandering as slowly as he could through the corridors of the workshop, he unavoidably came to the front door, only to find there was no one there.

It wasn't like Cwen to invite strangers into the house. It wasn't like Cwen to invite anyone to anything. Had she been taken? Had a murderer arrived to offer himself to The King's Investigator, only to take Cwen hostage? His inner panic, which always stood ready for action, got him hopping on the spot.

'We're upstairs,' Cwen's voice called from above.

Upstairs? In Wat's business chamber? The one reserved for important clients, or Norman soldiers who treated the place as if they owned it? This must be a unique visitor.

Hermitage turned from the door and made his way up the crooked steps to the floor above. This room was broad and open, and sunlight streamed in through the windows of real glass that overlooked the front of the workshop.

Cwen was there, resting in the window seat and Abbot Abbo was beside her.

'Father!' Hermitage cried with joy. Perhaps this was a harmless visit after all.

Abbot Abbo stood to greet Hermitage, but his face was

---

[1] A Murder for Mistress Cwen and A Murder for Master Wat (easy to tell which is which)

dark and solemn. No, not a harmless visit, then.

Rather than mutual hugs of welcome, Abbo took Hermitage's hand, grasping it firmly in the manner of one offering comfort.

'I am sorry, Hermitage.'

'Sorry? Sorry for what? No matter the circumstances of your visit, it is good to see you again.'

'You are too kind. But I didn't know who else to turn to.'

Hermitage felt odd, being someone turned to. He didn't think he'd ever been turned to before. Yes, people demanded of him quite regularly, but that wasn't the same at all.

Hermitage beckoned that they should sit again, and he joined Abbo in the window.

'Right,' Cwen said, brightly. 'I'll be off then, leave you to it.'

Abbo nodded. 'That is probably for the best. There are words that must be for Hermitage's ears only.'

'That's fine.' Cwen was abrupt. 'I'll find out what they are later.' She stepped off towards the stairs. 'I'd better tell Wat as well. If there's been a murder you're probably going to need all of us.'

'In this case,' Abbo said, 'I think not.'

'Right,' Cwen said as she left, with what sounded very much like a snigger.

Once she had gone, Hermitage, open-mouthed, faced Abbo. 'A murder?' he asked. He knew there would be one but hearing it out loud was still disappointing.

'There has been a murder,' Abbo confirmed. 'Brother Pewlet.'

The name meant nothing to Hermitage. 'Pewlet?'

'Brother Pewlet of Leicester?' Abbo sounded surprised that Hermitage didn't know the deceased personally.

Hermitage tried to look as if he was struggling to recall

someone he didn't know. 'I don't think I'm familiar with him.'

'Brother Pewlet of Leicester? You don't know Brother Pewlet of Leicester?'

'I'm afraid not.'

'Well, I never. I thought everyone knew Pewlet.'

'Not me. But then, I have been rather out of monastic circles recently. And before that, I was at De'Ath's Dingle.'

'Ah, yes.' Abbo seemed happy to accept that as an excuse for anything.

'But he's dead?' Hermitage moved the conversation on.

'Oh, yes. Shot.'

'What was?'

'He was. Pewlet. He was shot.'

'Was he?'

'With a crossbow, we think.'

'Good heavens.' Hermitage gave this some thought. It was an unusual thing to happen. 'On purpose?' he asked.

'I beg your pardon?' The abbot looked as if he'd just started talking about something completely different.

'Was he shot on purpose, or was it an accident? Crossbows are pretty dangerous things.'

'They are,' Abbo sounded a bit confused. 'But we don't traditionally carry a stock of them in a monastery, let alone have a workshop of monks carrying out maintenance.'

'Ah, I suppose not. Shot on purpose then.'

'Precisely.'

'Any idea who did it?' Hermitage thought it would be very handy if Abbo knew the murderer as well as the victim. It would make the whole investigation process so much easier.

'Er, no.'

'Ah.'

'That's why I've come to you.' Abbo was now sounding as

if he thought he had come to the wrong King's Investigator.

Hermitage nodded to himself as he thought about this. 'Normans,' he said.

'What about them?'

'They have all the crossbows. And they shoot people. It could have been a Norman.'

'I don't think it was a Norman.'

'Not a Norman?' Hermitage couldn't immediately think of anyone else who did killing these days.

'No. Because I know why Pewlet was killed.'

'Gosh.'

Abbo left a significant pause. 'His thinking.'

Hermitage also left a significant pause, mainly because he didn't understand. 'He thought he'd been shot, so he was?'

'No, no.' Abbo's familiar impatience was surfacing. 'He was shot because of what he was thinking.'

'I see,' said Hermitage, but he didn't.

Abbo just looked at Hermitage, clearly waiting for something else. 'Don't you want to know what he was thinking?'

'Oh, yes, that would be good.' Hermitage was still struggling with the concept of being shot for what you were thinking. How could anyone know what you were thinking, unless you told them, of course? But even then, what you said might not actually tally with what you were thinking. That happened to him quite a lot.

Abbot Abbo got up and went over to the stairs, clearly checking that there was no one in earshot. He returned to his seat.

'Cathari,' he said.

Hermitage's jaw dropped. 'No.'

Abbo nodded.

'He told you this?'

'He did. We were old friends from years ago. His family knew my family and so on. He was always a thoughtful and enquiring young man, exploring ideas as others would an interesting path or forest. He confided in me that he was considering the Cathari heresy, purely from the point of view of an observer. He said that some of their arguments had merit.'

'Really?' Hermitage couldn't believe that.

'Only as arguments. I am sure that he was not persuaded, but if others thought that he was coming to heretical conclusions; well, it does not bear thinking about. It would be very worrying.'

'I'll say.' Hermitage was worried himself, and they weren't even his conclusions.

'Had he told anyone else?'

'That I do not know. But he was an innocent and would talk about such matters freely.'

'But who would take such a drastic step against an innocent discussion?' Hermitage asked. Most of his discussions were innocent, and he wouldn't want dangerous people leaping to conclusions over them. Let alone bring a crossbow to the next meeting.

'That is just what we need to find out.' Abbot Abbo seemed happy that they had reached agreement. 'And who better to do so than the King's Investigator?'

'Hm,' Hermitage nodded. 'Ah,' he said, as he remembered who that was.

He knew that he would have to do this. Abbot Abbo was one of his oldest friends. He had already helped the old man out in his own troubles when he had found himself declared dead by a devious contrivance.[2] And this was a murder. Just the sort of thing he was supposed to deal with. And the murder of a fellow monk; what more compelling reason for his engagement could there be?

That didn't stop him thinking about how he might avoid the whole thing though. He would rather not have anything to do with people with crossbows who went around shooting enquiring monks.

His deliberations were interrupted by a clattering on the stairs, and he turned to see the head of Wat the Weaver appear, grinning as usual, his unruly mop of dark curly hair seeming to make light of everything around him. He was followed by Cwen, who was sipping from a goblet of something or other. She hadn't brought one for anyone else.

'Well, well,' the weaver called, happily. 'If it isn't our favourite dead abbot, Abbo. You're looking well.'

Abbo grunted an acknowledgement. 'Master Wat. Still in business, I see.' He sounded disappointed at this.

'Oh, positively thriving. Who knew there was such demand for holy works and the like.'

'Anyone who asked, I suspect,' Abbo replied. 'The world never really needed images of the nature you produced.'

'Ah, but people did.' Wat's smile never twitched. 'Even church people.'

'The church has its problems,' Abbo accepted. 'And I met a fellow coming down your path who seemed to be having problems concealing something in his jerkin.'

'Really?' Wat sounded puzzled. 'Probably wanted to keep his tapestry dry.'

'It's not raining.'

'There you are then.'

---

[2] The Case of The Cantankerous Carcass is the one you're looking for.

Hermitage barely followed this. He still suspected that some trade in Wat's old tapestries was going on under his nose, but he had never managed to spot it. He thought Hartle, the weaving master, was behind it. One day he would make a slip and that would be that. Hermitage would deal with the matter as strongly and as firmly as required; he would express his heartfelt disappointment and steer Hartle to the better path.

'Been a murder then?' Wat confirmed what Cwen must have told him. 'In a monastery. Your monastery, I assume?'

Abbo nodded. 'I have been given charge of a very modest house not far from here. It is entirely suitable, and a peaceful place, until recently.'

'Until you started getting dead monks.'

'A single dead monk. And that is just what Brother Hermitage and I are discussing.' The Abbot was quite clear that this was a discussion for the two of them, and that Wat and Cwen could go now.

Wat sat down and looked very interested.

'We've done dead monks before, haven't we, Hermitage?'

'Oh, er, yes.' Hermitage cast his mind back and recalled the death of Brother Ambrosius at the monastery of De'Ath's Dingle. That seemed long ago and in a different world. As he thought about it he realised that it was long ago, and, compared to the house of Wat the Weaver, De'Ath's Dingle was indeed another world. And not a very nice one.[3]

Then there had been Father Ignatius, although he was a priest really, and not a monk, so probably didn't count. He had been impaled on a sundial though, so it was definitely murder.[4]

---

[3] And this is The Heretics of De'Ath
[4] The Case of the Clerical Cadaver, they do go on, don't they?

'This is a matter of some delicacy,' Abbo explained, patiently. 'It is not the sort of thing that a weaver and a, erm..,' he looked at Cwen.

'Another weaver,' Cwen filled in the gap. 'That's two weavers.' She helpfully added up.

'Erm, yes, quite, two weavers. Anyway. It is a matter of delicacy and not really appropriate for the attention of two weavers.'

'I should think not,' Wat agreed, much to Hermitage's surprise. 'You're in charge of a very modest house where the monks get murdered. Sounds very delicate to me.'

Abbo sighed at Wat's impertinence, which was only enhanced by the weaver's smile that seemed to consider the whole thing some sort of joke at the abbot's expense.

Hermitage could understand why the abbot wanted Hermitage to deal with this alone; the question of the heresy was about as delicate as a delicate thing could get. Such matters really were best kept within ecclesiastical circles.

But then there was the crossbow. Crossbows really weren't ecclesiastical at all. He had come across one once before, but Wat had been a great help in that circumstance.[5] And in recent times he had come to rely on Wat and Cwen, not only for support in trying times but for helping to spot killers when they were staring Hermitage in the face.

He didn't care for the prospect of contradicting his friend, but he cared a lot less for the prospect of seeking out a crossbow-wielding monk killer without Wat and Cwen at his side. The problem was how to persuade Abbo that the three of them would be best.

Before he could even start to consider how to formulate his

---

[5] Yet another one; The Garderobe of Death. There's a footnote for every one, so you have been warned

argument, there was another rattling of the stairs, a more urgent one this time, and Hartle burst into the room. He looked alarmed and exhausted from a quick run that a man of his age really shouldn't be tackling.

'What's up?' Wat asked urgently. Perhaps he thought the tapestries were on fire.

'A monk,' Hartle gasped.

'No thanks,' Cwen said. 'We've already got two.'

'No, no,' Hartle panted. 'There's a monk in the workshop.'

'I knew it would be trouble when we started letting them in here,' Wat winked at Hermitage. 'What does this one want? Tell him we don't do works like that anymore.' He faced Abbot Abbo. 'The fellow probably wants one of the nun specials; very popular in the less modest monastic houses.'

'Not this one,' Hartle explained. 'This one's a huge bugger with a big stick. Keeps saying we've taken his abbot hostage.'

They all turned to face Abbo.

'Brother Nult,' Abbo said, with weary resignation. 'I told him to wait in the tavern.'

'Ern probably sent him up here,' Wat said. 'Doesn't do trade any good, having monks in your tavern. Rats is one thing, but not monks.'

'I had best go and calm him.'

'If you could hurry,' Hartle urged. 'Him and Gunnlaug were squaring up to one another when I left.'

'Gunnlaug?' Abbo asked.

'Extra-large apprentice,' Cwen explained. 'He should be able to deal with your Nult. As long as he doesn't have a knife,' she added with a smirk.

'I've got his knife,' Abbo replied.

Cwen raised her eyebrows. 'What sort of monastery are you keeping? If you let the monks keep knives, it's no wonder people get hurt.'

'This one was shot by a crossbow,' Hermitage blurted out.

Abbo sighed at him, but at least he hadn't mentioned the heresy.

'A crossbow?' Wat sounded absolutely staggered by this revelation. 'A monk with a crossbow?'

'It wasn't a monk, obviously,' Abbo objected to the suggestion.

'I imagine you don't know who it was if you've come to find Hermitage. And if monks have got hold of crossbows, none of us is safe.'

'And,' Cwen took up the discussion. 'If you think Hermitage can deal with a crossbow-shooting killer without us to help him, I think you've come to the wrong Hermitage.'

'Another murder?' Hartle complained as if Hermitage was bringing them in on the soles of his sandals. 'Perhaps we could deal with the stick-waving monk in our own workshop first? That would be helpful.' He urged some action.

Hermitage could only smile weakly at the abbot as they all headed for the stairs. He had taken Cwen's words to heart and found them eminently sensible. When they got back from dealing with Gunnlaug and this Nult fellow, he would think about how to raise the suggestion that Wat and Cwen might like to deal with this murder, while he stayed at home

.

Caput V To the Monastery of The Murdered Monk

When they hurried to the workshop they found Gunnlaug and Nult getting on very well. They were both great hulking individuals, probably quite capable of fighting off a bear with a crossbow. This could mean that they had a lot in common and so, instead of destroying the looms and tools of the workshop, they were testing out the weight of Nult's club and the monk was promising to show his knife if he could have it back.

The look on the abbot's face said that this was very unlikely.

Abbo walked quickly over to Nult and engaged in a very intense and whispered conversation. It was clear that the abbot was explaining exactly why they were in the workshop of the infamous Wat the Weaver. Nult appeared to be listening, but he was also casting his eyes all over the place, perhaps hopeful of spotting a tapestry that was a bit more illustrative than he was used to. Or at least illustrated some things he'd never seen before.

Once the non-existent situation was resolved, they retreated to Wat's chamber once more, Abbo insisting that they must prepare for departure straight away. He dared not loiter as this killer, whoever he was, was still on the loose. He also dared not loiter in a place like this. It was bad enough that Nult knew; what if anyone else found out?

He was also quite adamant that Hermitage must deal with this matter alone. The sensitivities were simply too great to let anyone else be involved at all, let alone Wat the Weaver.

Hermitage gave this serious thought. He even looked serious and strode up and down the room a bit. He came to his conclusion and posed a simple question, which he put to the abbot.

'No, Hermitage,' Abbo replied gently. 'I won't be able to stay with you through every hour of the day and night. I have my duties as abbot to consider.'

Hermitage acknowledged this with a nod. 'Wat and Cwen are pretty much indispensable then,' he explained. He didn't like to say that there was no way in God's own heaven that he was going to go after someone with a crossbow on his own, instead, he made it sound as if it was simply a matter of getting the investigation completed effectively.

'There is too much to do in an investigation for one person to be able to complete it. Sometimes two or three things need to be done at the same time. You know, chase that person, find that one, get that body taken away. I must have help.'

'Nult here knows as much as anyone.' Abbo looked to his subordinate, who was polishing his club. 'In fact, he knows more now,' he sighed.

'And I am sure Brother Nult would be a great help, but he has not dealt with investigation before. The whole business would be most inefficient.'

He considered that it would be more inefficient if the investigator in question was pinned to the ground with a crossbow bolt. And it sounded like whoever it was had the crossbow, knew how to use it. Wat explained that. He said they were usually great, unwieldy things and it took some skill to use one at all, let alone hit the thing you were aiming at.

'You can't have forgotten that business with the crossbow in the garderobe?' Wat asked.[6]

'How could I?' Hermitage even remembered some bits of

---

[6] And sometimes two footnotes for the same book; The Garderobe of Death; essential reading for all crossbow/garderobe enthusiasts.

that awful experience when he woke in the middle of the night; and not the nice bits.

'So, you know a crossbow is a lot of trouble. Must be a serious killer to use one on a monk.'

To Hermitage's ear, this sounded like another very good reason for Wat to be involved in the investigation. The more people there were to aim the crossbow at, the less likely anyone was to get hit.

'I don't think such a killer would hesitate for a moment before firing his weapon at the King's Investigator,' the King's Investigator said nervously. 'If the man has already murdered an innocent monk, his standards of behaviour are obviously very low. The risk of being held accountable for his actions would almost certainly make him a desperate man. Shooting his investigator would only be natural.' Although he made this argument, he didn't like the sound of it at all. 'Wat and Cwen are experienced in investigation and would know what to do if anything, erm, unfortunate happened to me.'

'He could be a desperate woman,' Cwen suggested.

'No,' Nult butted in, talking more to his club than to the people in the room. 'I almost had him, but he got away. Definitely a man.'

'I don't think that the killer will still be around.' The Abbot dropped his voice and hissed at Hermitage. 'For reasons we have already discussed.'

'Oh, yes?' Wat asked brightly. 'And what reasons are those?'

Abbot Abbo didn't even grace this with a reply.

'Must be something pretty interesting,' Cwen speculated. 'A killer sneaks into a monastery with a crossbow. Shoots a monk and then escapes. And there's no way he's coming back because of "reasons".'

'I imagine he doesn't want to be caught and taken before the authorities,' Wat offered. 'You know what those church authorities can be like. Very nasty. Very authoritarian.'

'True.' Cwen looked thoughtful. 'But a monk? I mean, it's a bit odd, isn't it? They haven't got anything worth stealing. What do you kill a monk for?'

'A couple of shillings?'

'Well, yes, but why?'

'Just don't like him?'

'With a crossbow? And monks are easy enough to avoid if you don't like them. Just stay away from monasteries.'

'Maybe he was someone a bit more interesting than just a monk?' Wat nodded to himself as he thought. 'Sorry Hermitage,' he acknowledged. 'You know, a noble's younger son who's been sent to take the habit. And then the older son decides that his life would be a lot neater without any brothers at all. We could find there's a whole family fallen to the crossbow killer.'

'Oh,' Cwen said. 'That sounds neat. The "crossbow killer".'

Wat warmed to the idea. 'We could have many a good night down at the tavern, speculating about Abbot Abbo and the crossbow killer.'

Abbot Abbo looked a bit alarmed at this.

'Or it could be the abbot's monastery,' Cwen sounded as if she was about to tell a tale of mystery full of wandering spirits. 'Maybe there's all sorts of things go on there that we wouldn't even dream of. For all we know, monks could be shot once a week.'

'That's right,' Wat snapped his fingers as if realising the truth of it. 'And that will need even longer in the tavern. We might ask the priest what sorts of things a monk would get killed for. Or what might go on in a monastery where that sort of thing happens. Couldn't reflect very well on an abbot, I'd have thought.'

'All right.' Abbo spoke loudly and held the palms of his hands up. 'You can come.'

Hermitage looked up, wondering what had changed the abbot's mind. Not that he wasn't grateful.

. . .

At least Abbot Abbo was right that it was only a short distance to the monastery. Brother Nult was a comforting presence on what could be a dangerous road, and the four of them were happy to stride along in his wake.

Hermitage had never been very good with directions, but he thought they'd headed north from Derby, into the thick of the Sherwood forest.

The abbot urged them to caution as he had heard that the king's court was in Nottingham just at the moment. That meant that any bit of woodland in the vicinity could be crawling with Normans intent on hunting and killing all the living creatures. Deer and boar were favourite, but they never hesitated if a person got in the way.

The Normans had made it very clear that this place was no longer Sciryuda, the woodland of the shire. Now it was Sherwood, the forest of the Normans. And anyone caught doing pretty much anything in their forest, other than walking through it minding their own business, was going to be in serious trouble. They were very keen on hunting; very keen indeed. They hadn't conquered the country to have the locals wandering about killing their deer and boar and the like.

It didn't do any good to point out that the deer and the

boar and the like were local and, being here before the Normans, were probably actually Saxon deer and boar and the like.

It didn't do to point anything out to a Norman at all, really. So, people kept quiet, let the Normans get on with what they wanted, and only killed the deer and the boar and the like when no one was watching.

Even this was curtailed as people came to realise what serious trouble entailed. It all seemed a bit extreme for the sake of a few animals when there were hundreds of the things around, but serious trouble involved a lot more death than folk were generally prepared to tolerate.

The hunting by locals decreased and the numbers of the deer and the boar increased until they became a positive nuisance: But still not as big a nuisance as a Norman with a sword in his hand, sitting on a horse complaining that you've killed his deer.

Through the winding paths of the forest, the abbot led them, until he came to one spot, no more remarkable than any other, at which point he led them off, away from the main thoroughfare.

'Who knew there were monasteries so close at hand,' Wat said as if disappointed that he was only now finding out, as he'd quite like to have paid a visit.

'A modest house.' The abbot repeated his description. 'The monastery of Woodhouse.'

'Convenient,' Cwen noted, looking at the preponderance of trees.

'And hidden away in the woods,' Wat added. 'Not the sort of place you'd come across by accident.'

'Indeed not,' Abbo replied with some significance.

Hermitage pondered what the significance might be.

Monasteries away from the beaten track could easily vanish from sight. Unless people were making a specific journey, such places could go unvisited for months on end. And to think that this place had been visited by a killer with a crossbow, a most unusual individual in his own right.

'I say,' he said.

'What do you say, Hermitage?' Cwen asked.

'Our killer would have to go to a lot of trouble to find this place.'

'That he would.'

'When I say our killer, I don't mean the person who's going to kill us; I mean the one we're looking for.'

'I think we get that.'

'So, he really was coming here specifically. To this monastery.' He knew the abbot had said Pewlet was killed for his Cathar thinking, but he couldn't believe that was a reasonable motive at all. If people went around killing one another for what they were thinking, where would it end? There wouldn't be anyone left at all in a few years. And who decided what thoughts deserved execution? No, a system like that was simply unthinkable.

'He could have gone somewhere a lot more convenient if all he wanted to do was kill a monk.'

'Or just waited by the side of the road until one walked by,' Wat suggested with a slight gleam in his eye.

'Quite.'

'It is as I said,' Abbo said, quietly, as if worried that the trees might hear. 'Brother Pewlet was sought out. No one else in the monastery was injured.'

'Apart from me,' Nult put in.

'Really?' Hermitage asked, thinking this might be significant.

'He walked into the door,' Abbo explained.

'I didn't walk into it, it was put in my way.' Nult turned to face them as he walked and pointedly rubbed his head.

'By the killer?' Cwen asked.

'That's right.' Nult clearly took some pride from banging his head on a door put there by a killer, rather than any old run-of-the-mill door.

'But you didn't see him?'

'It was dark.'

'You didn't notice anything about him?'

'In the dark?'

'Did he speak to you?'

'Nope.'

'He's hardly going to say "excuse me".' Wat gave a little snort. 'Not after he's just shot a monk.'

'I'm trying to find out as much as we can.' Cwen's implication was clear; she was useful, Wat was not. She turned back to Nult. 'You didn't feel his clothes?'

'No, I did not.' Nult was mightily offended. 'I don't go round feeling people's clothes in the dark.'

'He didn't brush against you?'

'It was a killer,' Nult explained, impatiently. 'It wasn't Brother Hengard.'

'Brother Hengard?' Cwen asked Abbo.

'A completely different problem.' The abbot waved this one away. 'I don't think we can solve Brother Hengard. A killer is quite enough of a challenge.'

Cwen just shook her head. 'So, this killer at the door didn't say anything. He didn't make any noises, he didn't push you out of the way. Nothing at all?'

'No,' Nult insisted. 'Nothing at all.' He glared at her as if she was accusing him of something. 'I even loosed a rock at him.'

'A rock?' Hermitage asked, now picturing an awful scene.

'From my sling.' Nult produced a sling from his habit. 'I mainly use it for the rats.'

'Charming,' Wat said. 'Off the beaten track and full of rats.'

'You didn't hit him?' Cwen stuck to the main subject.

'No,' Nult was now sounding quite cross. 'It was dark, as I keep saying. I can't see people in the dark and I can't hit them with a rock.'

'But the killer could hit the monk,' Hermitage mused, mainly to himself.

Cwen nodded. 'He must have been close. If it really was that dark, what are the chances of hitting a monk with a crossbow.'

'With a crossbow itself, quite high, I'd have thought.' Wat put in. 'With a bolt, more of a problem.'

Cwen gave him a very good glare. 'If you're not going to be helpful, shut up.'

Wat shrugged.

'In fact, shut up anyway.' She directed her attention to Hermitage. 'Perhaps the monk knew his killer?'

'Knew him?' Hermitage thought that knowing killers was not the sort of thing a decent monk should do. He was King's Investigator, he'd met more killers than most and he wouldn't associate with any of them.

'I mean knew who he was. Recognised him.'

'In the dark?'

'Perhaps they spoke?' Cwen seemed to think she was on to something. 'Our killer says "Hello," what did you say his name was?'

'Pewlet,' Abbo said, with clear disappointment that the

deceased's name wasn't even remembered.

'Yes, that's him. Hello Pewlet old friend. Oh, hello, is that you? Yes, it is, why don't you come over here. Oh, all right. Point, shoot, dead. There you are.' She held her hands out, glad that she'd explained it all.

'It still doesn't explain why he was killed.' Hermitage couldn't accept that Pewlet knew his killer; that he knew any killers at all, come to that. But he didn't have a sensible alternative.

'Well, no,' Cwen admitted. 'But why would anyone who knew Pewlet want to kill him?'

'Why would anyone want to kill him at all? That's the question,' Wat spoke up again, but sounding sensible this time. 'This monastery, out of the way in the woods. One monk picked out in the dark and then the killer escapes? I'd say someone was after Pewlet specifically. Instead of trying to think who the killer was, we think about why anyone would want to kill Pewlet.' He cast a serious, questioning look at Abbo.

'The son of that noble?' Cwen asked.

'Could be. Although, from the look on dear Abbot Abbo's face, I'd say there was more to it than that.' Wat smiled with satisfaction.

'Which is not a discussion for the middle of the woods,' Abbo instructed. 'We have not far to go now. Further consideration can wait until we are settled.' He said no more and walked on behind Nult.

'Are you sure you didn't get him with your sling?' Cwen asked Nult. 'After all, it was dark. You might have hit him and not know? We could be looking for someone with a big lump on their head. That would make it easier. Man with crossbow and lump.'

'No,' Nult confirmed. 'I missed. I know I did. I could hear the rock fly away and hit the gate. And he wasn't making any complaint when he limped over me and out of the gate.'

Cwen was so silent it caused Nult to turn his head towards her.

'He what?' she said in her scary voice.

'Wasn't making any complaint.'

'I got that bit. Wasn't making any complaint when he what?'

'Went out of the gate,' Nult insisted.

'You said he limped out of the gate.'

'Right, yes, limped out of the gate.'

'Are you saying he had a limp?'

'Did I not mention the limp?'

'No, you did not.'

Nult tried to make light of this, without success. 'Ah,' he said. 'He had a limp.'

'Thank you. Now we're looking for a crossbow killer with a limp, who knew Pewlet. Can't be many of them about.'

'Unless there's lots of people want to kill him,' Wat said with a smile. 'Which we'll find out when we sit down with the Abbot and he explains all about Brother Pewlet and what made him so popular with killers.'

Hermitage knew that this was a discussion they were going to have to have. He worried about how Wat and Cwen would deal with the details of the Cathari heresy. They would doubtless be horrified, and the situation would need careful handling.

Caput VI Heresy is Inadmissible

'They think what?' Wat burst out laughing when Hermitage had finished his sombre explanation. That wasn't the response he'd expected at all. His words had been horrifying even to his own ears, and he was speaking them.

Abbo had indicated that Hermitage could do the explanations, the ideas doubtless being too sinful to even pass through an abbot's head.

They were sitting in Abbo's chamber in the monastery, which, it turned out, was very well named. The whole place was indeed made of wood, much of it seeming to be entire trees of great age. This place had clear Saxon origins and had doubtless been undisturbed on this spot for many years.

Over those years the wood had mellowed and softened, and the furnishings and passage of thousands of monks had blended it into its landscape. It was a warm and comfortable place, now seeming to grow from the ground, rather than being placed upon it.

The room they were in had a window looking out towards the chapel and a simple desk and chair, along with a small altar for the abbot's private devotions. More chairs had to be fetched along with wine and food after their journey, but there was still room for them to spread out as Hermitage explained all about the Cathari.

Cwen was looking thoughtful. 'So, there are two Gods?' she asked.

'No, no, no.' Hermitage should have known that this was a bad idea. In fact, he did know that it was a bad idea, but there was Brother Pewlet to think about. 'Of course there aren't two Gods. There's only one God. That's perfectly clear.'

'But you said...,' Cwen was frowning.

'The Cathari believe that the devil created the earth and all things physical.' He dropped his voice as he said this, so very wrong was the idea. Even the walls of the monastery should not be forced to listen. 'God created all things spiritual. They think that the God of the Old Testament and the God of the New Testament are different.'

'Isn't there a lot of smiting and the like in the old bit?' Cwen asked.

'The old bit,' Hermitage repeated, with a sigh. 'Yes, smiting and a vengeful God.'

'Which could be the devil.'

'No, it couldn't,' Hermitage almost shouted. 'There is only one God and the Cathari are heretics. It's simple; they're wrong.'

'I see.' Cwen didn't sound convinced.

'And, because of their heretic beliefs, they want nothing to do with the physical world and shun all pleasure and comfort.'

Cwen looked around the bare wooden walls of this monastery stuck in the middle of the forest. 'Don't you do that as well?'

'It's not the same at all,' Hermitage explained, carefully.

'And the church does not look kindly on these Cathari?' Wat checked, still smirking slightly.

'Of course not,' Hermitage thought that would be obvious.

'And Pewlet was one?'

'No, he wasn't.'

'I'm lost.'

Abbo took up the discussion. 'Brother Pewlet was not a Cathari. As far as I know, there are no Cathari in this country at all. Their heresy is mainly in the east, but that does not stop us knowing of their beliefs. So that we can be on our guard if nothing else. Pewlet knew them and, being a thoughtful brother, he considered them.'

'And that's enough to get you shot, is it?' Wat asked.

Although it sounded very blunt, it was the question Hermitage wanted answered. Well, he knew the answer really, it wasn't enough to get you shot. Or, at least, it shouldn't be.

'Normally, no,' Abbo said.

'Normally, eh? That's comforting.' Wat rolled his eyes.

'But Pewlet confided in me that he had found some of the Cathari reasoning to be sound.'

Hermitage butted in. 'In the sense of a sound argument, not that they were right.'

'There's a difference?' Cwen asked.

'Oh, yes. Let me give you an example. Men fight horses, is a perfectly reasonable statement, isn't it? It's not nonsense. The words are proper words and they have been put together in the correct order.'

'Sounds like nonsense,' Cwen said.

'I saw a man fight a horse once,' Wat put in. 'Of course, he was drunk. The man, not the horse.'

'That's not the point.' Hermitage was in danger of losing the point. 'If I said the man is a horse, that would be nonsense. It's simply not a statement that makes any sense.'

'Of course,' Wat was going on. 'The horse might have been drunk as well. You can take a horse to water, but it would rather have beer.'

'All Pewlet meant,' Hermitage pressed on in the face of all this difficulty, 'was that some of the statements of the Cathari are not nonsense. I imagine he concluded that a lot of them are, but some maybe not.'

'Did they have horses?' Wat asked.

'Can we forget the horses,' Hermitage pleaded. 'The Cathari may well argue that the world was created in six days. No one would disagree with that. We know that's true. When they then say that it was done by the devil, well, that is nonsense. Doesn't make sense at all. But Pewlet didn't believe that bit.'

'How do we know?' Cwen said. 'He's dead.'

'Because no one would.'

'Apart from the Cathari.'

'Well, yes, but then they're the heretics.' Hermitage was glad they'd come to a sensible conclusion at last.

'So, it's all right to shoot heretics, yes?' Wat sought confirmation. 'Whether they've got horses or not.'

'Well, no,' Hermitage said.

Abbot Abbo didn't look quite so sure.

'It's not all right to shoot anyone. But Pewlet wasn't a heretic anyway.'

'Someone might have thought he was,' Wat pointed out. 'If he went around saying how these Cathari were making some good arguments.'

Hermitage had to admit that this was a possibility. He didn't like to raise the whole area of the more authoritarian elements of the church, who probably thought that shooting heretics was too good for them.

'And let's be honest,' Wat said, leaving a helpful pause. 'Who is worried about getting rid of heretics, apart from the church authorities?'

'I hardly think the church authorities would go around with crossbows shooting possible heretics,' Hermitage dismissed the idea.

'And I can't think of anyone else who'd want to,' Wat replied. 'Anyone who'd even know what a Cathari is, let alone want to put a hole in one.'

'Who do you think did it then?' Cwen asked Abbo, quite rudely, to Hermitage's mind.

'That's why I came for Brother Hermitage. He finds out who killed people. Or so I thought.'

'He does,' Cwen confirmed, her teeth clenched. 'But part of all that is finding out why it was done. People don't just pop up and do it. Unless it's a battle or something, but then Hermitage doesn't do battles. You may not know who did it, but you think you know why it was done; because Pewlet had heretical thoughts. That narrows it down to people who want to kill heretics.'

'Heresies such as the Cathari are an abomination to all,' Abbot Abbo lectured Cwen. 'Any right-thinking person would want to be rid of them.'

'A right-thinking person with a limp and a crossbow then? That's who we're looking for.' Cwen sniffed.

Wat took a more conciliatory approach. 'Come on Abbo,' he cajoled. 'You must suspect someone in the church or at least someone connected to it. I'm not saying our limping crossbow killer was a priest or a monk or one of the others.'

'Others?' Hermitage had to ask.

'Yes, you know, all the others. Novitiatings, nuns, bishops, all that lot.'

'I hardly think a bishop is going to limp around with a crossbow.' Feeling ashamed of himself, Hermitage found the image quite amusing.

'Exactly,' Wat agreed.

'Exactly?'

'A bishop wouldn't do it himself. He'd get someone to do it for him.' He snapped his fingers. 'The castigatori.'

'The castigatori?' Abbot Abbo was incredulous.

'Don't sound surprised. We met them, didn't we Hermitage?'

Hermitage nodded.

The abbot explained, with little patience. 'The castigatori are humble and pious men who travel the country ensuring that the establishments of the church maintain proper order and procedure.'

'The ones we met were nasty, devious, violent and seriously lacking in piety or humility.'[7]

'I can just see them with a crossbow,' Cwen added. 'They held me captive and wanted to take Wat in front of some bishop or other.'

The abbot looked as if he was not in the least surprised to hear this.

'So,' Wat went on. 'If some bishop in charge of heresy heard about Pewlet, he might well send one of his castigatori to get rid of the problem.'

Abbo shook his head, sadly. 'Not in a monastery in the middle of the night. If "some bishop in charge of heresy", as you so neatly put it, wanted to deal with Brother Pewlet he would simply summon him. No need for crossbows, limps or anything else. I would receive a missive telling me to send the Brother and off he would go.'

'Never to be seen again, eh?' Wat suggested.

'I do believe your trade has warped your ideas,' Abbo said.

'Warped,' Hermitage said, with a smile. 'Like a loom has a weft and a…,' he trailed off and his smile departed as he saw no one else was interested in the amusing play on words.

'You have to admit that murder for heresy is a pretty special field of expertise,' Wat pressed on. 'Not the sort of

---

[7] It's The Tapestry of Death. You might as well read the full list at the start of the book.

thing the average man digging turnips concerns himself with.'

'True,' Abbo accepted. 'But there may be those who see it as their divine right to take action, where the body of the church has no such intent.'

'I see.' Wat said this very slowly and nodded at Hermitage. 'And you know of such people?'

'Of course not.' The abbot sounded insulted by the suggestion. 'But there are always individuals who take things into their own hands; sometimes regardless of instruction to the contrary.'

'And if one of these hands has a crossbow?' Cwen said.

Abbo gave the slightest of shrugs. 'I merely suggest that it could be a possibility.'

'So, why not go to the body of the church and report your suspicions?' Wat asked. 'You've got a dead monk to show them.'

Abbo steepled his fingers and seemed to be considering his words very carefully. 'If this is the case, and I make no accusations or suggestions, it might also be true that some person or persons in authority is, in some way, connected to one of these individuals.'

'Or is one of these individuals,' Wat concluded.

Abbo said nothing.

Hermitage just looked from one face to the other. They looked back as if giving him the time to catch up. 'Someone in the church thinks that they can shoot heretics,' he said. 'Without permission.'

'Or even thinks that it's their duty to do so,' Cwen added.

'And if the King's Investigator could expose them, the full authority of the king would be brought to bear, instead of some even higher up bishop who would bury the whole thing. Along with the dead monk.' Wat looked quite impressed if this was Abbo's approach.

'Puts Hermitage in a rather dangerous position, don't you think?' Cwen said.

Hermitage didn't like the sound of that at all. Where was the danger?

'If this person, or people, don't want to be revealed, they might decide that shooting a King's Investigator is next on the list.'

Ah, there was the danger.

'I hardly think so.' At least Abbot Abbo sounded confident. 'The church is as much in fear of the Normans as anyone. Trying to kill Hermitage would be like trying to kill King William himself.'

'And there's a few who have tried that,' Wat said, unhelpfully.

'Just so I can get this straight,' Hermitage said. He thought he had it quite straight already, but it was always worth checking. Perhaps there was some detail he'd missed. One that might take some of the danger away. 'It is possible that some person or group within the church has taken it upon themselves to shoot heretics.'

'Not necessarily shoot them,' Cwen said. 'Perhaps it was just shooting this time. Could be poisoning, stabbing, anything, really.'

'Wonderful. These shooting, poisoning, stabbing people did for poor Pewlet and we need to find out who they are.'

'Well, you do,' Abbo said. 'In your official capacity.'

Hermitage felt even more horror that the abbot had thought he could do this on his own.

'But they might not have actually done the shooting on this occasion, they just got someone else to do it for them.'

'Paid someone, probably,' Wat said. 'A hired killer.'

'Hired killer, I see. And they might be important people of the church.'

'But secret,' Cwen said. 'Not wanting to be found out.'

Hermitage nodded to himself. He was quite impressed that he hadn't already jumped out of the window and run away. 'A secret group within the church is hiring killers to murder heretics and we just need to find them.'

'And the actual killer,' Cwen added. 'After all, he's the one who did whatever you do to a crossbow to make it shoot.'

'Pulled the trigger,' Wat said.

'Really?' Cwen sounded quite interested.

'Oh, yes,' Wat sounded quite keen. He adopted the pose of a crossbowman. 'Click, whoosh, thud.' He then clutched his chest and stuck his tongue out, presumably indicating that he'd been shot.

Hermitage tried to ignore the performance. 'We then take it all to,' he swallowed, 'King William, and let him deal with them?'

'That's it,' Abbo smiled as if Hermitage would get on with it straight away. 'In fact, the king's court being in Nottingham at the moment could be very useful. We could get the information to him quickly.

'Before someone click, whoosh, thuds us,' Cwen said.

Abbo ignored her. 'The king could take it in hand straight away.'

'What if he doesn't want to?' Hermitage asked.

'Who doesn't want to what?'

'What if King William doesn't want to take a secret church group of heretic murderers in hand? What if he doesn't care? He doesn't care about much.'

'I'm sure he will. It is important.'

Hermitage hoped he looked worried, and that it was

66

catching. 'You'd be surprised at the things King William thinks are important. A secret group of killers might be just what he's looking for.'

'His immortal soul would be in peril,' Abbot Abbo pointed out.

'As I said, I think you'd be surprised at things he thinks important. And if he doesn't want to do anything about them, we're left with a secret group of killers who are probably quite annoyed. With us.'

'I'm sure it won't come to that.'

Hermitage wasn't sure at all. 'The first thing we need to do is find the limping crossbowman. Only through him will we find out anything.' He hoped that finding the limping crossbowman would mean they didn't need to find out anything else at all. Perhaps it was just something personal after all. He was warming to the idea of the noble's son. No group, no secrets, no one wanting to kill anyone else at all, Pewlet having been done.

'And how do we do that?' Abbo asked.

'Erm,' Hermitage scrambled around in his head for an idea. 'Make enquiries,' he said.

'Make what?' Cwen turned her nose up.

'From inquiro, the Latin to seek, search. We ask around. Someone may have seen a limping man with a crossbow. There can't have been many about on the night in question.'

'Excellent plan.' Abbo was impressed. He got up as if it was all decided and he could leave Hermitage to sort the whole business out. The others rose, realising that they were being invited to go away. Abbo beckoned Hermitage to draw close and whispered in his ear. 'It seems that you and your, erm, friends have this all in hand. I'm sure you understand that it wouldn't do for me to be seen in the company of erm, these particular friends?'

Hermitage was puzzled and looked it.

'Wat the Weaver?' Abbo said as if no more was necessary. 'I know Pewlet has been murdered, and this must be resolved, but I am confident that you will manage.'

Hermitage was glad that one of them was confident.

As they moved to leave the room, the door opened, and the prior put his head around the door.

'Ah, Prior Thulred. I'm glad it's you. You can meet Brother Hermitage and, erm, some other people.' He nodded into the room.

'I'd like to,' Thulred replied. 'But we are having some trouble at the main gate, I think you had best come.'

'Trouble?'

'Someone demanding entrance.'

Hermitage felt his insides go soft. Had the secret group found them already?

'We are an open house,' Abbo explained. 'All are welcome. What's the problem?'

'That's what we've tried to say, but the monk in question says he's not having any of that.'

'A monk? Why on earth is a monk demanding entrance to a monastery at all? Especially one that's not even shut?'

'He says he needs to be officially received.'

Abbot Abbo just shook his head at this. 'Perhaps it is some senior abbot,' he said to the others. 'Many of them have strange ideas.'

'Not an abbot.' Thulred seemed very flustered by the experience he had had with this new arrival. 'He's very loud and says that he's the King's Investigator, Brother Simon?'

Caput VII Investigatori

Abbot Abbo cast a questioning look at Hermitage. 'Brother Simon?'

'Oh, my,' Hermitage gulped.

'Is there another investigator?'

'Well. No, not really.'

'Not really?'

Wat spoke up. 'Brother Simon thinks he is the King's Investigator.'

'He thinks he is?' The abbot obviously wasn't finding this helpful.

'He was appointed by a fellow called Nicodemus, who didn't have the authority to appoint him in the first place and then, when the king found out, Harold, that is, he was unappointed.[8]'

Abbo's eyebrows rose. 'Nicodemus eh? I know that name.' It didn't sound as if the knowledge was of the good kind.

Wat smiled. 'I'm sure you'll find out all about it. Brother Simon is, how can I put it? An idiot. A pompous one at that. God knows what he's doing here, but if anyone is going to demand entry at an open door it'll be Simon.'

Abbo just shook his head in bewilderment. 'Thulred, you had best go let him in.'

'That's what I've been trying to do. I think the abbot had better do it.'

Abbo gave Thulred a very blank expression but then beckoned that the prior should lead the way.

Hermitage found himself harbouring thoughts of a sinfully

---

[8] All of which is nearly explained in The Heretics of De'Ath

pleasurable nature. Brother Simon was a most difficult fellow and was very hard to manage. Abbot Abbo was the immovable object to Simon's irresistible force; it would be fascinating to see how this turned out.

Stepping briskly to the main gate, wearing his impatience and irritation like extra habits, Abbot Abbo came upon Brother Simon, waiting to be received. The man was gazing around at the condition of the monastery and the look on his face betrayed his thoughts; "Oh, dear, oh, dear, oh, dear".

As Hermitage beheld him once more he couldn't help his first impression returning. It was as if monastic orders had opened their doors to the animal kingdom, and the weasels were the first to arrive.

He knew that it was possible for a man's nose to grow with age, spreading out and becoming more bulbous. Surely they never actually got longer, particularly not when that man had started with the biggest nose in Christendom in the first place?

Brother Simon's protuberance, always more like the beak of some deformed goose, seemed to have spent the last few years subjugating the rest of his features. It was as if the whole of his head was being slowly sucked in until one day there would be only a nose. Once the eyes disappeared Simon wouldn't have anything to look down his nose with.

'Who are you?' Abbot Abbot demanded, very brusquely.

That put Brother Simon off not one jot. He stood proud and as tall as he could get. 'I am Brother Simon, the King's Investigator,' he said, without really looking at anyone.

'No, you're not,' the Abbot replied.

That did put him off.

'I most certainly am.' Simon's high and mighty were supporting one another admirably.

'No, you aren't. Brother Hermitage here is the King's Investigator.'

Brother Simon did now bother to look at the people he was talking to. That put him off even more. He peered at Hermitage as if trying to recall an insignificant face. When he turned and saw Wat grinning at him, he almost jumped backwards.

'Ah, Father,' he called to the abbot. 'Beware.' He even went so far as to raise his arm and point at Wat as if at some evil spectre. 'You are duped.'

'Not by you, I'm not.' Abbo folded his arms now. 'You are not the King's Investigator, Brother Hermitage is. I have witnessed his work first-hand and can testify to his skill. I hear that you, on the other hand, call yourself King's Investigator, never having been appointed by a king.'

Simon waved this away as he regained some of his composure. 'The king himself does not handle such matters. There are people at court to deal with this sort of thing.'

'That fraud, Nicodemus?' the Abbot enquired. 'I think it is you who have been duped.'

Simon just shook his head sadly at this poor old man's befuddlement.

'And I imagine that impersonating the King's Investigator without authority is a very serious offence.' The abbot went on, not really talking to Simon. He managed to ignore the man completely and talk as if he wasn't there.

That really did put Brother Simon off. Being the centre of attention was not so much an occasional pleasure as a way of life.

'King William does like Hermitage,' Cwen mused. 'Last time we met, Hermitage solved a really nasty murder right on the king's doorstep.'

'In his camp,' Wat added with a supportive nod. 'Very grateful, he was.'

'And now some fellow called Simon is found wandering the country, claiming to be William's investigator?' The abbot sounded quite worried about this. 'It is probably our duty to send word to the king, let him deal with it.'

'He deals with things so well,' Cwen agreed on the course of action. 'So well that they seldom come back to bother anyone a second time.'

'Many of them can't walk after they've been dealt with,' Wat added. 'Which makes it much more difficult to go anywhere anymore.'

Despite this horrifying conversation, horrifying to Hermitage, anyway, Simon seemed to be only increasing in confidence, which was strange.

'Ah, my poor fellows,' he sympathised. 'Would that it was so simple.'

The abbot looked at him as if he was waiting for a drunken novice to explain where he'd got the mead from in the first place.

'The details of my appointment are irrelevant. It is my business that takes priority.'

'That's neatly dismissed the fact that he was never appointed and isn't the King's Investigator,' Wat noted.

'My mission this day is not of the king's bidding.'

'But then none of your missions has been,' Cwen pointed out. 'In fact, I'm not sure you've actually been given a mission at all. From what I hear, you make them up yourself.'

Hermitage found it remarkable that all these revelations about the true nature of Brother Simon seemed to wash over him like water off a duck's back when there wasn't any water; or a duck. It seemed that any word of criticism or question appeared to Simon's ears to be in a foreign language; a really obscure one that nobody spoke. He genuinely seemed not to understand what was being said to him.

Hermitage thought that this would be a remarkably useful skill to acquire. Whenever anyone criticised him, which happened quite a lot, he took it to heart, gave it considered thought and vowed to improve in the future; even if the criticism was entirely unjustified or plain wrong.

He had heard about people who didn't care what others said about them; he'd never met anyone who was actually incapable of hearing it.

Simon held a hand up to indicate that Cwen should be quiet; never a good move by anyone.

Cwen clamped her teeth. 'If I punch him on his massive nose do you think he'd bleed to death?'

The Abbot made a calming gesture, which Simon acknowledged with a slight nod.

'It would be unseemly for you to strike a monk,' Abbo reprimanded gently, much to Cwen's disappointment. 'Brother Nult would be much better at that sort of thing.' He looked intently at Simon. 'If our Brother here does not come up with a very good explanation for his arrival.'

Simon did swallow now. Probably because being punched on the nose worked in all languages and was very hard to ignore.

'I am sent,' he recovered his condescension. 'By an important gathering of the church. A great conclave, if you will, that has trusted me with its task.'

Hermitage glanced at Wat and the others. Was this the secret group of heretic murderers? He couldn't help but think that if they'd chosen Brother Simon to deal with their business, they might not be as dangerous as he'd thought.

Mind you, they had shot a monk, or so it seemed, that was dangerous enough.

'I understand that a monk died here recently,' Simon went on.

'Monks do,' Abbo replied.

'This one was shot. With a crossbow.'

Abbo frowned. 'You are remarkably well-informed.' He peered hard at Simon as if trying to see his innermost thoughts.

Hermitage suspected that these would be largely about Brother Simon and wouldn't help much.

'Walk up and down for me,' the abbot instructed.

'I beg your pardon?'

'Walk up and down for me. Just here. Now.'

'I see no reason at all...,'

'DO it!' the abbot barked with all his authority.

Recovering from the surprise, Simon did as he was told and took a few paces up and down. As he did so he looked as if he was magnanimously pandering to the whims of an old man.

'Hm.' The abbot scowled. 'No limp.' He nodded to Hermitage and the others.

They saw the reason for the test.

'I don't think he could handle a crossbow,' Wat said. 'Probably shoot himself instead of anyone else.'

'What are you talking about?' Simon demanded.

'Just seeing if you're the killer,' the abbot explained as if it was quite natural. 'Turn up here, knowing all about a monk who's been shot? It's very suspicious, isn't it, Hermitage?'

'Oh, er, yes,' Hermitage said, agreeing that it was.

Simon sniffed at the impertinence. 'I am charged with discovering details of the event and reporting back to the conclave.'

'I see,' Abbo nodded. 'And how did they know?'

'How did they know what?'

Abbo sighed. 'How did they know a monk had been shot? It only happened two days ago. I have been to summon the King's Investigator, the real one, and no one else has left the place.'

Simon simply gave a knowing nod.

'Well?' Abbo wasn't satisfied with a nod.

'These things are known,' Simon said, with a twist of mystery.

'Obviously, they're known. Otherwise, you wouldn't be here, would you?' He turned to Wat. 'You were right about him.'

Wat shrugged.

'My question was how are they known? By what means did the knowledge of the death come to the conclave?'

'That is hardly for the likes of you and me to know.' Simon tried to put the abbot in his place.

'Not for the likes of you, no, I can see that. I, on the other hand, am the abbot of this house and I do need to know. I need to know how some conclave was aware of the death of a dear brother before anyone else.' He paused. 'Unless they had something to do with it, of course.'

Brother Simon looked rather lost, for once.

'I don't suppose anyone told you what you were doing or why,' Wat said as if so much was obvious. 'Knowing how Brother Simon works.' He nodded to the abbot, ignoring Simon. 'As soon as someone in authority tells him to do something, he does it. And if they give him a nice title to go with it, so much the better. This conclave probably said he could be King's Investigator again if he just did one little job for them.'

Cwen joined in. 'Pop along to the monastery in the woods and find out what you can about a dead monk, just been shot with a crossbow. Who did it? Oh, don't worry about details like that. Just come back and tell us what you find.'

'And what is it you're supposed to do then?' Wat continued. 'We know there's a dead monk. Are you to go back and say yes, there really is a dead monk? Perhaps they're checking that the job got done properly, and you're just the idiot to do their bidding.'

Simon was once again shaking his head at the poor understanding these people had of significant issues. 'I can waste no more time on these bizarre speculations. I have important business, to which you are not privy. I have neither the duty nor the inclination to explain anything.'

'Nor the ability,' Cwen stifled a laugh, but not very well.

'I don't suppose it's occurred to you,' Wat said slowly as if being helpful. 'That the people of this conclave are the ones who had the brother here murdered. And that when you take word back that it all went well, they'll kill you as well.'

'Tying up loose ends,' Hermitage put in, enthusiastically. He'd come up with the idea from Wat's weaving. It fitted investigation quite well.

Wat nodded, sagely. 'You'll be the only one who can connect the members of the conclave to events here. Better you were out of the way, really. Much neater.' He smiled at Simon. 'After all, we don't know who they are, you haven't told us.'

There was the slightest twitch at the corner of Simon's mouth.

'Aha.' Cwen was still looking at him intently, most of her intent being towards his nose. 'You don't know either.'

'What?' Simon dismissed this babbling.

'You don't know who the conclave is either. You probably just thought they looked important so did what you were told. What did they do, keep their cowls down and talk in whispers? Or maybe you never met them at all?' She was clear that this was unbelievable. 'What did they do, send a secret message?'

The twitch on Simon's face said that this was a bit close to the truth.

'Proverbs fourteen, verse fourteen,' the abbot said.

Wat and Cwen looked puzzled.

'The foolish will be filled up by his own ways.' Hermitage gave the passage.

'Couldn't have put it better myself,' Wat said, which was rather blasphemous.

'Shall we tell you what we think?' Wat asked, sounding very polite. 'Would you like to know what we've thought about the murder? Or would you just like to go back to your conclave and see what they'd like you to do next?'

'Like die,' Cwen said.

Simon sighed that he was willing to accommodate whatever rambling nonsense they'd come up with.

Hermitage gave Wat a warning glance not to go into too much detail about the heresy. He hoped that was the message he conveyed, and not that he'd got something stuck in his eye.

'We think that this conclave of yours likes to get rid of monks who know too much. Or ones that know the wrong things. Or ones who just ask questions. They sent a killer with a crossbow and now they've sent you to check that the job has been done. They sound like pretty dangerous people to us, and we're going to try and find out who they are, using the King's Investigator.' He nodded towards Hermitage, who smiled.

'But I'm sure that all of this is of no interest to you, who know far better than us that they had nothing to do with it. In fact, you know better than everyone. Still, you've got our thoughts now. Do what you will with them.'

Simon's smile said that he had spent quite long enough accommodating these ill-informed people and their quaint views.

'Well, if that is all, I had best be on my way.'

'That would be the very best, yes,' Abbo agreed.

'Ah,' Simon raised a finger. 'The name of this monk.'

'The murdered monk?' The abbot looked and sounded deeply angry. 'The young brother who has been taken from us by the actions of men of evil? Men who do the work of the devil and who will surely go to hell, along with those who associate with them?'

'Er, yes,' Simon seemed to wonder what the abbot was going on about.

'Brother Pewlet. Remember that name. Burn it into your memory.' The abbot pointed an accusing finger at Simon.

'Of course,' Simon said as if remembering one name was not going to be difficult. He gave them all looks that said he was truly puzzled by their bizarre and disrespectful treatment. He had sympathy for them, but a man in his position had more important things to deal with. All that; in one look.

Turning his back, he gave no wave of acknowledgement or thanks; he simply left.

'At least he didn't demand to be let out of the open door,' Wat observed.

'That brother.' The abbot pointed again, his finger now shaking slightly. 'If anyone deserves to come to an ignominious end.'

'Father!' Hermitage was shocked at the idea.

'I know, I know. But the likes of Brother Pewlet lost to us while a.., a thing like that still walks abroad. And thinking the best of himself while he does it.'

They stood and watched the departing back of Brother Simon for several moments before the abbot turned back to the monastery.

'I've just had an idea,' Cwen said, without moving.

'Oh, yes?' Wat asked. 'I think he's too far away to be hit by a rock.'

'No, no,' she said, with some impatience. 'Why don't we follow him?'

'Follow him?' Hermitage asked, thinking it sounded rather rude. 'What do you mean, follow him?'

'You know what following things is. They go somewhere, and you go along afterwards. Follow. Probably from the Latin followamus, or something.'

'No,' Hermitage was thoughtful. 'The Latin would be sequitur. Not the same at all.'

'It doesn't matter,' Cwen snapped. 'What we do is the following. We want to know who this conclave is, he's going to the conclave. We follow we find out.'

'Gosh,' Hermitage was impressed. 'I'd never have thought following people would be part of investigation. It's a bit intrusive, isn't it? I mean we haven't asked if he'd mind or anything.'

'Did Pewlet get asked if he'd mind being shot?'

'Probably not,' Hermitage had to admit.

'Asking Brother Simon's permission for anything is not going to worry me,' Wat said. 'Sounds like a good idea. Coming Abbo?'

'It is an excellent idea.' The abbot had quite a devious smile on his face; for an abbot. 'I must stay here and tend the monastery, but you follow him. Follow him to this conclave, discover them, expose them and bring them to justice.'

They all nodded.

'Especially Brother Simon,' the abbot even snarled now. 'That monk needs more justice than most.'

Caput VIII The Followers

The day was well on its way to the close of business before they quickly gathered their things and set off after Simon. The abbot's travel to and from Derby had taken the entire day and so it was evening before Brother Simon even arrived. The clouds had left the sky and the bright moon once more lit the night, making travel easy. Even so, they could expect the so-called investigator to stop somewhere before long.

'Don't you think he's going to spot us?' Hermitage asked. 'The three of us tramping along the trail behind him is not going to go unnoticed.'

'I'm not sure Simon would notice a host of angels behind him,' Wat said. 'Unless they were there to praise him.'

'Wat, really,' Hermitage scolded the borderline blasphemy.

They weren't within sight of Simon, so he would hardly wonder what three people were doing behind him if he turned around. They had seen him take the path back to the road from the monastery and when they got there, saw signs that he had turned south; fresh sandal prints sat in the dust and dirt of the track - it being fortunate that sensible people kept off the road after dark.

'I say, this is like real tracking,' Hermitage was quite excited.

Wat just looked at him.

'Come on Wat,' Cwen rebuked him. 'Investigation, from the Latin, vestigare, to track.'

'Is it?' Wat asked.

'Dear oh, dear, do you never pay attention?' She rolled her eyes at Hermitage.

Wat just looked puzzled by the criticism. 'I did notice that

Simon had no pack,' he said. 'Which means that he needs somewhere to stay. He can't just make camp at the side of the road.'

Hermitage was quite impressed with that thinking. The only thing he'd noticed was Simon's nose.

'Not that I can imagine him making camp anyway,' Wat went on. 'Unless the animals of the forest were going to come out and do it for him. Which is probably only right and proper, considering how important he is.'

'And considering how important he is,' Cwen continued the reasoning, 'he will probably impose himself on some unsuspecting local and demand that he be given accommodation. And food and drink and anything else he wants.'

Hermitage could see that this might well be the case.

As they walked on along the path there was no sign of any activity at all. No one would be travelling at this time of night, but neither was there sign of any campfire made by those who were between towns on their journey. It was quite common for travellers to band together of an evening and create a little encampment. By this means they shared the work and the fire and avoided the attentions of any robbers who would not fancy their chances against a large group; unless one of the group turned out to be the robber, in which case the others would wake in the morning to find all their possessions gone.

Of course, there were always Normans to worry about; they didn't care whether the group they were attacking was small or large. But then there was no point worrying about Normans at all. They would do whatever they liked, no matter what precautions you put in place.

'Over there,' Cwen pointed off into the woods to their

right.

Just off the track, there was a hovel. Either that or the falling leaves of a hundred autumns had decided to settle into a hovel-like shape. Timbers had fallen from the trees to land upright in the ground, making walls. Sticks and smaller pieces lay across the top to form the roof. This was clearly not the hovel of a master carpenter. The whole thing could be easily cleared away with a good strong broom.

This entire construction could have been mistaken for an accident of nature if it wasn't for the slow plume of smoke that wound from the centre of the roof. A fire seemed a very courageous thing to start in a house built mainly of kindling, but it was a sign of habitation.

'Do we knock?' Hermitage asked, not sure of what they were going to do.

'On what?' Cwen asked. 'If we knock on that thing it will fall down.'

'And we don't want Simon to know we're following, do we?' Wat asked Hermitage to think about this.

'Ah, no. We don't.'

'Although,' Cwen was thoughtful.

'What is it?' Hermitage asked, encouragingly. 'Another idea about investigation? The last one was very good.'

'What if he did know we were following?'

Hermitage considered this. 'I think he might ask us to stop.'

'And if we say no.'

'Knowing Simon, he will just sit down somewhere and refuse to move until we stop following.'

'We only want to meet this conclave of his. That's a reasonable request, isn't it?'

'To normal people, it might be,' Wat said. 'Brother

Simon's not normal though, is he?'

Hermitage had to agree. 'He sees the conclave as his secret. He's hardly likely to share it with anyone. He's probably been sworn to protect them and already thinks we're the worst of the worst. Well, Wat is.'

Cwen nodded her agreement at that. Wat seemed quite happy with it as well.

'But,' Cwen went on as if coming to the nub of her idea. 'What if we let him know that we are following and that if he doesn't take us to his conclave, we'll do something horrible to him. Well, Wat will.'

Wat seemed to think that he could manage that.

Hermitage was horrified. 'Cwen! You mean we threaten him?'

'Erm,' Cwen thought about it. 'Yes, that's it. Threaten him. Tell us what we want, or else.'

'That's awful.'

'So's he.'

'I know, but we cannot stoop to his level.'

'I can,' Wat offered.

'We'd probably only have to twist his arm or something. He's so hopeless I think he'd give up at the first hint of trouble.' Cwen pleaded her case.

Hermitage could hardly believe what he was hearing. He'd been quite encouraged when Cwen recalled the origin of investigation. Now here she was, suggesting that they do physical harm to someone with information. If that was investigation, he would have nothing to do with it. Of course, he wanted nothing to do with investigation anyway, even when it was done nicely, but this really was too much.

'Where would it end?' he asked, very reasonably. 'If the investigators go around threatening and frightening those they are investigating?'

'Quicker investigation?' Cwen suggested.

'Corrupt investigation,' Hermitage corrected. 'He might say anything, just to get you to stop twisting his arm. How would we know that it was true?'

'It would be a start. And if we found out he was lying we could come back and twist the other arm.'

'Or a leg,' Wat offered. 'Or something a bit more personal.'

'No,' Hermitage was firm. 'It's bad enough that we're following him without permission.'

Wat and Cwen exchanged looks of hopelessness.

'And now we're going to sneak up on him and listen to what he's saying without asking as well,' Cwen said, nodding towards the hovel.

'We're going to what?' Hermitage was getting more and more worried about the course of this investigation. Following people, threatening them, prying on them? It was all completely outrageous.

'Of course,' Wat said. 'We don't even know for sure that he's in there, do we?'

'I suppose not,' Hermitage had to admit.

'So, we sneak up and check that he is.'

Well, that seemed vaguely reasonable. It would be a waste of their night if they waited outside a hovel, only to find that Simon was in a completely different hovel altogether.

'And as we've sneaked up to do that, we might as well have a bit of a listen while we're there.'

Hermitage wasn't happy with that step.

'You know what Simon's like,' Cwen said. 'He'll be boring a total stranger into the ground with tales of how important he is, and what great work he's doing.'

'And the owner of this place probably thought he was in a

bad enough way already,' Wat smiled. 'You live in a pile of leaves in the forest and then have to put up with Brother Simon.'

'He'll probably tell this poor hovel owner all about the conclave and the crossbow and everything.' Cwen said.

Hermitage had to admit that this was very likely. If Simon was in there. 'Very well. But first, we check that he's in there. If not, we have to move on.'

'Well, yes.' Cwen couldn't see why they'd do anything else.

Sneaking up on a house made of leaves, across a wood covered in leaves, during the still of the night, was not a straightforward process. There were bound to be twigs and branches under the leaves that would snap at the press of a foot, alerting the hovel that someone was approaching.

Halfway to the hovel Hermitage found himself wondering what this looked like; a monk and two weavers sneaking up on a pile of leaves in the middle of the night. Luckily, there was no one there to observe.

And luckily, they didn't have to go much beyond halfway before they heard Simon's piercing tones, droning in the hovel like hornets who had realised they'd just made the most boring nest in the history of hornets.

'He's definitely there then,' Wat noted.

'And we hardly have to listen in,' Cwen said. 'I should think even the squirrels have had enough of this by now.'

Nodding towards a nearby oak, Wat led the way over so that they could sit with their backs to the trunk and still hear the goings-on in the hovel. Well, the going-on. There was only one, and Simon was in charge of it.

He was, indeed, telling the hovel owner how important he was, and illustrating this through a comprehensive list of all the people who had ever spoken to him. Hermitage frowned as he heard Simon regale the woodland with tales of his close relationship with King Harold.

As Hermitage had been there at the time, he knew King Harold had only had a few words for Simon, and they had not been good ones.

He sighed at the others. 'The fellow is just dishonest.'

'Not only dishonest,' Cwen nodded at this thoughtful analysis. 'Most dishonest people are entertaining, in a way, as long as you know they're dishonest. You can smile at the bald lies and inaccuracies, knowing that you don't have to take them seriously. Brother Simon can lie and bore your breeches off at the same time. It's very disappointing.'

Wat reached into his pack and delved about, before emerging with some bread, dried meat, fruit, cheese, nuts and a skin of wine.

'Where did you get this from?' Hermitage gazed with wonder at the feast, only now realising that he really was quite hungry.

'This?' Wat asked. 'Just basic rations. Never go anywhere without it. And if we've got to sit and listen to Brother Simon all night, we should at least be comfortable.'

They did get very comfortable and sat eating and drinking quietly, resting against the oak tree, the warm night drifting around them as they listened to Brother Simon, who was boring like a woodworm.

As the last drops from the skin of wine, and the last shell of the last nut were disposed of, Cwen sighed, contentedly.

'Is he ever going to get to the point?' she asked. 'We've already been here hours and he still hasn't got to the present day.'

'He's got to sleep sometime, surely,' Wat said, with a yawn.

'Probably talks in his sleep as well.'

'Oh, God. We don't have to listen to that as well, do we?'

'One thing does surprise me,' Cwen said.

'Oh, yes, what's that?'

'The hovel owner.'

'What about him?'

'He hasn't killed Simon yet.'

Wat nodded that this was a very good question.

'I mean, if you were trapped in a hovel with Brother Simon all night, wouldn't you do something drastic?'

'Perhaps he's killed himself?' Wat suggested. 'Or he's been dead all the time and Simon hasn't noticed.'

'Could be.' Cwen didn't seem to think that was a ridiculous idea at all. 'Or he was already on his last legs and Simon's arrival kicked them out from under him.'

All their ears pricked up as they heard Brother Simon go on. 'Even now,' he was saying.

Even now, sounded very promising. They shuffled a little closer to the hovel.

'Even now, I am carrying out the most vital mission for the country. Obviously, I can't tell you anything about it.'

'Ha,' Cwen scoffed, quietly.

'But once I have delivered my news to Breadsall, great events will unfold.'

'Breadsall, eh?'

'Didn't we walk through Breadsall?' Hermitage recalled their journey to get here.

'We did,' Wat confirmed. 'Reasonable sized place. Got a church and a hall.'

Hermitage was impressed at the magnificence.

'That's easy then,' Wat said. 'We don't have to follow him anymore. We can go to Breadsall and wait for him. He'll never know we were here.'

Hermitage couldn't help but think that eavesdropping on a private conversation, and then using the information to your advantage was rather unpleasant. But then he thought that following Simon at all was a doubtful activity. He tried to focus on the plight of poor Brother Pewlet. The crossbow killer could well be in Breadsall and so the sooner they got there the better.

Then he thought that there might be a crossbow killer in Breadsall and so going there at all might need more thought.

'Hardly a place for secret conclaves, Breadsall.' Cwen was not so enthused about the place. 'Dull as a ditch, as far as I recall.'

'What do you want?' Wat asked. 'The Breadsall festival of the secret conclave? Not very secret, I'd have thought.'

Cwen snorted at him.

'Do we go now?' Hermitage queried. 'Or wait until morning.'

'Go now, I say,' Wat replied. 'There's no knowing what time of the morning Simon wakes up. Must be pretty early to get all his talking in before sunset. I'd rather get to Breadsall, settle in, and wait. One of us at a time can stay awake, in case the hovel owner finally comes to his senses and throws the man out.'

'We don't know exactly where he's going though,' Hermitage said. 'He's only said Breadsall. But where in Breadsall?'

'For heaven's sake, Hermitage. It's only got a church and a hall, and we're looking for a secret church conclave. Have a guess.'

'The church,' Hermitage said, after considering the question.

'Well done. We'll go to the church and find some shady

spot to hide out.'

This was getting worse and worse. Following people, listening to them, threatening them and now hiding so you could watch them without them knowing. This behaviour was just as bad as the people who were being investigated. How could anyone tell the good people from the bad if they all did the same thing? A simple analysis of facts, presented in a sensible order and considered with a suitable amount of time, that was investigation.

He just had to accept that the chain of events had led them here. With such doubtful links in the chain though, he had little confidence that it wouldn't break before the end.

Wat put the wineskin back in his pack and stood slowly, being careful not to make too much noise. Hermitage and Cwen followed and prepared to sneak back to the path and head off to Breadsall.

'You know,' Cwen commented. 'I've not heard the hovel owner say anything at all. In all the time we've been here. I can't really believe even Simon would talk to a corpse. Not for this long, anyway.'

'Would you say anything? Stuck in a small room with Brother Simon? It only encourages him if you answer back.'

'You'd think he'd start off with the occasional "oh, really" or "that's interesting". Before he got on to "will you shut up" and "please leave me alone now". But nothing. Not even a cough.'

'Do you think we should see if he's all right?' Hermitage asked.

'I'm not going in there,' Wat was very clear. 'Besides, he really would know we're here if we poke our heads through the door. Or the wall.'

Hermitage accepted that this was sensible. Even though it

meant leaving some poor peasant to the undivided attention of Brother Simon.

'Well.'

They heard Brother Simon speak as they passed by the hovel.

'I had better be getting some sleep. An important day tomorrow, as I am sure you will agree.'

They paused and listened intently, to see if there was any reply, or whether Brother Simon really had been talking to himself all this time.

'I'm seventy-two,' a cracked and elderly voice rang out. A very loud voice. A very, very loud voice for someone who lived in the quiet of the forest and only had one person to talk to; and that person was probably standing right next to him.

'I see,' Brother Simon's reply sounded cautious.

'Lived here all alone, all these years,' the old voice boomed on. 'No one visits. No one to talk to.' The man sounded quite happy to have had the company. At least that was something.

'I mean to say,' the elderly one shouted to the woodland. 'Who wants to spend their time talking to an old deaf man, eh? What would be the point in that?'

Caput IX Babes in The Wood

The wait for Brother Simon in Breadsall was as quiet and peaceful as it could be. It was not a large place and in the middle of the night, no one was doing anything at all. The street was deserted, the houses quiet, and the church and hall shut.

Wat scouted around until he found a suitable spot towards the back of the church, on the edge of the wood, from where they could see the road to the north.

'This place is like a grave,' he commented. 'I think we'd notice a rabbit walk down the path, let alone a monk weighed down by his own importance. I think we should all get some rest.'

Hermitage had no problem agreeing to that. The food and wine and the night-time walk had readied him for sleep.

As they settled among the bushes, moving sticks and debris out of their way to create comfortable spots, there was a rustling in the trees behind them.

'Probably a deer,' Cwen said.

'Or a boar,' Hermitage suggested, with some trepidation, knowing what boars were capable of.

'No,' Wat sounded confident. 'I'm sure the snakes will scare the boar away.'

'Snakes?' Now Hermitage was awake.

'I'm fooling you. There are no snakes,' Wat was not concerned.

Unfortunately, Hermitage's wood was now full of snakes just waiting for him to fall asleep. And as soon as they'd bitten him to death, the boar would come and eat the remains. 'Perhaps we should sleep in the church,' he suggested. 'That way, we'd know for sure when Simon arrived.'

'Are you allowed to sleep in churches?' Cwen asked.

'A lot of people do,' Wat replied, his eyes already half-closed as he lay comfortably. 'Usually when the priest is talking.'

'I am a monk,' Hermitage reminded them. 'I'm sure it will be all right.'

'And it will be all right when Simon comes in and sees us snoring in the apse, or whatever it's called.'

'Ah.' Hermitage hadn't thought of that. 'We could hide somewhere?'

'Hermitage,' Wat said, with some resignation. 'If you would rather sleep in the church, please do. I'm sure Simon wouldn't pay any attention to a habit. But if he saw Cwen and me, he'd run a mile. And if the secret conclave turns up, I think one of them will notice three sleeping bodies at their meeting.'

'Hm.' Hermitage really did want to go and sleep in the church, but he felt that doing so was a betrayal of his friends, somehow. Maybe he should just stay awake all night and look out for the snakes and the boar. Who, even now, were probably planning their attack together.

He cautiously settled himself for a good long worry about the animals of the forest, but before he could get to the meat of the problem, he was asleep. He then dreamed about the animals of the forest who were treating him as the meat of their problem.

After the sort of sleep that felt like it was nothing more than a nodding off, but may have been hours, the rustle from the woods returned. This time accompanied by a giggle.

'Laughing boar, eh?' Wat noted, without opening his eyes. He rolled over and wearily got to his feet. Turning his head left and right as if to get his bearings, he suddenly stepped quickly into the depth of the bushes and vanished from sight.

The rustling got quite violent as Cwen looked on, without getting up.

After a couple of worrying moments, Wat emerged once more, one hand holding the scruff of the neck of a young boy, the other doing the same for a girl. They wriggled and protested at their treatment, but Wat's grip was firm. They could only be about eight or nine years old and were really no match for a weaver who was used to dealing with much bigger people who wished him personal harm.

Despite the fact one was a girl and one a boy, the children were almost identical, not only in looks, shape and size, which was small and thin, but also in condition, which was dirty and dishevelled. They carried similar expressions of outrage at their treatment, with the clear understanding that they wouldn't put up with this sort of thing in another ten years.

'Gerroffus,' the boy protested.

'We weren't doing nothing,' the girl chimed in.

'Not doing nothing, eh?' Wat asked. 'Apart from skulking around in the woods at night. Up to no good, I imagine.'

'No.' The boy replied with such speed that the answer was clearly yes.

Wat deposited them before Hermitage and Cwen and loosened his grip. He stood close though, making it quite clear that he would only go and get them again if they tried to run away.

'Yeuch,' the girl commented, with some disgust. 'It's a monk.'

The boy nudged his companion and turned up his nose as he nodded towards Cwen. 'And a girl.'

The girl looked at Cwen, looked at the boy and then punched him on the shoulder, with all her might.

'Ow,' the boy complained.

Cwen nodded her approval at this quite appropriate reaction and looked ready to add a clip round the ear of her own.

'What you up to?' the boy asked Wat, as he rubbed his shoulder. He was obviously accusing the weaver of something very distasteful.

'Never mind what we're up to. What are you up to? In the king's wood at night?'

'King's wood?' the girl sneered at the name.

'That's right,' Wat confirmed. 'It's the king's wood now. You know that. And this is the King's Investigator.' He nodded towards Hermitage.

The children's eyes widened, and their jaws dropped as they reconsidered their position.

Hermitage tried to look solemn and serious but didn't do very well. He couldn't for a moment believe these two urchins had the first idea what an investigator was, but it sounded significant.

'We weren't doing nothing,' the girl protested, more sincerely now.

'You said that.' Wat looked at them both. 'What nothing was it you weren't doing, exactly? Looking for the king's deer, or rabbits? Catch some ferrets and take them home?'

'We wouldn't.'

'More like you are a couple of ferrets, sneaking around looking for something to steal. Going to get into the church, were you? Or the hall?'

'No, mister, no,' the boy now appeared to be taking their situation very seriously.

'Who are you, anyway?'

The two looked at one another as if debating whether to give this vital information away.

'Herbert,' the boy said, his eyes cast down.

'Agnes,' the girl added.

'Well, Herbert and Agnes, I assume you're brother and sister?'

They nodded. 'We're twins,' Herbert said, proudly.

'And does your father know you're out?' Hermitage asked, as severely as he could manage.

Herbert and Agnes considered the ground. 'We ain't got no father. And our mother's ill. We've come looking for herbs and the like.'

Well, thought Hermitage, that was remarkable. Here were twins, and the mother had survived their birth. That didn't happen very often.

'Didn't sound like you were looking for herbs and the like. What herbs?'

'Crosswort, mainly.' Hebert said. 'Mother's got a bad head.'

Agnes proudly produced a red kerchief, the one that would be used to bind the Crosswort to the head and get rid of the pain.

'Hm,' Wat seemed reluctantly prepared to accept this. 'So, why all the giggling?'

'We saw you here. We wondered what you was up to.'

'So you stopped to have a look.'

Herbert nodded. 'Three people in the woods at night do some funny things.'

'You've seen them, have you?' Cwen asked, her anger having dissipated.

'We see everything,' Herbert confirmed.

'I bet you do.' Wat was encouraging now. 'Smart children

like you.'

Agnes and Herbert nodded their agreement to this.

'See all the comings and goings, eh?' He raised his eyes towards Hermitage.

Ah, what a good idea. If meetings had taken place here, these children would certainly have seen them. It was hard to believe that a secret conclave could meet in a place like Breadsall without being noticed by someone.

'We saw some Normans the other day,' Herbert reported, with some awe.

'They didn't stop,' Agnes added, with disappointment. She gave Hermitage a sideways glance.

'Brother Hermitage here has met the king,' Wat said. 'Spoken to him.'

The children's awe was at risk of running out.

'And King Harold before that,' Cwen added.

There was really nothing that could be said to this. In fact, they nudged one another and then bowed to Hermitage.

'Oh, no, no,' Hermitage began.

'That's right,' Wat interrupted. 'There's only one King's Investigator in the whole country, and Hermitage is it.'

'Don't forget the imposter,' Cwen reminded Wat.

'Oh, yes.' Wat nodded his thanks. 'There's some fellow called Simon who goes around saying he's the investigator, but he isn't.'

Even Hermitage noticed the flash of recognition that crossed the children's faces.

'Wanders around saying as how he's the King's Investigator and he's on some secret mission.'

Hermitage had to admit that only Brother Simon would feel the need to announce to the world that he was doing something secret.

'We've seen him, we've seen him,' Herbert almost bounced for joy.

'Well done,' Wat congratulated them.

'He was here earlier. Told Mistress Winson how she had to give him some bread because he was the King's thingy, on a secret whatnot.'

Agnes looked very sombre. 'No one tells Mistress Winson to give them bread,' she said, in dark tones. 'I bet he's still getting the crumbs out of his habit.'

Herbert leaned over and put his hands against his sister's ear as he whispered some words to her. Whatever the words were, they resulted in fits of laughter from the pair of them along with vivid impressions of someone trying to walk while a loaf of bread was impeding them in some way; some rather intimate way, from the looks on their faces.

'And did he meet anyone else here?' Wat asked, trying to get them to stick to the question. 'Any other people going around doing secret things?'

'There's not no one like that around here.' Herbert made this perfectly clear.

'No big meetings in the church?' Cwen prompted. 'Monks and priests and the like coming and going?'

Agnes and Herbert looked at one another and gave clear signs that they thought these newcomers were completely mad.

'We've got a priest, but he doesn't move much at all,' Agnes explained.

They then blew out their cheeks, stuck their arms out at their sides and waddled around in circles, clearly impersonating a very large person who had trouble walking.

Hermitage admonished them with a pronounced "tut".

'Hm.' Wat looked very thoughtful at this. 'Where's the

conclave then?'

Hermitage thought that it was hardly likely to be gathering in the street, that not being the best location for a secret conclave. 'I expect that they are very discreet, making sure they don't get seen, that sort of thing.'

Wat held his arms out to bring Hermitage's attention to the full extent of Breadsall; one church, one hall and some hovels. 'They'd have to be six inches tall not to be noticed in this place. I think a conclave of just two people would be the most excitement Breadsall has ever seen.'

'Of course,' Hermitage suggested. 'It could be that Brother Simon is not entirely accurate.'

'I think that goes without saying.'

Hermitage couldn't immediately think of anything in life that could go without saying. 'I mean, he may be, what can we say, making it up?'

'Making it up?' Cwen dismissed the idea. 'I've only just met this Brother Simon and from what I've seen I don't think he could make up a pile of logs in a log shed full of logs with a picture of how to make a pile of logs.'

'It would require some qualities I've not seen from Simon,' Wat went on. 'Imagination, intelligence, that sort of thing.'

'And why would he do it anyway?' Cwen asked. 'To get his nose into the monastery and the death of Pewlet, I can understand. To try to bore a deaf man to death in his own hovel?'

Hermitage had to accept that Simon making it up seemed very unlikely. It was a complicated and far-fetched story. His experience of the man told him that the Brother had trouble recognising the truth when it was standing in front of him ringing a bell, never mind a whole world full of lies and deceptions.

'More likely,' Wat said, 'that someone else has made it up and told Brother Simon. He's then believed every word.'

'Which still leaves us with the same problem,' Hermitage pointed out. 'Who's behind all this and why? Brother Pewlet is still dead, whether Simon knows what's going on or not. Someone sent him to the monastery. They could be a conclave, they might not be. We still don't know.'

Agnes and Herbert had been watching this discussion with fascinated expressions.

Herbert whispered the question that they had clearly both agreed upon. 'There's a dead monk?'

Hermitage nodded with all due solemnity. 'There is indeed. A young fellow called Pewlet.'

'Cor,' Agnes said. 'Can we have a look?'

'A look at what?'

'Pewlup the dead monk.'

'It's Pewlet, and no, you may not.' Hermitage was appalled at such an idea coming from such young mouths.

'Aw, go on,' Herbert urged.

'He's miles away,' Wat said.

'And it is simply not appropriate for young children to be gawking at the body of a brother.'

'We seen dead people before,' Agnes argued.

'Monks are no different,' Cwen said.

'Don't they glow and fly up to Heaving?'

'Heaven,' Hermitage corrected, feeling no little despair at these two.

'Yeah,' Herbert agreed. 'We've never seen that.'

Hermitage was tempted to say that he thought it unlikely that they ever would if this was the best example of their behaviour.

'There is something you can do though,' Wat said, a

scheming look on his face.

'What? What?' Herbert was all enthusiasm.

'You can look out for us.'

Herbert frowned now. 'But you're here. What's the point of looking out for you when you've already arrived?'

'No, no.' I mean you can look out for something for us.'

'Is it a dead monk?' Agnes asked, sounding quite keen.

'Not yet,' Wat replied. 'It's Brother Simon. He's still walking about at the moment and will be here soon. He knows us and if he sees us he might not do what he's planning to do.'

Agnes and Herbert scowled as they tried to follow this.

'And we want to know what he does,' Wat concluded.

Herbert and Agnes engaged in a hurried conclave of their own. Once they had come to their conclusion they turned to Wat. 'This thing the monk is going to do?' Agnes asked.

'Yes?'

'Is it very bad?'

'Yes,' Wat said blankly. 'We don't know what it is exactly, but it is probably very bad.'

The children grinned. 'We'll do it.'

Herbert had an extra thought, a rather hopeful one. 'I don't suppose it's rude as well, is it?'

'I doubt it,' Wat said. 'Knowing Brother Simon.'

Coping with this disappointment, the children agreed that they would keep watch for Brother Simon.

'Just watch what he does, who he meets and anything else that goes on,' Cwen instructed. 'You don't need to talk to him but if he does talk to you, don't mention the dead monk.'

'Right,' Herbert agreed.

'And when you get the chance, come and tell us,' Wat instructed.

The twins nodded, clearly looking forward to their role in whatever it was that was going on.

Hermitage felt bad that they were dragging two innocent children into this sorry business. Getting them to spy on a monk who may be involved in a murder was truly awful. Perhaps there was another way. Then he thought that the monk in question was Brother Simon and that young Herbert and Agnes were anything but innocent. Still, it wasn't right.

As they prepared to retreat further into the woods, so as not to be spotted by Simon when he arrived, Agnes interrupted. 'Hold on,' she said.

Hermitage thought that perhaps the girl had realised what they were getting involved in and was having second thoughts. There was one dead monk in this tale already, a dead child did not bear thinking about.

They turned to face Agnes who had put her hands on her hips and was looking very stern. 'If we do this for you?' she asked.

'Yes?' Wat said.

'What's in it for us?'

. . .

'What's in it for us?' Hermitage repeated for about the seventh time as they made themselves comfortable in a small hollow in the woods, out of sight of Breadsall. 'That small child, living a quiet life in this humble place has been asked to spy on a monk who may be involved in death, and she asks what's in it for her.'

'You've said that, Hermitage,' Cwen sighed.

'It needs saying. And it needs thinking about.'

102

'I wouldn't get in Agnes's way if I were you.'

'Not only did she want to know what was in it for her, Wat promised money.'

'Children like money,' Wat explained his decision.

'You are taking the young to corruption.'

'I think those two have already got there.' Wat smirked.

'What if Simon is involved in the death of Pewlet? We have now put two children in danger.'

Wat gave a hollow laugh. 'If Simon's involved in any way other than being the fool, I'll eat a tapestry. And if anyone is in danger, it'll be Simon. At least with those two watching out for us, we can all get some more sleep.' He settled himself again and looked as if he had not a care in the world.

'I'm not so sure,' Hermitage looked cautiously around at the same world and saw cares everywhere. He wasn't sure if he should be more worried about the boar and the snakes sneaking up on him, or about Agnes and Herbert.

Caput X Writing on The Wall

Hermitage was rudely awakened with the dawn.

'Get up you lazy monk,' Agnes said, as she kicked him again.

The child appeared to float up and away from Hermitage as Wat took her scruff once more and pulled her backwards.

'That's no way to treat the King's Investigator.' The weaver shook the child, to see if it would help the lesson go in.

'It's no way to treat anyone.' Hermitage pulled himself to his feet and gave Agnes a very fierce look indeed.

Wat dumped the child at the foot of a tree and gave an imperious gesture that her brother should join her; and that they should both stand there until they were told they could do otherwise.

'What did you see?' Cwen asked.

'The monk,' Herbert announced, proudly.

Hermitage looked around quickly, imagining for a moment that they might have brought Simon back here.

'Just the monk?'

'Just him. It was the same one as got Mistress Winson's loaf where he didn't want it.' Herbert sniggered.

'No one else?' Hermitage couldn't understand this. It wouldn't be much of a conclave if Simon was the only one there.

'Nope.' Agnes grinned, apparently still happy at the chance to kick a sleeping monk.

Hermitage, Wat and Cwen just exchanged puzzled looks.

'Perhaps the conclave has not yet gathered?' Hermitage offered. 'Simon could be waiting for them to come to him. A time may have been arranged for a meeting.'

'He's gone,' Herbert said.

'Gone? Gone where?'

'I don't know. You only told us to look out for him. You didn't say anything about wanting to know where he went.'

'That'd be extra,' Agnes said. 'We can go after him if you like. For more money.'

Hermitage gave Wat his fierce stare now. 'Which way did he go?'

'Back north.'

'He did nothing while he was here? Met no one, spoke to no one?'

'There's no one about,' Herbert explained. 'And people here have met him once already. They wouldn't want to do that again.'

'He must have done something,' Hermitage insisted. 'Did he just walk into town, turn around and walk out again?'

'Oh, no,' Agnes said. 'He went to the church.'

'Aha.' Now they were getting somewhere. 'And who did he meet at the church?'

'No one.'

No, they hadn't got anywhere after all. 'So, he went to the church. Did he go in?'

'No.'

'He just looked at it and left?'

'Well, he made some marks on it. Then he left.'

'He made marks on the church?' Hermitage was becoming convinced that Herbert and Agnes hadn't seen anything at all. In fact, they could have been making up the whole business of seeing Simon in the first place. And that was Wat's fault for corrupting them with money.

'You're making this up.'

'We are not.' Herbert was offended. 'He did make marks on the church, he did. And then he went off. We saw it, so

105

that's what happened.' He folded his arms as if he wasn't prepared to talk to Hermitage anymore.

'All right, all right.' Cwen stepped between the children and the monk. 'What do you mean he made marks on the church? What sort of marks?'

'You know, marks.'

'Er, no. I don't know, I haven't seen them. What sort of marks?'

'The usual.'

'The usual?' Hermitage couldn't help his exasperation at all this boiling over. 'The usual sort of marks people make on churches. Is that what you're saying?'

'No.' Herbert sneered at Hermitage for being so stupid. 'The usual marks people make all the time. You know.' He waved his hands around in the air making loops with his finger and thumb together.

'Writing,' Wat said. 'You mean he wrote on the church?'

'That's it.' Herbert sounded pleased to be reminded of the word as it had completely slipped his mind. 'He did writing on the church. He wrote on the church.'

This didn't help Hermitage one bit. You couldn't write on a church; it made no sense at all. The quill would break, for one thing. And how would the ink stick to the walls?

'I think you'd better show us.' Wat indicated that the children could leave their tree and lead the way back to town.

The short walk back to the church was accompanied by the constant complaint of the children about how stupid grown-ups were and how no one ever believed them.

Hermitage was quite confident that this was because they lied most of the time. He was certain that no one had written on the church, Agnes and Herbert had simply made it up. Or they'd seen something completely different and got it wrong.

After all, if they couldn't even remember the word for writing, how could he be sure that they'd seen any?

When they got to the church, Agnes and Herbert took them straight to the writing.

'Ah,' Hermitage said. 'You mean he chalked a word on the door.' He peered at the letters that had been put at the bottom of the door at the rear of the church. Put there by a rather shaky hand with what was obviously a stone of chalk or something similar.

'Is that not writing then?' Herbert asked, impudently.

'Well, yes, it is, but...,'

'There you are then.' Agnes held out her hand to indicate the writing that they could all see. 'He wrote on the church, didn't he?'

'Not in the usual sense of writing,' Hermitage began to explain.

'Yes,' Cwen agreed. 'He wrote on the church. Well done.'

The children beamed at Cwen and stuck their tongues out at Hermitage.

'Oh, really,' Hermitage huffed.

'And look at what he wrote,' Wat nodded down at the letters.

'Yes,' Hermitage agreed with the significance of Wat's comment as he read the two words. 'Brother Pewlet.'

'The dead one?' Agnes asked, full of enthusiasm once more.

'The dead one,' Wat confirmed.

'Where is he?' The children's heads swung around, eagerly awaiting the presentation of a monk's corpse.

'Just here.' Hermitage pointed at the writing.

'Where?'

'The writing.' Hermitage was impatient. It was quite a new experience for him. He got frustrated by people quite often, but seldom impatient. Perhaps it was a special quality of children that gave him the urge to point his finger at them very firmly. 'That's what the writing says. Brother Pewlet.'

Agnes and Herbert gazed at the marks in wonder. 'Them squiggles say things?'

'Of course, they do. How can you not know what writing is?' He could understand that these two would not know how to read or write, but to not even know what writing was? That was just ridiculous.

'We've seen it, obviously.' Herbert defended himself. 'The priest's book has lots of it.'

'And does Mistress Winson have a sign outside her bakery? One with writing on?'

'Nah.' Agnes dismissed such sophistication. 'She's got a picture of some bread.'

Hermitage shook his head. 'That's what writing is. It's a series of special pictures that take the words we speak and, erm, write them down. So that other people can read them.' He wasn't sure that this was the best explanation of writing, but he hadn't thought one would be required. He also didn't know whether the children really knew this and were just laughing at him. 'Have you never been shown your letters?'

'Why?' Herbert thought this was a perfectly reasonable question.

'So you can read.'

'Read what?'

'Writing on churches?' Hermitage suggested.

'That doesn't come along very often.'

Although it was really nothing to do with the matter in hand, Hermitage could not resist dealing with this. Ignorance of writing was just unthinkable.

'Look,' he said, as he picked up a piece of chalky looking

rock from the floor. Perhaps it was the one Simon had discarded. He stepped up to the door and drew a neat 'A' on the main panel of the church door. That's an 'A.'

'Ay, what?'

'Just A. Whenever you want to use the letter A, that's what you'd write. And everyone would know it was A. A for Agnes.'

Agnes looked very confused.

'Agnes is spelt with a letter A. That's your letter.'

Agnes suddenly looked enthralled and went up to run her fingers over the letter, much of which smudged under her attention.

'And what's Herbert?' Herbert asked.

'What do you think? What letter would Herbert begin with?' Hermitage immediately saw that this was a very stupid question. If you didn't know the letters in the first place, how could you know which was which? 'What sound does Herbert begin with?'

'Herb.'

'And Herb begins with H.'

'Aitch?' Herbert asked. 'Aitchbert? That ain't right.'

'No, no. We call the sound of H, aitch.'

'Why?' Herbert asked.

Hermitage didn't know. What infuriating things these children were.

'We just do,' was his best explanation.

'Sounds pretty silly to me. If Agnes can have Ay why can't I have Herb? Herb for Herbert.'

'Because there isn't a letter Herb.'

'Make one up.'

'You don't just make up new letters.'

'Why not? What if you want to make a sound no one's

made before?'

'We've got all the letters we need. We can make up any noises with the letters that there are. If we made up new letters all the time, no one else would know how to read anything.' Hermitage was in danger of getting thoroughly confused over all of this.

'What about Graarrgh?' Herbert challenged the theory.

'What about Herb,' Hermitage responded. 'That's made up of four letters.'

'It's only one noise, why does it need four letters?'

'Because it does.' Hermitage's ability to teach small children anything at all had just run out. 'All right.' He surrendered. He decided that getting just one letter into each of these heads would be a triumph. He drew an H on the church door.

'Coo,' Herbert breathed. 'It's like Agnes's A, except not joined up at the top.'

'Erm, yes, I suppose it is.' Hermitage hadn't really thought of it like that before. 'That's the first letter of Herb.'

'They can be our secret marks,' Agnes announced. 'If ever we want to leave secret marks, these could be them. I'll have A and you have H.'

Herbert nodded happily at this.

'It's not actually very secret,' Hermitage pointed out. 'Anyone who can read can see that it's A and H.'

Herbert looked smug. 'There's no one here who can read.'

'Apart from us, now.' Agnes beamed.

'We could charge people for doing their reading for them,' Herbert schemed.

'It's only A and H,' Hermitage explained. 'There are eighteen other letters to be learned as well.'

'Eighteen?' Herbert was astounded. 'Why, that's more than

lots.'

'That's if we stick to English. Writing should be in Latin, really. In that case, there's another twenty-one.'

'Twenty-one? That's hundreds.' Agnes and Herbert looked horrified at the prospect.

Wat raised a warning hand. 'I don't think we've got time to do numbers as well as letters.'

'What about the priest?' Hermitage asked. 'He'll be able to read.'

'Nah.'

Hermitage gaped. 'What about the words from his book at mass?'

'He just says the same words every time. He's learned them.'

Hermitage sighed at the state of the world in general, while Agnes and Herbert danced about, practising their secret letters.

'Education of the young is all well and good,' Wat said. 'Well, actually, it isn't really. Very bad idea, in my experience. Teaching children anything only leads to trouble. But this isn't catching us a monk killer.'

In his engagement with letters, Hermitage had almost forgotten why they were there in the first place.

'And why has Simon just written Brother Pewlet on the door and then left?' Cwen asked.

'It's obviously a message.' Wat carried on as Hermitage was still deep in his concern for children, the priesthood and everything else he could be concerned about. 'This conclave, or whoever it was that sent Simon on his mission, will come along and read the message and know that Pewlet has been done for. I wondered why Simon wanted to know the name. They'd clearly sent him to confirm the job has been done, and this is his report.'

Cwen folded her arms. 'So, we have to wait and see who comes along to read it? That could be a bit tricky; spotting people having a crafty read.'

'We just need to spot anyone reading at all, it not being a common activity in these parts.' Wat nodded his head towards Agnes and Herbert. 'And whoever it is, they're going to be a stranger.'

'When the road gets busy there could be all sorts of people wandering about. We'll never spot our conclave person.' Cwen gave the children a sour look as if this was their fault.

Hermitage came back to the problem in hand, instead of the many in his head. 'And what are we going to do when we find him? If we do notice someone reading the name, what do we do? Accuse them of murder? It's not much to go on, reading a word on a church door. There could be a perfectly innocent traveller who thinks, oh, that's odd, there's a name written on the church door over there. I wonder what it says? Next thing is we've descended on him.'

'We find out what's going on,' Cwen explained.

'How?'

'All sorts of ways. Threaten him, twist his arm, follow him, spy on him.'

'Oh, dear, oh, dear.'

'If he's a man with a limp and a crossbow we'll be all right,' Wat said.

Hermitage scowled at the levity. 'The man who killed Pewlet is hardly likely to come along to read his victim's name.'

'Well,' Wat held his hand out to the church door. 'Unless you've got any better ideas, we just have to loiter here and watch who comes by.'

112

'And if we get nowhere, we've still got Simon,' Cwen smiled rather nastily.

'What good will that do?' Hermitage despaired.

'He's someone to threaten, he's got arms to twist and we can still follow him.'

Hermitage shook his head. 'This really isn't what investigation should be about at all.'

'Oy!'

They were all distracted by a sudden cry from Agnes.

Looking around, Hermitage spotted her in the middle of the street. She was pointing down the road that led out of town.

'It's Rolf,' Herbert called, clearly offended by the presence of another boy of their own age, who was sauntering down the road. 'Clear off, Rolf.'

'Now then,' Hermitage urged a Christian greeting.

'It's Rolf of Eaton,' Herbert explained as if the reason for his offence was obvious. 'Get out of it Rolf.'

'Make me,' Rolf cried back.

'Come any closer, and I will,' Herbert retorted.

'Go on,' Agnes encouraged. 'Punch him on the head.'

'Children, children,' Hermitage pleaded. 'This is not the way to behave.'

'It is Rolf of Eaton,' Herbert repeated, obviously frustrated by Hermitage's lack of basic understanding.

'So I gather. But he can be allowed to pass. There is no reason for trouble.'

'It's Rolf of Eaton,' Agnes now added to the argument. 'He smells.'

'You mean you smell,' Rolf replied, sticking his tongue out.

'Oh, for heaven's sake. You're clearly as bad as one another.'

Wat and Cwen looked on with amusement as Hermitage attempted to resolve the conflict of three eight-year-olds. They clearly thought he was on safer ground dealing with murder.

'Master Rolf,' Hermitage spoke to the new arrival who was now close by. 'If you have simply come to offer insults, you should pass by or go back to Eaton.'

'Wouldn't want to stay here,' Rolf retorted. 'Whole place smells. Everyone knows that Breadsall smells.'

'Not as stinky as Eaton,' Agnes pointed out.

Hermitage drew himself to his full height and stood between the two parties, although he didn't look very confident.

Rolf peered around him at Herbert and Agnes. 'Don't want to stay here or I'll end up smelling as well.' Rolf walked on past.

'That's right, run away,' Herbert called out.

'It's all right,' Rolf replied. 'I'll get you on the way back when you're not hiding behind a monk.'

Agnes and Herbert now stuck their tongues out and Herbert reached down to find a rock he could throw at Rolf.

Hermitage stepped over and took the stone from the boy's hand. 'He who is without sin,' he quoted.

Herbert looked puzzled.

'Let he who is without sin cast the first stone,' Hermitage completed the explanation.

Herbert nodded his understanding. He then quickly reached down, picked a new stone and threw it at Rolf.

Caput XI Explain Yourself

'You've got some explaining to do.' The dark and dour figure from the conclave confronted the limping crossbow killer.

The limping crossbow killer made sure his hand was close to his crossbow. It wasn't uncommon, in his line of trade, to have to deal with the people who refused to pay after he'd done their bidding. Frequently, they threatened to report him to people in authority if he ever came near them again. A simple recitation of his list usually sorted that out; the list of people in authority who now had a lot less authority and one more crossbow bolt to their name.

And people always knew how to get hold of him. It was important that he be contactable, after all, how was anyone going to arrange for a killing if you couldn't get word to a killer when you wanted one? The drawback was that people could also get hold of him to complain afterwards. And they did.

Actually, he thought that anyone who hired a killer was a pretty despicable type and shouldn't really have the temerity to moan about it after the event. And of all the events there could be, death by murder was probably the most eventful. It wasn't the sort of thing anyone owned up to - apart from soldiers and other professionals - so how people managed to complain that their murder hadn't been done right, was beyond him.

Doing the deed itself was fine. That was noble and manly. Well, some of the ones he'd done were anything but noble or manly, but he had to make a living, after all. Shooting an unarmed monk in the dark was probably lower on the noble and manly scale than most. But paying someone else to do your killing for you? Well, that was just weak and shameful. If you couldn't kill the people you wanted yourself, you didn't deserve to have them die.

Still, it was all part of the business. He'd just let them complain and then go about his work. His customers, having discovered how convenient it could be to have an obstruction in their life removed, frequently returned with further commissions. It didn't do to antagonise them too much. Unless they really went too far, of course, in which case they were at risk of receiving his services for free.

The man from the conclave had had no problem making contact with the killer once more and arranging a meeting. There was no telling what was going to come; it could be complaints, it could be repeat business. This time, it seemed to be complaints.

They were huddled behind a large oak tree in a stretch of forest that pressed the boundary of Breadsall.

No grand conclave hall this time. No summoning to be gazed upon by a dozen hoods in all their finery and importance. This was a grubby little conversation under a tree. Repeat business seemed unlikely.

'Pewlet.' The man from the conclave made it sound like an accusation. His own hood was on, but it was slightly skewed, and the man had to keep tugging at it so he could see through with both eyes.

'Pewlet.' Crossbow killer shrugged as the name meant nothing to him.

People would insist on giving him the names of people who were to be dealt with, and they never understood that this was useless. What was he supposed to do? Go into a crowd asking for names? And then, when he'd got the right one, shoot them? A description was what he needed. A very good one, preferably, to avoid any little mishaps.

'We have received word that you killed Brother Pewlet.'

'I killed the man whose description you gave me. I killed the man who was in the place you told me he would be, and who was in the company of the abbot you said would be there. It's no good blaming me if you've changed your mind.'

'No good blaming you?' The neck sticking out from under the hood took on several shades of red all at the same time. They appeared in blotches as if warring with one another for total control. 'You're the one with the crossbow.'

'That I am,' the killer reminded his accuser.

The red neck from the conclave calmed slightly. 'I'm not saying that we didn't want Pewlet dead. Of course, we did. But not yet.'

'I can go back and ask him if he'd mind not being dead, but I think it's a bit late.' It was always annoying when people changed their minds completely. He'd go for his money and there would be shock that he'd done what he'd been paid for. "I didn't want him dead, not really", they'd bleat. "Just frightened a bit".

The killer would assure them that the victim had been frightened, quite a lot as it happened, and then he had been dead. And now it was time to pay.

It was not uncommon for the husband/wife/son/daughter, or whoever was paying, to say that they now wished they were dead as well. Of course, the killer would be only too happy to arrange that but would need payment in advance.

The red had returned to the neck and a shaking finger pointed at the killer. There were clearly words waiting to be said, unhelpful, angry words that wouldn't get them anywhere. With a visible effort of self-control, the finger withdrew.

'All right,' he said. 'All right. Pewlet is dead. What's done is done.'

The killer liked the sound of that. He might use it. "What's done is done". It had a nice ring of finality about it. He might even whittle the words into his crossbow or get someone who knew what the words were to do it for him.

'You're going to have to go back and get the right person this time.'

The killer liked the sound of that as well. It opened a whole new area of trade. Get paid to kill someone, do the wrong one, then come back and get paid again to do it right. It wouldn't do to use it too often, he'd end up with a reputation for killing the wrong people and that would never do. Still, once or twice might be worth a try.

And he was seldom asked to kill people in a particular order. It was always amazing what went on in some people's heads. Good, traditional family business sometimes went that way. The father would have to go first, followed by the eldest son and so on. All the way down to the one who was paying for all the killing in the first place; who would then end up being done by some uncle or other.

He couldn't imagine that the same system worked for monks. How could it matter what order you killed monks in? They all looked the same and did the same things.

'You'd better make sure you give me the proper description this time. I don't want to be coming back here in a day or two for you to be saying I should have done this one before that one.'

'I'll even give you the name of this one.'

'Names are no help. "Are you Harthacanute of Godalming? Oh, good, I've got something for you. Just stand still for a moment"? It doesn't work like that. They try to run away.

Makes it all very difficult.'

'Oh, I do apologise for inconveniencing you.' The man from the conclave didn't sound very apologetic.

The conversation, which had started to grow in volume, came to a sudden stop as there was a rustle on the other side of the tree.

The two men waited in silence to see if it was some animal, or whether they had company. The hand went to the crossbow in case this was someone else who needed dealing with. If it was, he would add it to the bill. If it was a boar, he would do it for a meal.

It was worse than a boar or a potential victim; it was a nun.

The killer shivered in his boots.

'Have you told him?' The nun demanded in that way that only nuns seem able to demand. There must be something in their training that gave them the awesome power they possessed. Either that or you weren't allowed to become a nun unless you already possessed the awesome power.

'Where's your hood?' the hooded conclave man demanded, in clear shock at the nun's face being revealed.

'Ridiculous things,' the nun dismissed them. 'We all know who we are.'

'We know who we are, yes. Our killer here doesn't. Well, he knows you now.' The man seemed to conclude that this could be an advantage. 'Oh, please yourself,' he said. 'And, of course, I've told him. I'm dealing with it, aren't I?'

'You're taking a long while about it.' The nun glared with her powerful nun eyes.

There was no telling what sort of person was inside the nun's garb. The headpiece was bound tight to the side of her head as if daring her eyes to look sideways. Her habit dropped straight from shoulders to floor, and, as far as the killer could tell, there might as well be a brick wall in there.

Putting an age to the face was impossible. From the expression cast upon both men, this woman might well have been in the Garden of Eden, looking for serpents to punish. Now the serpent had been done, she could turn her attention elsewhere.

There weren't many faces from which a hired killer retreated, but this was one; along with every other nun he'd ever met. And he'd never had any business from a nun. He'd had lots of requests to deal with nuns, but he always turned them down as a matter of principle. The principle being that he would rather survive to the end of the day. He strongly suspected that the right stare from a nun could stop a crossbow bolt mid-flight.

'You've given him instruction?' the nun demanded.

'I was about to when you interrupted.'

'Get on with it then. We haven't got all day.'

The killer was happy to watch this conversation and be talked about while he stood there. There was no need for him to engage with the nun directly. Or in any other manner, come to that.

'How could you kill Pewlet, anyway?' The words withered the killer.

The killer said nothing but slid the crossbow quietly behind his back.

Fortunately, the nun was quite prepared to answer her own question. 'Idiot,' she concluded.

The killer was happy with idiot; if the nun left him alone.

'As you killed Pewlet first,' the conclave leader began again, quite fiercely. 'You're going to have to go back and do it right this time.'

The killer could tell that a lot of this outrage was for the nun's benefit. He wasn't about to leave another man to the mercy of a rampaging nun. Some behaviour was too low, even for an assassin. Instead, he just shrugged, indicating that another arranged death would not be a problem.

'Same place?'

'Same place.'

'And do it right, this time,' the nun added.

'Another monk?' The killer could not help but resist this challenge to his competency. 'A monk in a monastery, in the dark. I hope this one's got some distinguishing features.'

'This one's got a title.' The nun directed her ire to the conclave leader as if this information should have been given out the first time around. The killer couldn't help but agree. But titles were another problem.

'A title?' he asked as he sucked the air in through his teeth. 'Oh, tricky things, titles.'

The nun said nothing but just folded her arms and stared her silent question.

'People with titles have friends,' the killer explained. 'And relatives.' He knew very well that the monasteries of the country were full of the younger sons of the nobility, put there to avoid any awkwardness over inheritance of estates; and to keep them out of the reach of older sons who wanted to make inheritance absolutely clear.

'You arrange the death of someone with a title and there's a good chance one of their family will come after you. They don't take that sort of thing lightly, you know.'

'I hadn't realised our hired killer was so cautious,' the nun said to the conclave leader. 'There I was thinking that hired killers killed people.'

The sarcasm of a nun was of a different order to that of normal people.

'I'm not saying it can't be done,' the killer retorted. 'What I'm saying is that it's more of a problem. If I'd been told about the title in the first place, I might not have done your Pewlet. But I wasn't.' He was pleased to see that the nun had no reply to this. 'And I'd have charged accordingly. Killing a title is a much costlier business.'

The nun sighed; another unique feature of the nun that could get to a man and chill his soul from the inside out. 'I can't imagine they get better quality crossbow bolts.'

The killer tried his own sigh, but it was like the sleepy caterpillar that's just decided to make its cocoon in a wasps' nest.

'No, but it can mean trouble. The sort of trouble that follows a man. The sort of trouble that means he must lay low for a while. Leave the country even. All of that takes money. Makes it very difficult to seek out new business, when the nobility's on the lookout for you.'

'How much?' the conclave leader asked, with weary resignation.

The killer gave them his figure.

'Ha.' The nun did shock, contempt and amusement, all at the same time.

'Half now and half when the job's done.' The killer wondered if ignoring the nun might work.

'You should do it for free, considering you killed the wrong man in the first place. But, if we're feeling generous, half in total is twice as much as you deserve.'

Ignoring her didn't work. And he'd never known a nun to be generous. 'What is the title, anyway?' He thought that if it was a minor one, he might be able to drop the price; a bit.

The nun nodded to the conclave leader who leaned over to whisper the title so that the trees wouldn't overhear.

'What!' The killer stepped back in genuine shock. 'You are joking.' He looked at the nun and realised that of course, she wasn't joking. Nuns didn't.

'That's twice as much, to begin with,' the killer said. He hadn't realised that such high levels of society ended up in monasteries.

'Tell you what,' the nun offered. 'We'll give you half and you do the job. Then we pay the other half to a much cheaper killer to come and do you. That way you don't need to worry about people coming after you and we get all our money back.' Was that a smile that approached her lips; cautiously and from a great distance?

And this from a nun! Was there no depth to which they would not stoop? He began to wonder why the conclave hadn't sent her to do their killing for them in the first place. 'You know.' The killer had had enough of this. 'I think you finding another man for the job is an excellent idea. I'll leave you with dead Pewlet and wish you the best of luck. How's that?'

Now the nun did smile, which really got the killer worrying. A smiling nun was always a precursor to something quite horrible. 'Would that it was so simple. News of our activities must be confidential. You know about it, but it must stop there. If we do hire another to complete our sacred work, then we would have to let the Normans know who was killing monks in the first place. Let them deal with you.'

The killer saw her point. The Normans didn't really care who got killed, in fact, they did most of the killing themselves. But that was the point; they didn't like other people taking things into their own hands. When they found someone interfering in their business, they took steps; usually over the dead body of the one concerned. And despite his generally appalling behaviour, King William was reputed to be quite devout. Killing monks was probably something he frowned upon.

The killer breathed deeply. 'All right. I'll see to this titled monk for you, but that's it. Any more and you can do them yourself.'

The nun nodded. 'Agreed. And a reduced fee is quite reasonable in these circumstances, I think. Sort of buy one, get one half-price if you like.'

'I don't like,' the killer said, but he was keen to get out of all this as quickly as possible. 'You don't tell the Normans who's killing monks, and I won't tell them who's paying. And no one mentions any reductions for multiple deaths.'

There were nods all around at this, and an unspoken agreement that they could now go about their business. The killer knew that his own business was a dubious one at best, but he dreaded to think what these two got up to when they weren't arranging the assassination of monks.

As he left them and trudged away, he mused that while he had never accepted a commission to deal with a nun, he would take a bit of pleasure if this one ever became a bit less alive than she was now.

But there was the wretched conclave to consider. If he did the nun he'd end up having to do the lot of them. And that was a lot. Still, perhaps he could consider it a professional challenge. Pick them all off one by one, without the others noticing. He'd hadn't used his favourite poisons for ages.

Caput XII Nothing to See Here

'Useless,' Cwen snorted. 'We come all the way to Breadsall, follow Simon, find out what he's up to and what good is it? None.'

Hermitage had to agree that they had gained nothing from their trip. They had waited and waited to see if someone would turn up to read the name written on the church door, but no one had. Eventually, as the day drew towards midday, the priest himself had appeared from behind the door. And the children had been right; he was a very large fellow indeed. Getting through the door at all was a challenge, and it was quite a big door.

As he struggled to negotiate the entrance, grunting at it as if wondering what trickster had shrunk his door in the night, he puffed and panted and looked on the verge of giving up. If it was this hard to get out, it probably wasn't worth the effort as he would only have to get back in again afterwards.

He did make it, although what he was going to do thereafter was a mystery. The man looked incapable of walking anywhere at all, and so it proved. He took a few breaths of air and then turned to go back inside again, girding himself for the herculean task of fitting the irreducible object through the unexpandable space. Perhaps this was his daily exercise and he would now go inside for a rest. As he faced the door, he noticed the writing and let out a grunt of annoyance.

He scrubbed Hermitage's letters away with his hand but there was no way he was going to be able to read the word. It was far too close to the ground and if this priest bent down that far there was very little chance of him ever getting up again. Instead, he leaned on the door and used his sandalled foot to scrub the letters from the door.

Satisfied that he had at least smudged them to uselessness, he spared a glare for the empty street, challenging whatever miscreant had written on his door to show themselves.

Hermitage, Wat and Cwen quickly concluded that the priest was not the man they were waiting for. The way he had squinted up and down the only road of Breadsall made it clear that he could barely see the stomach in front of him, and that was the most visible thing for quite some distance. Coupled with the report from Agnes and Herbert that the man couldn't read, the three of them decided that all they could do was go after Simon once more.

Hermitage insisted that a straightforward question was all they needed. Why had Simon written the name of Pewlet on the church door?

Wat was all for adding that failure to answer would have dire consequences.

Cwen suggested that if they did the consequences first, the answer would come quicker.

'Where's he likely to have gone, though?' Hermitage asked as they headed out of Breadsall once more, following the directions the children had given. 'Hardly likely to go back to Abbot Abbo, I'd have thought. He was given a very brusque welcome there.'

Wat shook his head. 'Have you ever known Brother Simon show any sensitivity or the slightest sign of recognising when he's not wanted?'

'I suppose not.'

'And now he knows where the monastery is, he'll go there so they can offer him their hospitality.'

'He probably thinks the abbot will have come to his senses by now,' Cwen said. 'And will treat him with all the deference due to his position. I mean, your position.'

Having nothing better to offer, they made for the monastery in the woods. At least it was close, and Brother Simon may have passed by, even if he hadn't stopped.

When they got back and met the first brother on passing through the gate, it was perfectly clear that Simon had arrived, and had stayed.

Monks were generally patient fellows, more concerned with the life hereafter than the concerns of the everyday. Irritation might surface at some troublesome task; a planting that went awry, a repair to the monastery that failed, perhaps a turn at a tiresome duty had come around earlier than expected.

The poor brother who cast his eyes upon them looked ready to kill.

'Are you with him?' The brother barked like a dog.

'Let me guess; Brother Simon has arrived?' Wat asked. 'No, we're nothing to do with him. Except we want a word.'

'A word, Ha!' The poor monk sounded on the verge of hysterics. 'I've got one for you, but I swore never to say it once I took the habit.'

'Where is he?' Cwen asked.

The brother gave Cwen a look of surprise, doubtless not expecting to see a woman. It soon passed, as his mind returned to its current trial. 'Everywhere. He's everywhere. You just can't get away from him. You hide in the refectory, and he follows you in. What did I do? I ask you, tell me, please. What did I do?'

The poor monk had now approached Hermitage and was clasping at his habit.

'I don't know, brother,' Hermitage said, trying to stop the man tearing holes in his only article of clothing.

'The abbot called and said he had a task for me. Well, that's not so bad, is it? And then he tells me what it is, and I still don't mind. He says he's far too busy to deal with it himself and wants me to do it. It's a privilege.'

Hermitage, Wat and Cwen exchanged looks.

'And then I meet the task. In person.'

'You're to look after Brother Simon.' Hermitage understood now.

'Look after him?' The monk's eye took on a rather wild gleam. 'That's a good idea. I could look after him.' He rubbed his hands together. 'Properly. Make sure he's looked after, the abbot said that. Those were his very words. I wonder why the abbot hates me? Well, there's more than one way to make sure someone's looked after. You know what I mean? And who could blame me?'

'Brother, brother,' Hermitage laid calming hands on the man's shoulders. 'Don't worry about Brother Simon. We want to speak to him. Perhaps you need to go and have a rest.'

'Want to speak to him?' The brother was aghast. He shook his head. 'Rest, yes, rest.' He looked desperate to go and do something other than deal with Brother Simon. 'I will. I'll go and rest.' He half-turned to go and then spun back, pointing a finger at Hermitage. 'Don't you kill him while I'm gone,' he warned. 'I want to be there for that bit.'

'No one's going to kill anyone.' Hermitage was shocked by the suggestion.

'Oh.' The brother was very disappointed at that news. 'I thought that's what you'd come for.'

'Absolutely not. That would be a great sin.'

The brother thought about this for a moment. 'Not in his case, it wouldn't,' he said, as he wandered away. He continued debating questions around Brother Simon, but only with himself now. It was still a pretty lively discussion.

Hermitage thought that he might go and warn the abbot that one of his community was on the brink of doing something regrettable.

'We didn't ask where Simon is,' Cwen pointed out, looking around the space of the monastery for any sign.

'It's not a big place,' Wat said. 'If we walk around a bit we'll hear him.'

As they set off to see where Brother Simon might have got to, one of the very few groups of people ever to actively look for the man, another arrival peered around the gate.

This one hissed at Brother Simon's erstwhile attendant, who was now walking round in circles, still talking to himself.

Seeing a beckoning finger, the brother went over to the gate. He was invited outside to speak to this latest visitor, the place seeming to have become as popular as Hastings in October.

The monk was asked a very quiet question, which he refused to answer. He simply staggered backwards, through the monastery gate again, and ran for his cell, waving his hands around his head as if fending off a swarm of bees.

'I only asked,' the figure by the gate complained. He shrugged the burden that hung across his shoulder and walked into the monastery compound. Well, he limped.

...

Hermitage, Wat and Cwen wandered the building for some time, trying to discern the location of Brother Simon. This was so puzzling that they could only assume they had gone the wrong way.

'There must be a trail of irritated monks, ready to kill, following in his wake,' Wat said. 'Surely a man of his importance doesn't walk without an entourage; most of them wishing him harm.'

They arrived back at their starting point and looked around.

'Perhaps he's left again?' Cwen suggested.

'There'd be rejoicing and merriment if he had,' Wat said.

'We haven't looked this way.' Hermitage indicated the side of the monastery that went by the cloister.

Wat peered over. 'I see no signs of riot or commotion, but you never know.'

'That'll be him,' Cwen announced when they had only gone a few paces in what was obviously the right direction.

The whining monotony of Simon's voice slithered around the walls of the monastery and bothered the ears of anyone who stood still long enough. It wasn't clear who he was talking to, but he was talking. But then that was to be expected.

'This way,' Wat beckoned down a corridor and then led on.

Outside the door that obviously contained Brother Simon, Hermitage hesitated.

'Come on Hermitage,' Cwen urged. 'Let's frighten Brother Simon again.'

'What do we do if he won't tell us anything?' Hermitage was having second and third thoughts about this approach.

'Frighten him some more.'

Hermitage scowled. 'That is hardly the way to behave. I think we just explain the situation to Simon and reason with him to tell us what he knows.' He knocked politely on the door and there was a movement from inside, even though the drone never let up for a moment.

'And when he doesn't tell us what he knows, or we find out he doesn't know anything at all, can we frighten him then?'

'You go in and ask him nicely,' Wat suggested. 'And we'll do the frightening bit. Sort of good monk - bad weaver approach. That way you don't have to feel bad about being nasty to him, and we can do what we like.'

Cwen nodded her enthusiastic agreement to this plan.

'I don't know,' Hermitage said. He knocked again, not having had an invitation to enter.

'Well, you're about to find out.' Cwen smiled and kicked the door open.

The sight that met their eyes was not at all what they'd expected. Brother Simon was there; of course, he was, no one else could have produced that voice. But he was not in discussion with anyone, nor was he explaining his importance to the walls and the crawling things upon the floor.

He was on the floor himself and he was groaning. Unfortunately for Simon, groaning sounded a lot like talking, otherwise the investigators would have burst in more quickly.

Not only was he lying on the floor, but his blood was there with him, and not on his insides, where it ought to be. Alongside his groans, Simon was staring at his blood as if surprised that he had the same stuff as normal people.

'What happened?' Hermitage asked, rushing over to support Simon's head and shoulders.

'Don't tell me,' Wat said. 'You were just explaining your importance to someone, and they stabbed you. Got to say it was bound to happen sooner or later.'

'Wat!' Hermitage said. 'The brother here has been wounded. Perhaps we could get some aid instead of offering unhelpful remarks.'

Wat shrugged and closed his mouth. He obviously had several more unhelpful remarks ready for just this occasion. He looked around the chamber and found a cloth by a bowl of water. He brought it over.

Cwen stood by looking, clearly very interested in where this blood was coming from, and how much there might be. 'Is he going to die?' she asked, with interest.

Simon groaned some more.

'I hardly think so,' Hermitage felt some impatience with his friends' approach to this situation. 'He has been wounded, that's all. A simple binding should do the job.' He turned to Simon. 'Where are you wounded, brother?' he asked, in very loud and clear tones, it being common knowledge that everyone with an injury or illness becomes deaf at the same time.

Simon waved an ineffective hand towards his side, where his other hand was clamped.

Hermitage peered down. 'Oh, my. Oh, my goodness heavens.'

'What is it?' Cwen asked, her interest becoming a little disturbing.

'Look.' Hermitage directed Wat and Cwen to examine the injury.

'Well, well,' Wat said, with some satisfaction. 'A crossbow bolt, eh?' He looked at Simon as if criticising the man for being a monk and having a crossbow bolt stuck in him.

'He's been shot,' Hermitage concluded.

'Could well be,' Wat agreed. 'Unless he fell on it.'

'What would he be doing falling on a crossbow bolt? What would he be doing with a crossbow bolt at all?'

'Did you have a crossbow bolt?' Cwen almost shouted at Simon. She got a groan in reply. 'I think that means no.'

'Maybe it's the one that shot Pewlet?' Hermitage said. He thought that a bolt that had shot two monks really deserved to be burned and cursed.

'Certainly from the same crossbow,' Wat said.

Hermitage frowned at another unhelpful comment.

'There aren't many of things about, are there?' Wat reasoned. 'And a bit of a coincidence one turning up to do two monks in the same monastery.'

Simon's groaning had diminished slightly as he was tended to.

'Can we pull it out?' Cwen asked, clearly keen to do this bit herself.

'Can't leave it in there.' Wat was nonchalant about the whole situation, but then he didn't have a bolt in his side.

Simon now found the strength to grasp Hermitage's arm with his spare hand.

'Yes, brother?' Hermitage asked, gently.

Simon croaked in his ear. 'Fetch numbing balm from the brother apothecary.'

'A good idea, brother.' Hermitage nodded.

Simon didn't let go. 'And a strong sleeping draft.'

Hermitage agreed.

'As well as some pillows, clean bandages, fresh water and a large flask of wine.'

'Anything else?' Cwen asked. 'Haunch of venison, perhaps?'

Hermitage scowled at her and beckoned that she might be the one to go and find these things. When she didn't move he made it clear that she could swap places with him, and support Brother Simon's head. She left.

'What happened to you, brother?' Hermitage asked.

Simon indicated that he was doing his best to struggle against the pain and speak. 'Shot,' he said.

'Well, yes,' Wat agreed.

'A fellow,' Simon said.

'With a crossbow, I expect,' Wat went on.

Hermitage beckoned him to silence.

'Came in here,' Simon panted. 'Asked me who I was and then shot me.'

'Told you.' Wat could not resist.

'He asked if you were Brother Simon, and then he shot you?' Even Hermitage had to think that this was clear. He could well imagine that the brother might have upset someone who had a crossbow and was prepared to use it. He'd upset so many people, after all.

'No,' Simon breathed.

'No? He didn't shoot you?' Hermitage couldn't understand how the bolt got to be where it was if there hadn't been some shooting.

Perhaps the assailant had just walked over and stuck it in by hand? Crossbow bolts were probably more readily available than the weapons themselves. Still, it seemed an odd thing to do, to say the least. Surely a sword would be easier. It would be a lot of trouble and require a degree of cooperation for someone to approach you and then hammer a crossbow bolt into your ribs.

Simon managed to shake his head. 'He asked,' he said, and took a breath. Even in his weakened state, his chest seemed to swell slightly. 'He asked if I was the King's Investigator.' He breathed out. 'Then he shot me.'

Caput XIII Moving Targets

'What did I miss?' Cwen demanded as she returned to the room with a monk following behind.

This new arrival quickly appraised the situation and hurried everyone out of the way as he bent to Brother Simon. From a satchel at his side, he produced pots and bandages which he put in order before he examined the wound. He did glance at the face of Brother Simon and rolled his eyes as if saying that he might have known it would be him.

'The King's Investigator has been shot,' Wat said.

Cwen looked quickly at Hermitage, who smiled back.

'He looks all right to me.'

'No, not that one.' Wat nodded towards the recumbent and groaning Simon. 'That one.'

To his groans, Brother Simon had now added complaint. He appeared to be trying to give instruction to the monk who was treating him, while at the same time moaning that the man had no knowledge of his own craft. The squeak from Brother Simon as his carer tweaked the end of the crossbow bolt brought a halt to the lesson for the day. At least the monk had the grace to cross himself in repentance.

Cwen looked from one to the other. 'But he's not the King's Investigator.'

'You know that. I know that. Hermitage knows that. Even the king knows that. Our crossbowman clearly doesn't.'

'And Brother Simon does tend to tell everyone that he is,' Hermitage said. 'Whether they ask or not.'

Hermitage noticed that Wat and Cwen exchanged looks of worried realisation. He wondered what they'd realised.

'Of course, you know what this means?' Wat asked Hermitage.

Hermitage nodded. 'It means that this fellow with the crossbow thinks he has shot the King's Investigator.'

'And?'

'And I think he will find himself in serious trouble. We know that the king doesn't really take much interest in investigation unless he wants something, but I think he will take a dim view of his appointees being shot.'

'Oh, Hermitage.' Cwen sighed and smiled and shook her head.

'What?'

'Think about it? Do some investigation.'

Hermitage looked from one to the other. They clearly had some ideas in their heads that he hadn't grasped yet. He'd get there, he always did. He moved his chin about, which always seemed to help, somehow.

He pointed towards the door, imagining the crossbowman walking in. Imagining things had never been his strong point, but he was starting to get the hang of it. 'The man walks in if it was a man.'

'Doesn't matter, really,' Wat said.

'Very well. The person walks in. Asks Brother Simon if he is the King's Investigator. When Simon says yes, he gets shot.' Hermitage reasoned his way around this point. 'Presumably, if he had said no, he wouldn't have been shot.'

'Exactly.'

'So, the person with the crossbow came here not to shoot Brother Simon in person, but to shoot the…, oh dear.' He felt terribly pale suddenly.

'Got it now?' Cwen checked.

'I think so.'

'The owner of the crossbow came here to shoot you,' Wat spelt it out.

Hermitage sat down.

'Why would he want to shoot me?' Hermitage asked, with mounting panic. 'What have I ever done to him? I don't even know who he is. You can't go round shooting complete strangers, it's not decent.'

Cwen nodded to herself in thought. 'You are investigating the death of Pewlet.'

'Quite right too,' Hermitage said. 'It's bad enough monks being shot without investigators being targets as well.' He tipped his head towards Simon, who he now realised had taken a crossbow bolt for him. 'If the man, or woman, or whatever had found me before Simon, I would be the one lying there.' He swallowed.

'And if this man or woman or whatever shot Pewlet, he might not like being investigated.'

'Hardly grounds to go shooting the investigator, I'd have thought.'

'Perfect grounds, I'd have thought.' Cwen insisted. 'You said yourself that he might shoot the investigator.'

'Did I?' Hermitage recalled something of the like. But he now saw that it was a very stupid idea.

'If you find out who he is, you could report him to the sheriff, or the king, or his man, Le Pedvin. Then think how the crossbowman will end up.'

Hermitage could think. And it wasn't very nice. 'But killing me won't help.'

'I think it will. Without you to investigate, he'll get away with it. There isn't another investigator in the land, despite what Simon says.'

'Serve him right,' Wat chortled at the mess on the floor.

'Wat, really,' Hermitage protested. 'Simon may be an objectionable fellow, full of his own importance and without a care for anyone in the world, but he has just been shot instead of me.'

'At last,' Wat raised his arms to the heavens in praise. 'A redeeming feature.'

Hermitage slowly shook his head from side to side. This was simply too much to take in.

'What's going to happen when the man with the bow finds out he's shot the wrong investigator?' Cwen asked.

Hermitage now felt sick and wondered if the monk tending to Simon had anything in his sack that might help. 'He'll come after the real one.'

'Which will give us the chance to catch him,' Wat said, with bright optimism.

'Before, or after he's shot me?' Hermitage was despondent.

'Oh, before,' Cwen assured him. 'Definitely before. We'll make sure of that.'

'Mayhap he'll never know. He's gone away from here thinking that the King's Investigator is no more. That could be the end of it.'

Wat was shaking his head in that reluctant way people have when they have bad news that has just turned truly awful. 'But Simon's not dead.' He shrugged towards the investigator as if Simon couldn't even do being killed properly. 'It could be we disturbed the attacker before he could finish the job. The least he'll want to do is come back and put a proper bolt in Simon. Somewhere more immediately fatal.'

Cwen held up a finger 'We could use him then.'

Hermitage scowled deeply at this suggestion, whatever it was.

'Our man thinks Simon is the investigator and he's not quite dead. So, he comes back to make sure. He still doesn't know Hermitage is the real investigator. We simply put Simon up as bait and then catch our man.'

Wat nodded and smiled. 'And in that case, it doesn't really matter if Simon gets shot again.'

Even the monk dealing with Simon's wound was nodding agreement with this plan.

'I won't hear of it,' Hermitage said. 'Putting another man up in my place to be shot at, if not killed? It's completely out of the question.'

Cwen shrugged. 'You can do it if you like.'

Hermitage had managed to quickly conclude that this whole idea was the result of a fevered mind. 'There's no need for anyone to be shot at. We simply continue investigating the death of Pewlet and find our killer by the normal means.'

'Stumble about and hope something turns up?' Wat asked.

'Not at all,' Hermitage protested. Although he felt that most of his investigations did tend to go that way. 'There has now been an attempt on Simon's life, in error. When he is recovered he may be able to tell us about his attacker. It could be enough to identify him.'

'Limping man with crossbow,' Cwen said. 'I think we've got that much. As soon as we spot one we'll get him. Can't be many about.'

'There may be more clues to be had. His clothing, his face, something to tell us more about his identity.'

'That he has clothes and a face.' Wat nodded. 'Very helpful.'

Cwen was looking at Simon and pursing her lips. 'There must be more to it than this.'

'More than a dead monk and another with a bolt in his side?'

'It's a lot of trouble to go to. All for a bit of, you know,' she lowered her voice so that only Hermitage and Wat could hear. 'Heresy.'

Hermitage beckoned her to urgent silence.

'Well, isn't it?' she went on. 'One dead monk and now the killer comes after what he thinks is the King's Investigator? Hermitage is right, it is asking for trouble. And all for a bit of thinking funny.'

Hermitage indicated that they should stop talking in front of the monk dealing with Simon, who had now rendered the brother insensible with various herbs and was about to extract the bolt.

'I hope he's out of his senses,' the monk said.

'Because it will be very painful.' Hermitage felt sympathy for the injured man.

'No, because it might stop him talking.' With one swift pull, the man extracted the bolt, to only a slight moan from Simon, and he held it up for them to see.

Hermitage felt quite sick, but Cwen took it with interest.

The monk turned back to patch up the hole and stop any more of Brother Simon leaking onto the floor.

'What else do we know of Pewlet?' Cwen asked as she examined the weapon. 'He must have been pretty special to warrant one of these.'

'He was a lovely fellow,' the monk at Simon's side spoke up.

'You knew him?'

'Oh, yes. An educated and erudite brother. We had many a conversation on a number of topics, away from the mundane matters of the monastery.'

'Nothing about, erm, peculiar beliefs?' Cwen asked.

'Brother Pewlet read widely. He knew of many things outside of the ordinary, but he was as devout as you or I.'

'Well, you, probably,' Cwen clarified. 'So, why would anyone want him dead?'

'That is beyond any of us.'

'The abbot thinks it was because some of his knowledge was too wide.' Wat suggested.

The monk waved that away. 'There are always discussions, no one takes them seriously. Certainly not seriously enough for death. Brother Tundar firmly believes that God created the pixies that follow him about when he's in the woods. Nobody's shot him.

'Pewlet was completely harmless. He came as a guest of Abbot Abbo, having been a novice under him some years ago. He was reading a volume on the prophets that the abbot had acquired and was going to write a commentary. He liked nothing better than to spend the day alone with his books and was trouble to no one. In fact, the brother here,' he nodded towards Hermitage, 'reminds me of Pewlet in many ways.

Hermitage nodded sadly at this but then noticed that Wat and Cwen were looking at him again. 'What?'

'This Pewlet sound familiar, Hermitage?' Cwen asked.

'I'd never met the poor man.'

'Not even when you were a novice under Abbot Abbo as well?'

'Oh, I was never a novice under Abbo. I had already passed on to my first degree before I joined him in the monastery at Kilnsea.'[9]

'But you do like books and the prophets.'

'Oh, yes. But then, who doesn't?'

'And you're a good friend of Abbo,' Wat checked. 'And you look a bit like Pewlet, apparently.'

---

[9] The Case of the Cantankerous Carcass will take you there

'Well, yes, but I don't see what that has to do with anything.'

'And the killer came back specifically looking for the King's Investigator,' Cwen went on.

Hermitage wasn't getting it, again.

'Maybe the killer didn't mean to shoot Pewlet,' Wat said, slowly and clearly.

'Then he shouldn't have pointed a loaded crossbow at him.' Hermitage was outraged at such carelessness.

'He meant to point it at someone else.' Cwen was sounding a little exasperated.

'Really? Who?'

'You, Hermitage. He wanted to point it at you. And then shoot you. And then, when he didn't, he came back to have another go. This time he got Simon instead.'

'That's two monks shot instead of the right one,' Wat explained.

Hermitage thought about this for a moment. 'It's all bit far-fetched. Why would anyone go to the trouble of seeking me out to shoot me? And why would they mistake Pewlet for me?'

'Because from the sound of it, the two of you were virtually identical.' Cwen was even rather snappy now. 'Friends of Abbo, fond of a book or two, here to study. About the same age.'

'And then the killer asks for the King's Investigator by his title and shoots him.'

Hermitage tried to give this proposal genuine consideration, but it really was too much. 'Far more reasonable that a conclave of the church has taken against people with, erm, unusual thoughts, and has despatched someone to deal with them. Then, on discovering they are

142

being investigated, they try to eliminate the new problem.' He held his hands out to indicate that there was very little unreasonable about this sequence of events. Well, it was all completely unreasonable, obviously, but it wasn't without reason.

'It is still possible,' Wat admitted. 'But so's the other version.'

'Why didn't this killer simply come to your workshop in Derby and shoot me there, if that's what he wanted to do?' Hermitage asked.

'A bit crowded with people who might stop him,' Wat said. 'Perhaps they'd had word of a young, bookish friend of Abbo visiting him, and took their chance.'

'To shoot the wrong monk?'

'You do all look alike,' Cwen said. 'And if you're like Pewlet anyway?'

'It's simply ridiculous.' Hermitage dismissed the idea, although it felt as if it was going to loiter in an annoying manner.

'You are the King's Investigator,' Wat pointed out. 'The real one.'

'I thought...,' the monk at Simon's side frowned and pointed at his charge.

'Making it up,' Wat explained.

'Ah.' The monk seemed happy that this was likely true.

'And as King's Investigator, you've probably made a lot of enemies.'

'Enemies? How could I make enemies?' Hermitage was genuinely shocked by the idea.

'Oh, you know, catching killers, sending them to their fate, undoing their plans, that sort of thing,' Cwen suggested. 'Not going to make them very happy, is it?'

'Well, no. But that's only while uncovering the truth. Everyone wants the truth uncovered.'

Wat and Cwen were both shaking their heads.

'People don't behave like that,' Hermitage explained. He had to admit to himself that he had very little idea about how people behaved. Most of the ones he'd come across behaved badly, but even so. There was bad behaviour and then there was shooting people.

Wat and Cwen still didn't look convinced.

'Just think about it,' Hermitage urged. 'Going right back to the beginning, are you seriously suggesting that Prior Athan, for example…,' he stopped in the middle of his own thought.

'There you go.' Wat congratulated him on reaching a conclusion so quickly. 'Would Prior Athan want you shot? Does he want you dead? Hasn't he actually said so, on many occasions?'

'Not in so many words.' Hermitage's protestation was weak. Now that he had been forced to think about it, Prior Athan was just the sort of man who would want Hermitage shot. But then, Prior Athan wanted horrible things done to so many people, it might not be personal.

Perhaps the man had now left the monastery of De'Ath's Dingle and was making it his life's work to do harm to all the people he had promised to do harm to.

'Prior Athan didn't have a limp,' Hermitage pointed out.

'So?'

'If anyone did want me shot, and I will accept the proposal that Athan might be one such, he would do it himself. Why miss out by getting someone else to do it for him?'

Wat and Cwen had no answer to that.

'In fact, he wouldn't want to shoot me at all. He'd want to strangle me in his own bare hands. He has said that once or twice. No.' He was now happy with his conclusion, having argued his way out of the threat from Prior Athan. 'It is simply the case that Pewlet was the target, followed by the King's Investigator. This is not a case of mistaken identity.'

Caput XIV Conclavity

'How could you mistake his identity twice?' The screaming hood of the conclave was in full flight.

'You told me to kill the King's Investigator. I asked if he was the King's Investigator, he said yes, so I shot him. What more do you want?' Bargis retorted.

'He had a big nose, you said?'

'Massive. Biggest I've ever seen.'

'Brother Hermitage does not have a big nose.'

'Brother Hermitage?' The killer paused at the name, as it rang a bell somewhere in the recesses of his mind. Still, if he was this King's Investigator thing, his name was probably well known. 'You didn't say he was called Brother Hermitage. You said he was called the King's Investigator and this one said he was as well. I wish you'd make your mind up.'

'I have made my mind up. The whole conclave has made its mind up. You keep killing the wrong people.'

'Ah, well,' the killer lowered his excitable tone. 'The last one might not be dead, as such.'

'Not dead, as such?'

'Shot. Definitely shot, but I was disturbed before I could finish things off. As soon as he saw the crossbow he started running around the room, twittering his head off about how important he was, and how I couldn't shoot him. Soon put him right on that.'

The conclave leader paused for a moment. 'Big nose, you say. Thought he was important?'

'Very.'

There was a pause for a moment's thought. 'I think you've shot Brother Simon.'

The killer shrugged that it really didn't matter to him.

The hood now issued a single, cold-hearted laugh. 'Ha! Brother Simon is a man deserving of a crossbow bolt somewhere sensitive if ever there was one. But he's still not the one we asked for. And he's not even dead.'

'Not yet. But he can be quite soon. I never like to leave a job half done. Although it's getting tricky, with this mess.'

'Your mess. He'll have told people what you look like. Was Brother Hermitage there?'

'How should I know?' Now the killer felt entitled to be aggrieved. 'You keep sending me out with defective instructions. A quiet, bookish monk in Abbot Abbo's company, then a King's Investigator. Well. I did them both and you're still not happy.'

'Who disturbed you then?'

'Funnily enough, I didn't wait around to do the introductions. There were three of them though, from a listen I had through the window. Sounded like a monk, another man and a girl.'

'That's them.' The conclave leader breathed deeply as if all his wishes had just been granted. 'Brother Hermitage, Wat the Weaver and a girl called Cwen, who claims to be a weaver.'

'That was Wat the Weaver?' The killer was impressed. 'I'm not killing him. I like Wat the Weaver.'

'I bet you do,' the conclave leader sneered. 'Well now you know the monk we want, you can go back and do him.'

'Oh, no. I've had enough of this. It doesn't do to keep going back to the same spot. I don't mind finishing off the wounded, that's not too difficult, they don't fight back. But a fresh monk? No thank you. Not very sensible at all. I was lucky to get away this time. If you want him dead, go and do it yourself.'

The conclave leader's hood moved back and forth as if he didn't know whether to fall down and weep or explode. Such were the contradictions going on inside him that he was twitching. Eventually, he managed to say something. 'We must summon the conclave.'

'You can do what you like. I've killed and wounded enough people in this part of the country for now. Time to move on. I can do for the wounded one if you want, bit of poison, probably. But I'm not going to start a whole new one.'

'Oh, I don't think you're going anywhere.' The conclave leader gave a short nod and the killer felt strong hands clasp his shoulders, making it clear that he really was not going anywhere. The grip was so powerful and determined that there was only one sort of person it could belong to; a nun.

'What do we do with him?' the nun asked.

'Bring him before the conclave. The whole thing has gone wrong, again. We need to think.'

'Hmmf.' The nun made a noise that carried so much meaning. Contempt, disappointment, irritation; with everyone and everything. 'This was your plan, Athan,' she addressed the conclave leader.

Athan eh? The killer had heard that name mentioned while he was loitering around the most recent attempted murder. Still, this conclave didn't need to know everything he knew. In fact, he found that it was an important tenet of his trade; never tell anyone everything, and if you can manage it, never tell anyone anything.

'Thank you very much', Athan snapped, as he pulled his hood off and threw it to the ground. From the face that was revealed the killer rather hoped the man would put the hood back on.

'It was our plan, Sister Mildburgh,' Athan replied with

some vigour. 'The one agreed by us all. Now we have to come up with a new one.' He indicated, with a wave of the hand that they should leave the wood and head back to the building nearby to follow this through.

The killer really thought that this would be just the moment to make his apologies and leave, but it was clear that apologies weren't being accepted at the moment. Nuns never accepted apologies, anyway.

Sister Mildburgh half dragged her charge along as Athan led the way.

The killer had never had a sister so didn't know what they were supposed to be like; not like this, he surmised.

Leaving the shelter of the woods behind, they crossed an open stretch of ground before drawing up at the rear of a great house.

The killer had no idea who this place really belonged to but going inside was an unsettling experience. He had only been dragged through the corridors and into the single conclave room before, but that was bad enough. He'd been told that this was the home of one of the members of this bizarre group. If that was true, which the killer doubted, the man clearly had no family; or friends, visitors or staff to do any cleaning or repairs. A single person living in this great place would go mad. Unless they were mad to begin with, of course.

Pushing at the door, which was open now, Athan stepped on into the interior. Instead of the dark passages, he led the way up some rickety stairs to the first floor.

This was obviously the main room of the hall and was big enough for a good-sized community. The storerooms below would keep supplies and animals in bad weather, but this would be the main living space. And it would be a main living space for several people; probably a whole family including all the relations.

That it was now in a rather decrepit state, deserted apart from this conclave, roused the killer's suspicions.

A lone figure rose from a seat near the fireplace in the middle of the great room and came over to join them. From previous encounters, the killer knew that this was the man who claimed the house for his own. It certainly looked as if he had treated all the food and drink as if he owned it before he ate most of it. He wore the usual hood but even this looked as if it was under considerable strain to contain the head that it covered.

From his surroundings, the killer had the strong suspicion that this must have been the great hall of a significant Saxon household. He further suspected that the household in question would have gone off to fight with Harold. No one could own such substantial property if they didn't promise service in return. And recently, most of the Saxon service to their king had required a bit of death. A quick trip to Hastings first, of course, followed by death.

There must be empty houses up and down the land waiting for their owners to come back. When the owners did turn up, it was very likely they would have Norman accents.

Those capable of fighting having gone to fight, and lost, the rest would have fled to the north - or any direction that didn't have Normans in it. Easy pickings for anyone with the temerity to walk in and say the house was theirs. And when the Normans did turn up, a person with real gall might try to welcome the conquerors as saviours and hang on to the property that wasn't theirs in the first place.

Was this such a man? The large, round body that waddled over towards the killer certainly looked like a man of supreme confidence. People of supreme confidence tended to be so because they were completely blind to what was going on around them unless it was in their interest.

'So, we're all out in the daylight now, are we?' He addressed the question to Athan and Mildburgh, before reaching up and pulling his own hood off. This face seemed happy and was smiling broadly. Just as the killer suspected; not a clue what was really going on around him.

'We need to sort things out,' Athan said. 'We've had yet another failure.'

'Oh, dear.' The fat man didn't seem very concerned. 'Not another monk?'

'Brother Simon.'

'Don't think I know him.'

'And he's not even properly dead.'

'Well, good for him.'

'But not good for us. Simon saw our killer here, and Hermitage was with him.'

'Aha.' The fellow with all the food inside him seemed to think that was more concerning.

'And two others,' Athan added, with great weight.

'Two, eh?' There was real interest now.

'I imagine it was Wat the Weaver and that Cwen girl.'

'She's a weaver as well,' the large man explained, as an aside. 'Wat eh?' He gave it a moment's thought. 'Well, these things happen. Be a shame if old Wat got caught up in this, but there we are. The girl though, we can't go killing the girl.'

'Getting squeamish?'

'No,' the man replied. 'But I've got other plans for her.'

No one liked to ask what they might be.

'I'm not killing anyone else.' The killer spoke up.

'You've only killed one of them so far,' Athan pointed out,

critically. 'A shot and a miss don't count.'

'I didn't miss.'

'You didn't kill him, which is what I think you were paid for.'

'Enough.' The large man held his hands up for peace. 'Recriminations and arguments are not going to get anyone killed, are they? The right ones or the wrong ones. We need to think what to do next.'

'Exactly what I said,' Athan agreed. 'Gather the conclave again and we can decide.'

The rotund man sighed. 'I think you can let him go now, Sister Mildburgh.' He nodded towards the powerful grip of the nun, which was released. 'I don't think he'll be going anywhere. And with that limp, we'll soon catch him.'

'Not sure you will.' The killer nodded at the size of the other.

'Aha,' the man laughed. 'No indeed. But our dear sister here is very light on her feet, surprisingly. And quite fierce when she arrives anywhere.'

The killer had to accept that this was probably the case.

The man smiled broadly. 'As we all seem to be getting on first name terms, it seems, allow me to introduce myself. Briston. Briston the Weaver.'

The killer gave a slight nod. 'I don't use names.'

'Ah, but you must. We've given you ours, now we must have yours.'

'It's a rule I have.' The killer tried to sound apologetic.

'Very well,' Briston smiled some more. 'We'll just call you, what shall we say? Bargis?'

'Bargis?' The killer was shocked. 'How did you know?'

The smile never faltered. 'We're hardly likely to go and hire some killer without finding out a little about them.

Bargis the robber, I think you began with. Then off to Hastings? You probably thought the pickings would be easy there, all those fighting men dying where they stood, their valuables still about them. But ill fortune, a stray sword, or arrow, or both? And here you are, killer for hire. You know us, now we know you. Everyone happy.'

'Hardly.'

'But Athan is right. We must gather the others and have a good chat about what to do next.' He stepped over and put a very heavy arm around Bargis's shoulder. 'Now that you're part of the family, as it were.'

Bargis looked at the three of them and quickly concluded that this was no family he wanted anything to do with.

Briston whispered confidentially in his ear. 'Between you and me, it's only Athan and his companion who seem terribly keen on death, and all that. The rest of us would be perfectly happy with any alternative solutions to the problem at hand. Perhaps you might have some ideas, eh?' He gave Bargis a friendly punch on the shoulder.

Leaving him to his thoughts, Briston stepped over to the fire and the large pot that was hanging over it. Taking a metal iron from the glowing logs, he struck the pot several times, generating a loud clang; the one that usually indicated to those near-about that the meal of the day was ready.

The call did summon others to the hall, but they certainly weren't a happy, smiling band, just in from the fields.

First, some middle-aged, thin fellow in clerical garb entered and appeared to want to sidle into the place without being spotted. He seemed confused that people weren't wearing their hoods anymore.

'Nicodemus,' Briston nodded over. 'Doesn't say much, but what he does say is usually rather nasty.'

The next to arrive was a woman, quite old and small, but with a fierce fire burning within. Like the nun, Mildburgh, this looked like a woman to be avoided.

'Eadgyth,' Briston gave the name. 'Cwen's mother, would you believe?' Briston shook his head in disappointment. 'Family, eh?'

The last to enter the room was the most surprising of all. And it was the one who had given Bargis pause when he first saw him. He couldn't help but ask the question of Briston.

'A druid?' What the devil is a druid doing here?'

'We don't know, really,' Briston confessed. 'Athan and Nicodemus started all this off, sending word out that they were interested in meeting those with experience of the King's Investigator. When we'd gathered for the first meeting, the druid just turned up. He doesn't say anything at all, just sits there smiling at everyone, It's most disconcerting.'

'Right,' Athan announced. 'We are gathered once more.' He waved the others to draw close. Only the Druid seemed happy to do so. 'Come, come.' Athan encouraged and cajoled. 'We have news and we have decisions to make. The conclave must meet once more.'

Nicodemus and Eadgyth approached cautiously, like cats tempted by a fish with a dog sitting on it. Eventually, they found places to sit, each one as far away from the others as they could get.

Athan began, clearly thinking that this was the best he was going to get. 'The conclave is in session once more. The Conclave for the murder of Brother Hermitage.'

Caput XV What Lies Beneath

'Can't I keep him insensible?' the apothecary monk asked, plaintively. 'He's only bearable when he's insensible.'

Once the bolt had been taken out of Brother Simon, and the subsequent bleeding subsided, they had moved him onto the cot. Well, it was the cot set aside for visitors, but Simon had already pointed out that it was wholly inadequate and that he would need something far more suited to his station.

Several of the monks, having heard reports of Simon, had taken some pleasure in speculating exactly what sort of cot they felt suited the new arrival. None of the ideas was very nice, or very Christian, come to that. In fact, one of them included a few features that none of them had ever thought of, even in their darkest moments. They gave the proposer of these suggestions some very odd looks and advised him that he probably needed to confess to the abbot.

'We need to talk to him,' Hermitage explained. It was only to the good that Brother Simon had been rendered unconscious while his treatment was carried out. The removal of a crossbow bolt was the sort of thing even hardened soldiers winced at. No one could imagine Brother Simon coping with it at all.

Being manhandled off the floor and onto the cot had set the bleeding off again. There was no doubt that Simon would have been in great discomfort at this and would have let everyone know. He would probably also have complained about how he was being handled, which herbs he was given, how clean the cot was and why he wasn't being attended by the abbot in person.

The four people in the room stood looking down at the quietly sleeping man and could see the many advantages of keeping him that way.

'Please yourself,' the apothecary said. 'The herbs will wear off shortly, then you can talk all you like. Just one thing I ask.'

'Of course.'

'That I don't have to be here.'

Hermitage, Wat and Cwen gave him nods of agreement that said they'd rather not be around when he woke up, either. Still, duty was duty.

While they waited for Simon, Cwen did have a thought. 'Do we really mind if Simon got shot?'

'Cwen! Charity and fellow feeling, please.'

'And we do need to find out who shot him,' Wat said. 'Doubtless the same one who did for Pewlet. And wants to do for Hermitage.'

'That is pure speculation.' Hermitage quickly moved on from that idea. 'But Wat is right. Simon may have important information to give us that will help us identify his attacker.'

'We already know he's a crossbowman with a limp,' Cwen said. 'We can do some of your enquiry things; just go around asking if anybody's seen someone like that.'

'Go around asking?' Hermitage was rather appalled by the idea. That wasn't what he'd meant at all. 'What? Just ask anyone?'

'That's it.'

'Who?'

'Anyone. Everyone.'

'People we don't know?'

'Of course.' Cwen looked to Wat with an expression of despair.

'It's a bit rude, isn't it?' Hermitage asked. 'Going up to complete strangers and asking them things?'

'What did you think an enquiry was going to be?'

'Well.' Hermitage had certainly not seen it as in any way intrusive. 'I thought we'd just ask the abbot and the brothers.'

'The abbot we've already spoken to?'

'That's him.'

'Not going to get much new information, I'd have thought,' Cwen said. 'Think of it as investigation.'

'I'd rather not.'

'If we just knocked on a few doors and asked if anyone had seen a limping man, you never know what we might find out.'

'Now we're knocking on doors!'

'Well, yes. How else do we speak to people?'

'No, no, no. That's not the way to do things at all. We follow the trail we have. That will be much more effective.'

Cwen rolled her eyes. 'You follow the trail and I'll ask the next perfect stranger I meet.'

Hermitage hoped that he wasn't around when that embarrassing encounter took place.

They couldn't debate the idea further as Brother Simon started to moan; moan in the sense of response to pain, rather than just general complaint.

'Brother?' Hermitage asked, gently. 'Can you hear me?'

'No, mother,' Simon called out, without opening his eyes.

The others looked at one another with some alarm. None of them had ever thought that Simon had a mother. They turned their attention back to the patient.

'I don't want to go outside, it's cold.' Poor Simon was clearly in some half-dream.

Hermitage thought that they probably shouldn't be listening.

Wat and Cwen bent in closer.

'Is this my milk, mother?' Simon asked, his eyes fluttering.

Hermitage smiled. Brother Simon was clearly back in his

childhood, reliving happier days.

'It's not very cold,' Simon complained. 'And this jug is dirty.'

Wat slapped his hand to his forehead. 'He was born like it.'

'Why hasn't father lit the fire yet?' Simon asked the air. 'That wood he brought in was not properly seasoned, you know. And I did mention it at the time.'

The three of them looked at one another, torn between the propriety of not intruding further, which was Hermitage, and the desire to hear more, which was Wat and Cwen.

'Brother,' Hermitage said, louder this time.

'What?' Simon asked, now sounding in some distress. 'What do you mean, I am to go to a monastery? I'm your only son. And I'm only six.'

This was getting awkward and Hermitage really didn't know what to do.

Cwen leant forward, examined Simon's face, and then slapped it.

'What? What?' Simon called out, now roused to full consciousness.

'Cwen!' Hermitage almost leapt back.

'There you are,' Cwen said. 'I didn't think you wanted to listen to any more.'

'Ah,' Simon cried out in shock. It wasn't clear if this was at the three faces that were peering down on him, or at the fact that he woke to find he was in great pain. 'Where am I?' he demanded.

No, it was shock at finding that he was in such a miserable cot.

He tried to move, and then he discovered that he was in great pain. He called out again.

'You have been shot,' Hermitage explained, gently.

Simon looked him in the eye. 'You devil,' he said.

'Not by me,' Hermitage hurriedly replied. 'By another fellow. The one who shot Pewlet.'

Simon's mind had put a very confused look on his face, which was not surprising, considering the ordeal he had been through. 'Pewlet?' he said. 'Pewlet. I know that name.'

'I should think you do,' Cwen said. 'It's the one you wrote on the church door.'

'Church door?' Simon clearly thought Cwen was mad. 'And what's a woman doing in my bedchamber?'

'You've been shot,' Cwen pointed out. 'It would have to be either you or the woman.' She turned away.

'Do you recall the fellow who shot you?' Hermitage asked. 'Was it someone from the conclave?'

'Conclave? What are you rambling about?' Simon tried to move again but winced at the discomfort. He gently put his hand down towards the source of the pain and brought it back to examine the smear of blood on his fingers.

He fainted.

'Cwen,' Wat called. 'Come and slap him again.'

'No, no,' Hermitage protested. 'He will wake momentarily, I'm sure.'

'We might get some more of his family life before he does.' Wat sounded quite interested.

It was only a few moments before Simon wandered back to awareness. 'Ah,' he called out upon seeing Hermitage. 'The fellow who shot me.'

'Brother, calm yourself,' Hermitage tried to speak as quietly and gently as he could. 'You told us that you had been sent on a mission by a great church conclave and were asking about the death of Brother Pewlet. Then, you went to Breadsall and wrote his name on the church door.'

Simon frowned, deeply. 'How do you know this?' he demanded.

'Well, erm, you told us when we saw you here.' Hermitage tried a smile.

'And how do you know I went to Breadsall?'

'Ah, that. Breadsall. Yes. You see, we, erm,'

'Happened to be there at the same time, and saw you,' Wat spoke up. 'We were visiting and there you were. Writing Pewlet's name on a church door. Why on earth would you do a thing like that, eh?'

'Visiting? Visiting who?'

'My niece and nephew, Agnes and Herbert. Lovely children, you might have seen them. They're very good most of the time. Don't write on churches. You do. Why did you do that then? The priest wasn't at all pleased, I can tell you. Perhaps we'd better pop back and tell him who it was.'

Simon seemed to be put off his stride by this blatant accusation, followed by a threat.

Hermitage just hoped he wouldn't spot the blatant lie. Using the names of Agnes and Herbert was a very doubtful idea; after all, they were only children.

'And then,' Wat continued. 'After you'd written the name on the door, you got shot. What's that all about then?'

Simon appeared to have recovered some of his natural demeanour. And he used it to look down on Wat. 'That is not for you to know.'

'Fair enough.' Wat accepted this, happily. 'When the killer comes back to finish you off, we'll tell him where you are, shall we?' He made as if to leave.

'Comes back?' Simon asked.

'Oh, yes. Bound to come back. You not being dead and all. You don't shoot someone with a crossbow only to have them not die on you. That's what my old dad always said.' Wat winked at Hermitage.

Simon took a cautious look down towards his wound. 'Shot, you say?'

'With a crossbow. We've still got the bolt.'

It was clear from the look on Simon's face that the memory of the event had come back. The enormity of his situation seemed to descend on him from somewhere above, and he sagged into his cot. 'Why would they shoot me?' he wailed.

'You tell us,' Wat encouraged. 'Did you recognise the man who did it?'

Simon seemed rather offended by the question. 'I don't know anyone who goes around shooting people.'

'He knew you. Most people don't go round shooting strangers.'

'You'd never seen him before?' Hermitage asked, more gently.

'Never,' Simon shook his head. 'He was a rough and surly fellow. I thought he'd come to attend to my pack, bring me some fresh water and ask if I wanted anything to eat. You know, he'd been assigned to me as a servant for my stay.'

Now Wat rolled his eyes at Simon's assumptions. 'And then?'

'Then he asked if I was the King's Investigator.'

'And you naturally said yes.'

'Naturally.'

'And then he shot you.'

'Then he said, "at last", and then he shot me.'

'At last?'

'That's what he said.'

'At last, he'd found the King's Investigator?' Wat asked this question of Hermitage. 'Could mean that killing Pewlet was a mistake and he was after the King's Investigator all along.'

Hermitage shook his head. 'Or it means that at last he'd found the investigator and so he can get him off the trail.'

'Nobody said I'd be shot at,' Simon complained.

Wat gave him a hard look. 'No one told you you were King's Investigator in the first place. Apart from Nicodemus, who, as far as I'm aware, has never been the king.'

Simon looked at them both. 'You mean they were trying to shoot someone else?' He sounded quite relieved at this.

'They were probably trying to shoot Brother Hermitage.' Wat nodded his head towards Hermitage. 'Who is, after all, the real King's Investigator.'

'Oh, good,' Simon said.

'Pardon?'

'At least it means they won't be coming back for me, after all.' Simon even smiled.

Hermitage thought that this was not the appropriate response from a brother.

'They still might,' Cwen offered from the other side of the room. 'There's still the question of writing Pewlet on the church wall. These people probably want to make sure there's no one left alive.' She even gave a little cackle at this.

Simon turned a little paler than loss of blood accounted for alone. He gave them all a careful look as if making up his mind whether they were trustworthy or not. Or, more likely making up his mind how he could avoid being shot anymore.

'I was simply told to come here and find out the name of the poor brother who had been killed. I was then to report it to the church.'

'By writing it on the door?' Cwen sounded contemptuous.

'Those were my instructions. The church is obviously moving very confidentially in this matter.'

'Pah. You don't even know what the matter is.'

'Who gave you the instructions, brother?' Hermitage asked.

Again, Simon seemed reluctant. 'It was in a note,' he said, eventually.

'A note?'

'I was given a note.' He fished around in his habit and produced a small piece of parchment. He handed it to Hermitage.

'Who gave you the note then?' Wat asked.

'No one. I simply found it on the cot in my cell in the monastery I was staying at.'

Treating the thing with the respect any piece of parchment deserved, Hermitage opened it up and read.

'To the King's Investigator.' He raised his eyes at that.

'They know how to hook their fish,' Cwen commented.

'To the King's Investigator,' Hermitage went on. 'An important, but highly confidential conclave requires your personal attention. A brother has been killed at the monastery in the woods. Find out who it was and report by writing the name on the church door in Breadsall. Your service in this matter will not be overlooked.'

'Hook, line and sinker,' Wat concluded with a snort.

'Not signed, I imagine?' Cwen asked.

'No.' Hermitage examined the piece closely. 'And nothing else to identify it.'

'We've got no further then.' Cwen sighed. 'The parchment is no help, and neither is Simon. Mind you, I never thought he would be. We could cut him open and find nothing useful inside.'

'Cut him open,' Hermitage said, a thought popping into his head.

'Hermitage?' Cwen asked, very cautiously.

'You are not cutting me open. It's bad enough that I've been shot.' Simon looked rather worried. He also clasped his wounded side once more and fell into a swoon.

Ignoring the wounded man, Hermitage explained. 'No, no.' He held the parchment up to the meagre light coming in through a small window. 'It's about what might be underneath. This is not a new parchment, so little is these days. It all gets used several times over and the previous writing is scraped off to clear it. A palimpsest.'

'If you say so.' Wat didn't look any better informed.

'But,' Hermitage went on. 'Quite often, the old writing has not been scraped properly. Most people are very lax over this sort of thing.'

'Standards are slipping,' Cwen agreed.

'So, we may be able to see what was written before and get some idea where this parchment came from.' He now stood and went over to the window to let the maximum light get at the material in his hands, which was old and worn.

He held it up and turned it this way and that.

'Anything?' Wat asked.

'Yes,' Hermitage said, slowly, as he squinted and tried to make out the faint lines. 'It looks as if this piece has been used many times. It's hard to see which was the most recent. He moved his attention down to the bottom of the parchment, where there might be a signature or remains of an old seal.

There was just the faintest outline of something there, right at the bottom. And it looked as if it had been written over something else. He could just about make it out if he peered hard and tipped his head over a bit.

'Oh, my.'

'What is it?' Cwen asked. 'Can you read it?'

'I can. I am afraid that I can.'

'Well? What does it say?'

'It's the name of the person who last used this parchment.'

'Someone who could write then? That narrows it down,' Wat said.

'It narrows it down to just one person,' Hermitage took a breath. 'Nicodemus.'

'Ah.'

'The close and frequent companion of Prior Athan,' Hermitage added, for completeness.

'That's him.' Wat smiled, rather grimly. 'The Prior Athan who we know would like you dead.'

'Perhaps they're in it together?' Cwen said brightly. 'I mean, perhaps they're in it together,' she repeated in a darker tone. One that much better accompanied the look on Hermitage's face.

Caput XVI How to Tempt a Monk

'Just try killing him again,' Nicodemus suggested to the gathering. 'We nearly got him with the first go. Third time lucky, and all that.'

'I nearly got him,' Bargis pointed out. 'And I'm not in a mind for trying to kill the same man for the third time. That sounds like bad luck to me.'

'It sounds like a curse,' Eadgyth suggested. 'Maybe we can't kill him. Maybe no one can.'

The meeting had been debating for some time and really hadn't made much progress. Everyone had had their say, apart from the Druid who just sat there looking wise behind his great white beard. No one had anything useful to contribute, all they wanted to do was complain about the failure, attribute it to God or the incompetence of the modern killer.

At that point, Bargis had offered to solve the conclave's problems by killing all of them instead.

Briston brought things to some sort of order and managed to get the discussion back on an even keel.

'Are we still sure we want him, you know, dead?' he asked. 'He's probably worked out that someone's trying to kill him by now.'

'I wouldn't count on that,' Athan growled. 'And yes, we want him dead. He's a confidante of the king, he keeps meddling in perfectly reasonable business and disturbing plans he has no right to disturb. With him out of the way, we'll all be able to carry on without interruption.'

'I'd have all my silver now if it wasn't for him,' Eadgyth put in.

'You said it was your husband's silver anyway,' Briston

166

reminded her. 'And there seemed to be some doubt he was actually your husband.'[10]

'That's by the by. I had a lovely plan that was all going well until he turned up.'

'One plan?' Nicodemus arched an eyebrow. 'You're lucky he's only ruined one plan. Athan and I had a nice scheme going that he ruined. Even brought the king in on it and sent us into virtual exile. And then, a second time! We almost had our hands on the most marvellous treasure until Brother bloody Hermitage turned up.'[11]

'The King's Investigator is anathema,' Sister Mildburgh announced. And she looked very sure of it.

'Are you positive about that?' Briston asked.

'Of course. The king has no right to interfere in local matters. He can't go sending investigators all over the place, sticking his nose into the perfectly reasonable activities of ordinary folk.'

Briston raised his eyebrows at that. 'I think you'll find he can, considering that he's just invaded the whole country. And in any case, your little local activities didn't sound very reasonable at all.'[12]

'Those were for the people of Shrewsbury to deal with themselves. Where's our sovereignty if people from as far away as London can tell us what to do? We need to take back control.'

'Not sure I knew there was a King of Shrewsbury,' Briston noted.

---

[10] A Murder for Mistress Cwen, if you're still remotely interested by now.

[11] The Heretics of Death and The Case of the Clerical Cadaver. Books galore

[12] Hermitage, Wat and Some Nuns. So many notes, all at once.

Mildburgh turned her fearsome gaze upon him. 'You doubt our mission?' She looked around the room as if checking what support she would get if she asked Bargis to take on a new client.

'Not at all,' Briston assured her. 'I've lost out because of the King's Investigator as much as anyone. We know that he is very widely hated. Master Nicodemus's searches even secured letters from Normandy, asking to be rid of him.[13] If the king's own folk are behind us, what can be wrong? The only thing I point out is that we do seem to be having some trouble actually getting rid of the man.'

'The curse,' Eadgyth intoned.

'So, we give up?' Athan ignored her, his temper barely contained, as usual.

'No, no, no.' Briston held his hands out to calm the troubled waters. 'All I'm doing is confirming that we are still fully committed, that's all. Every one of us.' He cast a look at the Druid at this but got no response, again.

Grumbles and mutterings circulated the room as one or two seemed not to be convinced by Briston's assurances that death was still the favoured outcome.

'I have been giving this some thought.' Athan surprised his audience as none of them had considered him to be the sort of man who did thinking. 'And the situation is this. We have sent a killer, well, so-called killer.' He gave Bargis a glare that had very little effect. 'In fact, we have sent one killer twice, and have not achieved our goal.'

The conclave waited for his conclusion.

'So, it only makes sense to send two killers next time.'

Bargis seemed very ready to object to this.

'If one couldn't do the job we increase our chances with

---

[13] Hermitage, Wat and Some Murder or Other, read all about it

two. And the one who does it is the one that gets paid. A bit of competition might sharpen them up a bit.'

Bargis snorted. 'You can count me out. I'm not getting involved in a business like that. As I said, if you want him dead, go and do it yourselves. There's enough of you, for goodness sake.'

'We have been over this.' Nicodemus was getting weary. 'This is the King's Investigator, for all his faults. None of us can be involved in the death of a king's servant. We might have business to do with the court at some time in the future. I've met King William, and I wouldn't want to be explaining that to him when he hasn't had anyone to slaughter for a day or two.'

'But I can do it?' Bargis objected.

'You are a hired killer,' Nicodemus pointed out. 'I would have thought that it's a hazard of your occupation.'

Briston held his hands up again. 'Conclave, please. Let's have some order. There is a very practical reason why we cannot simply go sending more killers. Quite apart from the fact that we don't know where it would end. It's the thin end of a wedge at the start of a long road that leads to a slippery slope. In a month we could have a dozen killers wandering the roads, all getting in one another's way. And we still don't know that they'd be successful.'

The meeting gave some muted agreement to this.

'And we can't afford it anyway,' Briston added. 'We've already paid Bargis for the murder and our funds weren't high, to begin with. None of us is rich.'

'I bet you are,' Athan managed to get in.

'None of us is rich,' Briston repeated. 'We have put our resources together, scrimped and saved and found our last shillings to pay for one little murder. We simply can't go on endlessly buying killers.'

'He didn't even do the job,' Mildburgh complained. 'I don't know why we've paid him at all. We should get our money back.'

'You can try,' Bargis offered, putting his crossbow before him and appraising the conclave quite openly. He seemed to be concluding that none of them would put up much of a fight. He'd probably have to shoot the nun first, of course. 'You gave me descriptions of the people to kill, and I did them. It's not my fault you can't describe a victim properly.'

No one seemed prepared to pursue this with Bargis.

'At least we should get a reduction,' Mildburgh muttered.

'So, what's your idea then?' Athan spat at Briston's feet.

'I do wish you wouldn't do that.' Briston considered the mess on the floor.

'You say we can't afford another killer. You check that we still want to kill him anyway. I don't hear you coming up with anything useful.'

'Ah,' Briston looked thoughtful. 'I do have an idea, but I'm not sure you're going to like it.'

'Oh, yes.' Athan was sneering now. 'We give up. Move to Normandy?' He was full of ridiculous ideas. 'Become honest and upright citizens so that the King's Investigator won't have any interest in us anyway?'

The whole conclave laughed at that one.

'No.' Briston tried to hold their gaze. 'We take even more drastic action.' He smiled at the reactions around the room, most of which were that they couldn't think of anything much more drastic than paying a hired killer to murder a monk.

'More drastic?' Athan sounded intrigued.

'Exactly.'

'And what is this more drastic action?'

Briston left a pause while he made sure he had their attention. 'A trap.'

Several of them looked around the room to see where the trap might be.

'What trap?' Bargis asked. He was clearly contemptuous of any plan for murder that didn't require the employment of a professional murderer. 'What are you going to do, dig a hole?'

'Sort of.'

'A hole for an investigator.' Bargis snorted at the rest of the conclave.

'We've tried going to him,' Briston went on. 'Well, we've tried sending you to him and have failed. We've managed to kill a perfectly innocent monk and shot this Brother Simon.'

Bargis gave a little snarl.

'As the record of a hired killer, it doesn't look very good.' Briston observed, which quieted Bargis's mumbles.

'No. We've tried to kill him where he is, now we need to get him where we want him.'

Athan did not look impressed. 'And how do we do that, exactly? Ask him if he'd mind coming over for a chat? Him and those weavers? We'd have to do them all.'

'And you've said we can't afford Bargis anymore,' Mildburgh pointed out. 'I'm not sure we're up to multiple murder.'

'Nothing like that,' Briston assured them. 'What sort of thing attracts Brother Hermitage?'

'Books,' Athan said.

'Murder,' Nicodemus added.

'The chance to interfere,' Mildburgh threw in.

Briston wasn't happy with any of the suggestions. 'What we need is something that will get his attention. Something that will make him come to us, then we can do the deed. Or get Bargis to do it.'

Bargis folded his arms as if this was nothing to do with him. Which, as they had no more money, it really wasn't.

'The same Bargis who claims to have killed his target once, but did the wrong one, followed by a murder that didn't even leave the victim dead? You could hire a common street urchin to miss someone with a crossbow.'

'Now look here,' Bargis started to protest.

'When word gets out of Master Bargis's performance in this matter, he'll be lucky to get a job killing rats. Of course, if we managed to get the victim to come to us, and Master Bargis had the time and space to do what he does in peace, there would be a very good report.'

Bargis looked around the room with naked contempt. 'You bring him here?' he checked. 'To me. You see him and confirm that he's the right one?'

'Just so.'

There was a long pause while Bargis considered this. 'All right,' he said, eventually. 'But only this once and only because you told me to kill the wrong person in the first place.'

'Excellent.' Briston rubbed his hands.

'And just what is it that is going to attract his attention?' Mildburgh asked.

'I have it.' Nicodemus snapped his fingers. They all looked his way. 'A killer. Brother Hermitage likes nothing better than finding a killer. We know that he's looking into the death of Pewlet even now. If he suspected that the killer was here, he'd be bound to come. And we have one great advantage in this.'

'Oh yes?' Bargis asked.

'Yes. The killer really is here.' Nicodemus smiled at Bargis and held his hand out to illustrate exactly which killer of Pewlet he was referring to.

Bargis just frowned.

'We let it come to Hermitage's attention that the killer of Pewlet is here, and he'll come running like a chicken looking for his head.'

'Along with those weavers,' Athan said.

Briston did pause at this and pursed his lips. 'We'd have to think of some way of making him come in to confront the killer alone.'

Bargis nodded that he'd be happy with that.

'Brother Hermitage!' Athan made a noise like a laugh. 'Brother Hermitage doesn't confront killers. He gets other people to do that for him. Kings, armies, soldiers, those sorts of people. He just stands at the back and points and accuses people. If you tell him there's a killer in here, he'll run a mile.'

Briston scratched his head.

'There would have to be something here that he would come in for,' Mildburgh said. She had a very worrying look on her face; a combination of scheming, greed, and just plain sin. It was very unattractive in a nun.

'Such as?'

'These weavers?' Mildburgh asked.

'Wat and Cwen.'

'That's them. They all three go everywhere?'

'Have since I first saw them together,' Briston said. 'I've known Wat since we were boys; Cwen I met, erm, later; and the monk turned up at the end. Just in time to ruin a very carefully thought-out plan.'

'Just so,' Mildburgh waved Briston's problems away as insignificant. 'They care for one another then?'

'I suppose so. Hadn't really given it much thought.'

'What are you thinking?' Athan asked. And it sounded as if he was going to like it, whatever it was.

'Just that the monk would probably put himself in harm's way to save his friends.'

'We kill them?' Bargis offered, not for one moment believing that these people had any more money. 'Or threaten to?'

'Then we'd have to get them in here. Same problem,' Nicodemus objected.

'Not if we already had something else that was of value to them.' Mildburgh said, her eyes positively gleaming.

'That would be good, yes.' Briston didn't look convinced. 'But what do we have? We could send word that we have this whatever-it-is, and unless Brother Hermitage comes alone we'll do it harm.'

'That's just it.' Mildburgh did her look again.

'But we don't have anything.'

'Oh,' Mildburgh said. 'I think we do.' She moved her baleful eye to rest its weight on Eadgyth.

There was a silence in the room for a moment.

'What are you looking at me for?' Eadgyth demanded.

'Cwen's mother,' Briston reminded himself.

'What about it?' Eadgyth asked. 'I can't be held responsible for that.'

'I think you can. Quite definitively.'

'I see,' Nicodemus's eyes had narrowed. 'We tell Hermitage that we have Cwen's mother and that unless he presents himself, some harm will befall her.'

'Just a minute,' Eadgyth protested. 'I'm on your side.'

'We don't say exactly who has her, obviously,' Briston took up the plan, without acknowledging Eadgyth's concerns. 'Just that he has to present himself to a certain place at a certain time. Bargis here can do the rest.'

Bargis grumbled but was ignored.

'Doubtless, that idiot Simon has already spun the yarn of the secret church conclave.' Athan supported the idea. 'This is just the sort of thing secret church conclaves get up to.'

'Now, just a moment,' Eadgyth stood. 'I am not having any harm come to me just so we can get Brother Hermitage. My money's in this scheme as well, you know.'

'Don't worry, mistress,' Briston assured her. 'No harm will really come to you. We just tell Hermitage that it will, to make him come to your rescue.'

'Unless he doesn't come straight away, of course,' Athan pondered. 'That might require a small amount of harm. But we can cross that bridge when we get to it.' He tried a smile on Eadgyth but it worked about as effectively as his laugh.

Eadgyth looked around the room and gave them all piercing stares. 'You are forgetting one thing, of course.'

'Oh, yes? What's that?'

'This mysterious value that you think I have? It doesn't exist. Cwen is my daughter. When she's told that you're going to do me harm, she'll probably want to join in.'

'Ah,' Briston reassured her with a very horrible smile. 'But it's not Cwen we want, is it? It's Hermitage. And he's an idiot.'

They all concurred with that.

Caput XVII Bait

'They've got who?' Cwen asked with mouth open.

They sat in Abbot Abbo's chamber at the monastery, loaned to them for the purpose, while they received the messenger from the conclave.

Hermitage had always thought of Cwen as a serious and rather intense person. She was quick to anger and very clear about the way she expected to be treated. She could be critical and had little patience with most people, particularly those who didn't treat her the way she expected.

She was also fearless, intensely loyal and protective of her friends, even Hermitage, who she made it quite clear drove her round more bends than a shepherd on a mountain pass.

He further suspected that she and Wat were a lot closer than they made out. He had spotted them in quiet moments when her tenderness was on display; a tenderness she kept firmly under control the rest of the time. She seemed to consider it important that the rest of the world knew exactly which of the two weavers was in charge. It was doubly important that Wat knew it.

She did smile and laugh, of course, she did. There were genuinely funny incidents in the weaving workshop and Cwen's smile could light the room and even soften the hearts of those who'd been told they didn't treat her the way she expected.

Never, in his short years of her acquaintance had he seen anything like this.

Upon hearing the news that the messenger delivered, Cwen's mouth had dropped; Hermitage imagined it was the shock.

Then she stared at the messenger as if unable to take the

words in. After what felt like quite a long silence, there was a single convulsion of her body, which released a barked "ha".

Hermitage had thought that that would be that. But then he noticed that she was struggling to control the sides of her mouth, which were twitching and dancing like moths at a dance for moths.

After that, her breaths came short and sharp, each one jolting her slim frame as if vainly attempting to hold back some fit of coughing.

Eventually, she could control whatever was going inside her no longer. She opened her mouth and a stream of laughter burst into the room that was entirely at odds with all the issues they were currently dealing with.

Some creature, made only of laughter, had encamped inside Cwen and was now making its escape. And it was in danger of taking most of her insides with it.

She bent double and clutched her stomach while struggling to get air into her chest. And when she succeeded, it only came out again as another long waterfall of laughter.

The entire edifice that Cwen presented to the world had collapsed. The messenger's news had got straight to her heart and knocked down all walls of pretence. Her soul was laughing, and it wanted the world to know.

The smile that so seldom made itself known had now taken over completely. Her face was out of control, her eyes had drawn back their shutters and the real, untranslated Cwen was bouncing around the room like a baby being carried on a phalanx of fluffy kittens.

From her bent-up posture, she managed to drag herself upright, as if moving her head away from her stomach might alleviate the pain. And Hermitage saw that she was crying. Cwen didn't cry. Ever. Even when she trapped her fingers in the weft when the treadle came down. (That had been her explanation when she'd finished swearing at Hermitage for asking if she was all right.)

It is often said that tears stream down faces, and that might be the case when they are tears of sorrow and the face is drawn and sombre. In Cwen's case, the tears were bubbling like some fresh spring tumbling over sparkling rocks as they provided another escape route for the laughter that was possessing her.

And now the noises of her laughter took on a whole new form. From gasps for breath and the consequent shrieks as that breath was dragged into her lungs, she moved on to honks. It was as if each breath in took some massive goose with it, which subsequently honked its way out again, complaining loudly at its treatment. Shriek, honk. Shriek, honk. It was surprising that someone so slight could generate such a cacophony.

She even staggered about a bit, her legs obviously wanting to join in the hilarity.

Wat went over to her and took her arm, guiding her to a seat in which she could let the convulsions run their course.

Instead of bending double, her legs came up and she curled into a shuddering, laughing ball in the chair. The tears, clearly too copious for her eyes to cope with, were now coming out of her nose as well, but she seemed oblivious to the mess.

Hermitage and Wat could only stand and watch. Unfortunately, the laughter was so virulent that they couldn't help but catch some of it. What started as smiles at Cwen's laughter, became chortles in themselves.

As part of Hermitage laughed in genuine amusement, another part of him said that this was no laughing matter and that he ought to be ashamed of himself.

He exchanged a look with Wat that said neither of them really knew why they were laughing unless seeing Cwen so happy was enough.

The messenger wasn't laughing at all. He stood there looking at them all as if he had been deposited in a chamber full of loons.

As they watched, Cwen's condition gradually quietened, her body having simply exhausted all its power in laughter. She lay like some rag in the chair, limbs loose and body gently shaking.

She tried to wipe a hand over her face, but it didn't work properly, and she ended up gently slapping herself instead. She even found this funny and started to laugh again. Now, it appeared to be quite painful and so she forced herself to stop.

Managing to take a proper breath, she calmed herself and slowly moved around in the chair until she was sitting. She found her hands and beckoned to Wat that he should hand over his silken square, the perfumed one he put over his nose when things got too bad.

Very cautiously and with clear concern, Wat reached into his jerkin and found the material. He handed it over with great reluctance.

He was right to do so, as Cwen wiped her face with the thing and then blew her nose heartily. Another act she seemed to find quite amusing.

Wat looked on with horror at the state of his silk and indicated that she could keep it.

Taking several deep breaths and blowing out through her mouth, Cwen regained her poise and then looked at Hermitage and Wat.

'They've,' she said. And it was all she managed to say

before another expulsion of laughter burst into the room.

She put her hands out to her sides and made pressing gestures towards the floor as if this might help restrain the inner force that continued to well up.

This time she didn't look at them. Instead, she bit her lips and spoke, in a very squeaky voice, that was only barely under control. Even then, she had to say the words slowly, a good gap between each one so that the one before didn't trip her up.

'They've, taken, my, mother, hostage.' She paused as if considering her own words carefully, before adding her commentary on this development; 'Ha, ha, ha, ha, ha.' Then she collapsed again, and all the good work of the silk square was undone.

Hermitage, Wat and the messenger had to wait some considerable time before Cwen was able to engage sensibly. Even then, some word would set her off again and they'd have to sit back until the hilarity leaked away.

Her voice was high and squeaky as if this was all it could manage if it wanted to retain any semblance of control. 'Why would they do that?' She asked them all, her reaction contained to a simple snort of laughter now. 'I mean, have they really taken Eadgyth hostage?'

They turned to their messenger.

The young messenger was looking very bored at everything that was going on and simply sat beside his inquisitors, picking his nose.

'Yes,' Rolf of Eaton repeated for the hundredth time. 'Can I go now?'

'You can go when we say so.' Wat's look was enough to keep the child on the spot.

Rolf sighed a bored and slightly impertinent sigh.

'How long have you been in the pay of these people?'

'What?' Rolf looked at Wat as if he'd just spoken Latin.

'The people who sent you with this message. What else have they got you to do?'

'Nothing.'

'Nothing, eh? What sort of nothing, exactly?'

'I only brung the message, didn't I?' Rolf was defiant.

'Is that all? Who are they then?'

'I don't know, do I? Just people.'

'One called Nicodemus?'

Rolf just shrugged that he didn't know what their names were, and had no interest anyway.

'Tall, thin fellow,' Wat explained. 'Dresses like a priest but isn't one.'

Rolf gave no indication that he was going to give an answer, whether he knew one or not.

'But they said they wanted Brother Hermitage.'

'That's right.' Rolf was happy to confirm this. 'Stupid name for a monk.'

Wat half rose from his seat with a hand raised. Rolf cowered.

The boy did his sigh once more and repeated his message. He closed his eyes, so he could get the words right. 'Brother Hermitage is to come to the old house of Gifard to recover the Lady Eadgyth.'

'Lady!' Cwen snorted another nose full of humour that she failed to catch in Wat's silk, which was now completely sodden anyway.

'He is to come alone,' Rolf went on. 'And no harm will befall the lady.' He opened his eyes again, message delivered.

Cwen was now looking away as if taking her eyes off all this would help in some way. She'd also clamped a hand over her mouth and nose to stop any more of her head coming out.

Hermitage had a moment of revelation. 'It was you who told this conclave what was written on the church door.'

Rolf said nothing.

'I shouldn't think he can read,' Wat scoffed.

'No,' Rolf said proudly. 'I certainly can't.'

'He wouldn't have to. He clearly has a good memory, having recalled all the words of the message. He could simply recall the shapes Simon drew and then repeat them for the conclave. After all, Pewlet is a simple enough name.'

'Is that what you did?' Wat demanded.

'I'm good at drawing.' Rolf was proud of this now. 'I can draw a horse in the dirt with a stick.'

'I'll draw you in the dirt with a stick in a minute,' Wat threatened, which seemed to make little sense at all. 'Where did you go to see these people? The old house of Gifard?'

'Could be,' Rolf confessed.

'And who did you see? Come on. There's no point hiding it, Hermitage has been asked to go and meet them.'

'Just some man.'

'Some man.'

'I don't know, do I?' Rolf protested. 'Some fat man and an angry man. I don't know who they are, or what they want. I just done an errand, that's all. It's not my fault.'

'A fat man and an angry man.' Wat looked away in despair. 'Big help.'

'I don't think the child has anything else he can tell us,' Hermitage said. 'We know all he knows.'

'I very much doubt that.' Wat gave Rolf a threatening look.

Rolf stuck his tongue out.

Hermitage waved that Rolf might as well leave the room, which the child did, but not before stopping at the door and turning to point his bottom at them all.

'What an awful child,' Hermitage commented. 'We may need to have a word with his parents.'

'Who I suspect are dead,' Wat said. 'Unless they've just run away from home to get away from Rolf.'

'And this conclave has made use of a child to carry their messages.' Hermitage shook his head. 'That's very poor behaviour.'

'At least we know they're idiots as well.' Cwen was back facing the rest and was exercising some measure of restraint. She was still smiling very broadly but at least appeared to be rational now. 'Taking my mother as a hostage.' She contained a small fit of giggles. 'Who's going to want to ransom her? I wouldn't give you Rolf's stick for her, and I'm her daughter.'

'It's obviously a trap,' Wat said, as plainly as he could.

'A very bad one, with rotten old bait,' Cwen added with a beaming smile. 'Oh, dear,' she said, sighing to herself. 'This is the funniest thing in years.'

'Your mother is being held hostage.' Hermitage felt that he should point out the seriousness of the situation.

'No, she isn't.' Cwen dismissed this as if she'd just been told the cows were dancing in the fields.

Brother Hermitage frowned at them both and considered this impossible situation. Not only was it an impossible situation but even now that he was in the middle of it, he couldn't really work out how he'd got here.

'But,' was all he managed.

'The conclave hasn't been conclaved that could take my mother hostage,' Cwen explained. 'If she is a hostage at all, which I very much doubt, she's probably done it to herself. Wat's right. It's a trap. A ruse just to get you to go anywhere near them. There's only one answer to this. Leave her where she is.'

'Harm may come to her.'

Cwen thought about this for a moment. 'So?'

'So, we must rescue her.'

Cwen shook her head as if turning down a second turnip. 'No. There's no need to rescue her because she's not really a hostage at all. And if she is a hostage there's no need to rescue her because no one cares whether she comes to harm or not.'

'Oh, Cwen,' Hermitage gently chastised. 'She is the mother who gave birth to you.'

'We've only got her word for that. I was very young at the time.'

Hermitage didn't know what to say. If Eadgyth's own daughter was not interested in taking action, was it his place to interfere? Yes, of course, it was. There was a moral question, after all. You couldn't just let people go round taking hostages as they pleased. Where would it end?

'Pewlet,' he said, as he brought his mind back to where all this began. 'Regardless of the rights and wrongs of the hostage situation, all of this stems from the death of poor Brother Pewlet.

'If this conclave has anything to do with that, it is our duty to get to the bottom of it.' He was happy with this reasoning. 'What I can't understand is why a conclave of the church would be holding anyone hostage just to have a meeting with me? They've only got to ask.'

'Oh, for goodness sake, Hermitage.' Wat sounded quite exasperated. 'It's not a church conclave. It's Athan and Nicodemus and goodness knows who else - probably Eadgyth herself. They are out to get you because you keep interfering in their plans. This is all a ruse to get you to go to this house, where they will kill you.'

'They wouldn't.' Hermitage was appalled at the very idea.

'They already tried twice,' Cwen reminded him. 'And Wat's right. The Lady Eadgyth is doubtless in on it as well. Having lost all that silver she'd stolen in the first place, she won't be best pleased with you.'

'Whatever the details, these people had something to do with the death of Pewlet. They must be held to account.'

'Yes,' Wat agreed. 'They killed him by mistake, thinking it was you. If you go investigating all over them, they'll have a chance to get it right this time.'

'We'll all go,' Cwen offered. 'I'd like to see my mother held to account.'

'The message was that I must go alone,' Hermitage pointed out.

'Yes, it was, wasn't it? And you always do what you're told by hostage-takers, do you?'

Hermitage had to admit it had never happened before, so he wouldn't really know. But yes, as a principle, he did what he was told by most people.

'We know that this is a trap.' Wat was thoughtful. 'And if we plan it carefully it might be our trap, instead of theirs.'

Hermitage didn't like all this talk of traps.

'We don't know how many there are,' Cwen said. 'We could be heavily outnumbered.'

'We'll need to plan extra carefully then.' Wat smiled and rubbed his hands. 'We know where they are, and we know what they want.' His smile turned to Hermitage, which didn't settle him at all. 'If they've got Eadgyth as bait, we've got the King's Investigator, that must be better.'

'In fact,' Cwen added with a very worrying smile, 'we've got two of them.'

Caput XVIII Monk of the Day

'The others will come with him,' Briston stated the fact. 'We know they will. It's all very well sending some child with a message saying come alone, but he's not going to.'

'He is very stupid,' Athan pointed out. 'He's always done what people tell him in the past. Once, in De'Ath's Dingle, a band of brothers told him that it was washday for half of the habits in the place and so he would have to take his off and stay in his cell.'

'And he did?'

'Of course, he did. They sent him food and drink while he was waiting but I made them return the habit after a week. I suspect he would still be there, naked in his cell if I hadn't.'

'Got to wash a habit sometime.' Briston shrugged that this didn't seem a very clever trick.

Athan looked at him with disgust. 'No, you don't.'

Briston's shrug became a shudder. 'This is all very interesting, but Wat and Cwen are not quite so gullible.'

'And Cwen won't care about me anyway,' Eadgyth added. 'She's probably told him not to come at all.'

'Look.' Nicodemus got all their attention and explained as if to children younger than Rolf. 'Hermitage will come alone. It's the only honourable thing to do and he really is that stupid, take my word for it. Yes, the other two will try to persuade him not to bother, but he will insist. Then, they will say that they will go with him, but he'll say something like "oh, no, think of the poor Lady Eadgyth, I must go alone as I have been instructed.'

'Idiot,' Athan spat.

'Quite.' Nicodemus continued. 'But they will ignore him and come anyway, even if they follow without him knowing.

186

So, all we must do is prepare for the arrival of three people. Wat and Cwen will probably be sneaking around by some back path so that they can leap in and surprise us all.'

'We could always let them,' Athan suggested. 'And then do for them all. I've never liked that weaver. Too clever for his own good. As well as disgusting. Have you seen some of the things he does pictures of?'

'We've all seen the pictures.' Nicodemus sighed that they were getting off the topic. 'We are not doing for anyone else. It's the investigator we want. No one will miss him. We end up with a massacre of the weavers and people will come looking. You know how popular Wat the Weaver is in some circles.'

'Disgusting circles.' Athan was not convinced.

'And we don't touch Cwen,' Briston said. 'She's a talented weaver and I've got plenty of commissions she can help with.'

'Good luck with that,' Eadgyth said. 'Getting Cwen to do what she doesn't want? I think it'll be you who ends up done for.'

Briston had a retort on his lips but was interrupted.

'People, please.' Nicodemus raised his arms. 'We need to prepare.' They fell silent. 'Hermitage will come into the building alone, but there is no doubt that Wat and Cwen will be close at hand. All we need to do is make sure they are diverted.'

'Diverted?' Athan asked. 'What, by a jester or something?'

'Not that sort of diversion, for God's sake.' Nicodemus's patience was running very low and he started muttering to himself. 'If Brother Hermitage is an idiot, he'll be just one more to add to my collection.' He sighed. 'No, I mean diverted away from the main hall.'

'And how do we do that?'

'We don't, Bargis does.'

'Oh, does he?' Bargis said, taking a very high and mighty tone.

'You are the one with the crossbow,' Nicodemus pointed out.' I don't think they'll take much notice if one of us asks them nicely if they'd mind waiting in a storeroom while we kill their friend.'

Bargis folded his arms. 'Oh, you're going to kill him now, are you? That's all right then.'

'No, we are not going to kill him. You will lie in wait for Wat and Cwen. When they arrive you will capture them with your crossbow. Could you manage that?'

Bargis hefted his weapon to indicate that there were many things he could manage with it.

'Excellent.' Nicodemus showed not the least concern in patronising a killer with a crossbow who was standing right in front of him. 'So. You take them to the storeroom, lock them in and then come up here.'

'To deal with the monk,' Athan added, with unnecessary relish.

Bargis was observing them all and gently shaking his head.

'What is it now?' Briston asked, wearily.

Their killer had pursed his lips and looked as if he was calculating something very carefully; a remarkable achievement for someone who probably couldn't calculate the number of his own toes. 'The monk is all well and good,' he started. 'Well, it's not, but I have agreed, on this occasion, to help you out with the monk.'

Briston nodded. 'Mainly since the monk we asked you to kill in the first place is one we've just had to invite to our secret conclave, largely due to the fact that he isn't quite as dead as we'd specified.'

Bargis ignored this. 'And I am prepared to get the monk job finished. Now that I'm going to be shown which is the actual monk you want dead, instead of being given unhelpful descriptions that lead to a lot of wasted crossbow bolts.'

'One wasted crossbow bolt,' Briston reminded the hired killer. 'You got the one from Pewlet back. That's Pewlet the monk you killed by mistake.'

Again, Bargis managed to pretend no one else was talking. 'But capturing people and locking them in storerooms.' He shook his head and looked as if he'd been given all the tasks of Hercules to complete before bedtime.

'Oh, I see.' Briston sounded as if he finally understood. 'You can kill the wrong monk, shoot another one, another wrong one, and then finally kill the one we've asked for, but you can't lock someone in a room. Bit of a gap in your services, if I may say so. Be a very handy thing to learn, shutting a door and locking it. You never know when it might come in handy during a murder.'

Bargis waved the sarcasm away. 'I'm not saying I can't lock people in a room. Of course, I can. Very capable of locking people in a room when the need arises. Point is, I haven't been asked to lock anyone in a room, have I? I've been asked to kill a monk, and that's what I'm doing.' He got to the nub of the problem. 'Locking people in rooms is extra.'

'What?' Athan, Briston and Nicodemus all expressed their shock.

Bargis helpfully hefted his crossbow to let them know which way this conversation might go.

Briston rubbed his chin. 'Let me get this straight. You're saying that locking someone in a room to kill the person you're going to kill costs more.'

'There you have it.'

'Very well, we won't have the locking in then, thank you very much.'

'Won't have it?' Bargis suddenly looked on the back foot.

'No thanks. We'll let the weavers follow Brother Hermitage into the house and then you can do it while you're all together. Probably a much more friendly way to do it. They'd only be disappointed when they got out of their locked room to find their friend had been killed without them.'

'That's very reasonable,' Nicodemus agreed, speaking to Briston and ignoring Bargis. 'Of course, Wat and Cwen will probably cause a bit of a fuss. Around the time the shooting starts, I expect.'

'You could be right.' Briston nodded, knowingly. 'But then that must be the sort of thing killers are used to dealing with. I think we can probably leave him to it and come back when it's all over.'

'Now, just a minute,' Bargis began.

'I could do it,' Athan offered, with one of his horrible smiles. 'I could lock Wat in a room. I'd like to do that.'

'You'd need the crossbow,' Nicodemus pointed out.

Bargis clutched his crossbow close to his chest. 'All right, all right. God above you are the worst bunch I've ever had to deal with.'

Briston smiled at the compliment.

'Most people who hire a killer at least have the decency to be a bit ashamed about it. They don't start haggling.'

'Their killer probably doesn't try to charge them extra for every little thing.' Nicodemus bowed his head towards the killer in the room.

'Isn't this monk going to run a mile as soon as he sees you, anyway?' Bargis asked. 'In my experience, people tend to know who wants to kill them and who doesn't, and they try to avoid any meetings. He walks in here and sees you lot? Stupid or not, he's going to leave. Especially if he sees the hostage is one of you and not actually being threatened with harm at all.'

Nicodemus smiled. 'That would indeed be the case if he was able to recognise us.'

Bargis looked around the room. The people scattered about were easily recognisable. After this job, he'd never forget any of them.

Nicodemus gave a nod to the room and everyone reached for their hoods. Bargis sighed and shook his head 'For God's sake,' he muttered.

Each member of the conclave put theirs on and peered through the eye-holes at the front. There was a bit of a struggle as Athan adjusted his, having put it on so that the eye holes were at the back.

'Ha,' Bargis couldn't help but laugh out loud.

It was a strange gathering. It had been a strange gathering, to begin with, what with the religious folk, a druid and then Briston and Eadgyth. This same gathering with hoods on was just bizarre.

'I was right,' Bargis commented. 'One look at you lot and he will run a mile.'

'He won't know who we are,' one of the conclave said. It was hard to tell which one, due to the fact they all had their mouths covered and the voice was quite muffled. 'We will wear our hoods and will stand around the room while you deal with Brother Hermitage. There's one for you.' This figure held out a hood, which Bargis took with some disdain. 'We've even got a hood for our victim.'

It was now clear that this was Athan, who held up another

spare hood.

'Why?' Bargis asked.

'Why what?'

'Why have you got a hood for him? He's the one you want me to kill. Won't matter if he's got a hood on, will it?' He folded his arms.

'He won't recognise us.'

'You've got hoods on,' Bargis pointed out.

There was a rather awkward silence. 'Ah,' Athan had a new thought. 'It's so he won't know where he is.'

'You've just sent him a message telling him where to come.'

This was clearly a question the conclave had not considered in detail. If people in hoods could pass awkward looks, they now did so.

'Just put it on him,' Athan growled. 'It'll add to the sense of dread. His dread, obviously.'

Bargis snorted at this. 'If you ever want anyone killing in the future, would you like to think about it a bit more, before you hire your killer?' He shook his head as he considered the hopelessness of the gathering before him.

Athan, Nicodemus and Briston were fairly well disguised but Mildburgh looked just like a nun wearing a hood. There would be no mistaking her. And as for the druid, putting a hood on a large man with a voluminous grey beard dressed in white was not going to fool anyone. "Oh," people would say, "there's a druid with a hood on. You don't see that every day."

Bargis considered their plan and took it through its first steps. 'Hold on.' He sat on the edge of the table. He sounded rather critical. 'I thought I was holding Wat and this Cwen in a storeroom somewhere.'

Nicodemus removed his hood. 'You take them to the storeroom, lock them in, and then come up here.' He sounded very tired of explaining this simple process over and over again to what must be the most stupid killer in Christendom.

'Yes, I get that.' Bargis was making it clear that the people hiring the killer were even more stupid. 'But, if Wat and friend are following the monk, he will be in here, with you, before I've even captured them. Then, by the time I've locked them in and got up here, your monk will be long gone. If he's got any sense at all.'

'Ah, but he'll want to rescue the hostage.'

'Who isn't a hostage at all, and is one of you, standing there with your ridiculous hoods on.'

'Ah,' Athan said as he took his own hood off. 'I knew that bit of it was going to be a problem. From around his waist, he quickly untied the rope that bound his habit and stepped smartly over to the smallest conclave member of all.

'Here,' Eadgyth cried, as Athan threw the rope around her shoulders. 'What do you think you're doing?'

'Making you look like a hostage and harm is about to come to you.'

'Harm is coming to me.' Eadgyth wriggled and squirmed. 'I'm being tied up.'

'It's only for show,' Athan explained. The look on his face said he was quite enjoying it as well. 'This way, Hermitage will think you really are a hostage and waste time trying to free you. That'll give Bargis the chance to get up here and do the job.'

'Why me?' Eadgyth complained.

'Because you're the one we've told him is being held hostage?' Athan seemed astounded at the idiocy of his hostage. 'Be a bit odd if he comes to rescue Lady Eadgyth and finds big fat Briston the weaver tied up.'

'Do you mind?' Briston objected.

'For goodness sake!' Nicodemus threw his hood on the floor in frustration. 'We're supposed to be a mysterious conclave of the church, dealing with one of our own who has gone over to the Normans and ruined our lives in the process. This is getting like a mummers' play. Why don't we get a maypole and all dance around it while Athan wears a horse's head?'

The others regarded him with some concern.

'Calm yourself,' Sister Mildburgh snapped at him. 'It's perfectly clear. The Eadgyth woman will be the hostage, the rest of us will keep our hoods on so Hermitage doesn't recognise us.'

'What do you mean, the Eadgyth woman?' Eadgyth was not going to take this from a nun.

Mildburgh just gave her nun's stare, the one that expressed shock that anyone had dared speak to her without invitation.

'And you needn't look at me like that.' Eadgyth tried to shrug Athan off, but he had got on quite well with tying her up and was very satisfied with the results.

Nicodemus simply collapsed into a chair and held his head in his hands, his hood discarded on the floor. 'It would have been easier just to buy my own crossbow,' he muttered. 'Then I could have shot you lot with it afterwards.'

At that moment the door to the chamber burst open and Rolf strolled in as if he had just got back from robbing the bakers. He had a sly look on his face and appeared to be chewing something soft and sticky.

''I done it,' he called out, wandering across the room to Nicodemus. 'I told them what you said.'

'And?' Nicodemus asked.

'Dunno.'

What do you mean, dunno?'

'What do you mean, and?'

'What did they say? What are they going to do?' Nicodemus was starting to look quite happy that he had someone small and helpless on whom to take out his frustrations.

'Come and get her,' Rolf replied, impudently.

'Excellent.'

'I suppose.'

'You suppose?' Nicodemus gaped at the statement. 'Didn't you ask?'

'You didn't ask me to ask,' Rolf replied, quite reasonably.

Nicodemus buried his head once more and started having a conversation with himself that did not sound very positive.

'What did they do when you told them we had the hostage?' Briston asked.

Rolf sniffed, revoltingly. 'The girl laughed a lot. Nearly burst, she did.'

'Ha!' Eadgyth exclaimed.

'Well, when are they coming?' Nicodemus tried.

Rolf just shrugged again.

'Ah!' Nicodemus's cry was despairing. 'I come up with a perfectly good plan to get rid of the investigator and I surround myself with idiots.'

'Here,' Briston protested.

I even managed to get an idiot for a killer, who goes off and shoots at the wrong people.'

Bargis just gave a dark look.

'Never work with idiots or children. I should have known. And a druid! For heaven's sake a druid.' He waved a hand towards the druid who was sitting quietly in a corner. He still had his hood on but really did look like nothing more than a druid sitting in a corner with a hood on.

Nicodemus scanned the room. 'You lot wouldn't fool a fool.'

'We can always pay Bargis to do a little extra work when this is all over.' Briston was looking quite serious. 'After all, we wouldn't want to be associated with the death of the king's own investigator. William and his men might come asking questions. We could say Nicodemus did it.' He left a pause. 'So we had him shot.'

Nicodemus looked as if he wouldn't mind being shot, right now.

'You.' They all jumped as Mildburgh barked into the room. Her finger was pointing at Bargis. 'The killer fellow. Go outside and wait for the arrivals.'

'The name is Bargis,' Bargis said.

'Very good.' Mildburgh clearly wasn't very interested. 'The rest of you, get your hoods on and wait as well. You are all hopeless and if any one of you was in my nunnery you'd know all about it.'

'And who am I waiting for, exactly?' Bargis asked.

'A monk.' Mildburgh bit back. 'Like the one you killed only less dead. They're easy to spot.'

Bargis just grumbled.

'You let him pass and wait for two more people, a man and woman, and then do as you have been told.' Half to herself, she carried on. 'If everyone did what they were told the world would be a much better place.'

'You mean, if everyone did what you told them,' Bargis muttered as he left the room.

'How long do we have to wait?' Eadgyth complained, resigned now to sitting with her arms bound.

'As long as it takes.' Mildburgh dismissed the question.

'The Lord has taught me patience through the years. You are about to learn some as well. If we have to stand here all night, we will do so.'

'But,' Briston began.

'And no talking,' Mildburgh instructed. 'Can't have a murder victim coming to a lot of chatterboxes. Silence.' She clapped her hands to emphasise her order. 'And hoods on.'

They fell silent. Even Nicodemus, sitting in his chair, reached down for his hood to put it back on. As he did so, he cast a glance at Mildburgh. And, as the hood fell over his face, it cast into shadow the trace of a smile and muffled a sigh with more than a hint of longing.

Caput XIX Into The Valley of De'Ath

'I suppose they will be waiting for us.' Brother Hermitage was starting to feel a little nervous about his plan to rescue the hostage, right and proper though it was. 'Nicodemus and perhaps Athan.'

'They will,' Wat confirmed. 'That being the nature of a trap. And if your old friend Athan is there, it will be like a De'Ath's Dingle reunion.'

There wasn't anything in that sentence that Hermitage wanted to dwell on for a moment. 'I suppose there's nothing for it.' He girded his spirit in preparation for departure.

'Not so fast, Hermitage.' Cwen said. 'We need to plan this carefully.'

'We do?' Hermitage didn't usually plan anything carefully. He couldn't see what planning was required to walk to the Gifard house, apart from finding out where it was.

'Of course.' She looked to Wat and blew out a long, slow breath and shook her head slowly. Hermitage recognised the signs that said he had got something wrong. Again.

'We don't just go marching in there.'

Hermitage hadn't been going to march, he didn't really know how.

'We work out what we're going to do, where, when and how and then we do it.'

'I see,' Hermitage tried to sound enthused by this.

'It's obvious that they're going to be waiting for you and will want to kill you.'

Hermitage was about to object to this rash conclusion when Cwen raised her hands. 'Let's just assume that shall we? For the sake of argument?'

Ah, well. If it was for the sake of argument, then

Hermitage was all for it.

'Equally obviously, we don't want them to kill you.

He really did agree with that.

'So, what do we do?' She held up her hand and counted off the options on her fingers. 'One; don't go at all. Leave them to it, do nothing, keep our heads down and hope it all turns out all right in the end. Go home and wait for King William to come up with a proper murder for you to look at.'

Hermitage frowned at leaving the hostage and the murder of Pewlet uninvestigated.

'But there's Pewlet to consider,' Cwen acknowledged. 'Two; you go there to rescue the hostage, we wait here, they kill you, we come to collect the body.'

He wasn't keen on two.

'Three; and this is a good one. We send the King's Investigator to rescue the hostage.' She looked at Hermitage for signs that he understood what she meant.

'Brother Simon?' Hermitage was surprised at that one.

'Exactly. He's the King's Investigator, that's the person they want. We send him. We could even get him to change clothes with you.'

Hermitage frowned. 'What would be the point of that, we both wear the same.' He held out his arms to illustrate that he was wearing a monk's habit, but then they should know that.

'You do, but yours is, erm, how can I put it? More revolting than Simon's? His looks pretty new and neat and clean and so forth, while yours is, erm, lived in.'

'Lived in?' Of course, it was lived in, he lived in it.

'I bought him that, back in Lincoln.' Wat said. 'It was the best at the time.'

'But Hermitage has given it quite a lot of time since then.

More than its fair share, I'd say. The point is, that if Simon turns up wearing Hermitage's habit, and has his hood pulled down, they'll think it's him. Then he can find out what's really going on with Eadgyth.'

'Unless they shoot him on sight, of course,' Wat said.

Hermitage saw a problem with plan number three and put his hand up.

'Yes?' Cwen asked, pointing at him. 'The monk at the front.'

Hermitage looked around and saw that there wasn't a monk at the back. He tutted at Cwen's levity. 'I don't think Brother Simon would do it. He's not the most helpful of fellows. Particularly not to us. Why would he put himself in danger?'

'Obviously, we don't tell him he's going into danger.'

'Cwen!'

'We tell him that the great and secret conclave has sent for the King's Investigator. Of course, we recognise his importance now and he can even have Hermitage's habit for the meeting.'

Wat was nodding. 'Nice,' he said. Cwen smiled.

'It's outrageous,' Hermitage objected. 'We cannot trick the man into going to be shot. We can't trick anyone into going to be shot.'

'It's not much of a trick,' Cwen protested. 'Most of it's actually true.'

'Most of it being true is hardly sufficient. What's plan four?'

Cwen and Wat exchanged shakes of heads that a perfectly reasonable plan was being rejected. A plan that would see them kept safe and only had a slight risk of Simon being shot again, properly, this time.

'The same thing, except Simon's delirious from his wound and doesn't know what he's doing.'

'That's much worse,' Hermitage was even more shocked and was pleased to see Cwen lower her eyes.

'Alright. Five; you do go to this house.'

'As myself and in my own habit?'

'Just so. But we follow on. We keep you in sight and are there to make sure no harm befalls you.'

'Or the hostage.'

'Well,' Cwen didn't seem quite so worried about Eadgyth. 'We can worry about her later. We'll have to be very careful though. As Wat says, as soon as they see you they may shoot. Then we could be too late.'

'And if there's a lot of them,' Wat added, 'we could have our hands full.'

'It may only be Athan and Nicodemus.' Hermitage thought those two alone were quite enough.

'And Eadgyth,' Cwen added. 'We know she's there and she's doubtless in on this as well. That's three.'

'And who knows how many others they've got?' Wat said.

'Others?' Hermitage didn't like to think there was going to be a queue of people who wanted him dead.

He had to admit he was finding it hard to maintain the idea that this was all about getting the King's Investigator off the trail of Pewlet's killer. If that was the case, what was Nicodemus doing in the middle of it all? Wherever that man went, so went Athan. And wherever Athan went, there went ill-feeling towards Hermitage. Still, it was a bit of a leap from ill-feeling to a crossbow.

'Could be they've rounded up everyone from every investigation you've ever done,' Wat went on, with unnecessary enthusiasm. 'Well, all the bad people, anyway.

Or, like Simon, they've tricked a room full of fools into believing they're on some secret church mission.'

Hermitage pondered for a moment. 'How close behind me would you be?'

. . .

After a last look in on Brother Simon, they prepared to leave. Cwen was most disappointed that they found the wounded monk had taken several long steps down the path into delirium and was chatting and arguing loudly with a whole legion of people who were failing to meet his high standards.

Her disappointment was largely founded on the fact that in this state, he'd probably do whatever they told him, and could be quite useful. What a waste.

Hermitage put a firm stop to any such ideas as sinful and heartless.

Wat had pointed out that if they did manage to get him up and off to the Gifard house, he'd probably pass out from blood loss before he'd done anything useful at all.

Hermitage condemned that as just plain heartless.

Abbot Abbo was not much help, either. Despite them telling him what was going on, and how Hermitage was in danger, the best the Abbot could offer was directions.

Wat suggested that a small force of monks would be helpful. Or at the very least a small force of Brother Nult.

Abbo explained that there had been a bit of an altercation between Nult and some of the other brothers and that they were all now being punished by confinement to their cells.

When pressed, he had to admit that the altercation had been between Nult and all the other brothers and so everyone was locked in. He did say that if they could wait a day or two, he would see what he could do.

Hermitage shook his head and said that it was his duty to attempt rescue of the hostage straight away. If things went badly they would try to get away and come back to seek further aid.

Leaving the monastery, they found that they were almost in Breadsall before they came upon the outreaches of the Gifard house. Cwen warned Hermitage that he would have to go alone from some way out. They could follow through the trees without being spotted, but the people inside would doubtless be looking out.

Treading carefully through the undergrowth, the existence of the place soon became clear. Wood had been cleared and crops planted for some distance around to support those in the house. There was no way the three of them would be able to walk across this open ground without being seen.

'You wait here,' Cwen said, as they reached the edge of the woodland. 'Give us time to circle round to the back before you go in the front.'

Hermitage nodded silently, the prospect of entering this house having condemned his voice to silence. He wanted to say that he had not the first idea how long it took people to circle around a house, but it wouldn't come out.

Wat patted him heartily on the back. 'We'll go round and see what we can find. They shouldn't be watching the back. When we get there and know what we can do, we'll give you a signal.'

Hermitage just looked blank. What were they going to do, send him a note? In which case who would bring it?

'We'll make a bird sound,' Cwen explained.

Hermitage cocked an ear to the woodland, which was full

of bird sounds.

'Alright, a goose honk.' She demonstrated by doing a goose honk.

'That's nothing like a goose.' Wat made his own version of the honk.

'What are you, a troubled piglet?' Cwen snorted.

'Alright, we'll make a piglet sound.' Wat folded his arms.

Hermitage waved their disagreement away and indicated that he would recognise whoever made the noise, the woodland not being noticeably awash with the sound of either geese or troubled piglets. He suspected that the people in the house might grow suspicious if the non-existent pigs started shouting at one another.

'Don't worry, Hermitage,' Cwen reassured him, resting a gentle hand on his shoulder. 'The one thing we know about Nicodemus and Athan is that they're largely useless at everything they try. Holding my mother as a hostage is way beyond them. As soon as you get in there and see that all is well, get out again. We'll come in anyway and can deal with the whole Pewlet problem.'

Hermitage nodded. He could manage that.

'It'll only be a few minutes.' Cwen smiled. 'And then you'll be able to walk up and down in front of everyone explaining who did what and who the guilty party is. You know you like that bit.'

Hermitage tried a smile.

'With any luck, there'll be a limping man with a crossbow in there. How good will that be?'

Hermitage quickly concluded that it wouldn't be good at all, particularly if the crossbow was being pointed at him. He also doubted if Cwen and Wat would be able to reach him faster than a flying bolt.

With a last encouraging smile, Cwen and Wat stepped quietly off into the woods.

Left alone, Hermitage very quickly realised that everyone else's ideas had been better than his. All the suggestions that involved him not entering the house of the likely monk killers, were excellent. His proposal of stepping forth to rescue a hostage who very likely wasn't a hostage at all, he now saw as being intensely stupid.

It only seemed a very few moments before a distinctive sound echoed across the wood. The troubled piglet had taken a ride on the goose and both were now fighting.

Taking a very deep breath, so deep that it made his head spin, Hermitage took the first step out of the cover of the trees. He reasoned that the first step would be the hardest and after that, it would get easier. He was wrong about that as well.

Crossing the space like a scarecrow hopping away from a sparrow, he approached the Gifard house at a pace that would have the snails telling him to get a move on.

At the back of the place, Wat and Cwen had found a woodpile that provided good cover, so they could get quite close to the house without being seen. The last few feet of space were open and crossing this was unavoidable.

Having disagreed over whose goose honk was more realistic, they also argued over the best way to cross open ground. Wat was all for a sneak around the edge, while Cwen favoured the fast frontal approach and a dash for a door they could see. Doubtless, this was the entry to some storerooms and they would be able to access the rest of the house once they were inside. If they could get to the upstairs chamber just before, or at the same time as Hermitage, so much the better.

Wat decided to provide definitive leadership and beckoned Cwen to follow as he led the way around the open ground, keeping his head low and his knees bent. He made it across to the wall of the house and then scurried along towards the door. When he got there, he found Cwen, waiting for him, arms folded and a disappointed look on her face. He stood upright and tutted at her defiance.

Now, she indicated that he should follow as she put her hand to the door. It was a rough construction, being simple planks with cross-pieces, held together by wooden pegs hammered through. There was no attempt to make the door fit the opening it covered. This was the servants' door, after all, not for the fine folk who would use the front of the house. A simple wooden latch held the thing in place and this lifted with a slight squeak when Cwen moved it.

The door was a bit less keen to move, it having sagged on its hinges long ago. There was a clear trail in the ground where it had been dragged open and closed on many occasions. Cwen had to put her weight to it to get it to move and it ground itself against the rough earth and bent from top to bottom as it shifted.

Inside, the space was as dark as would be expected. There were no windows at this low level, the timbers and in-fill of the walls forming a solid barrier. It was also cool and smelled strongly of all the things that had passed this way. Slightly rotten wood was most prominent, but there was also the distant tang of fruit as well as a foundation of dung; this being the route for things to leave the house, as well as come in.

They paused and let their eyes get used to the darkness before they moved further. The room they were in was both a simple entrance and a store in its own right. A large pile of dry logs lay higgled in one corner, while some shelving opposite held what looked and smelled like apples. Apples that had shrivelled while waiting to be eaten by people who had long gone. The whole room had an aura of mustiness about it that spoke of absence, rather than the life of the great hall.

Looking about, Wat silently nodded towards another door, off in the back-left corner of the room. This was in much better condition, not being exposed to the weather. It also looked better made, as if more important people might want to use it now and again. It must lead to the rest of the house and so the two intruders gently and slowly made their way towards it, listening out for any warning that they would need to take extra caution.

Wat was the first to this door and lifted the latch allowing it to swing open easily on well-maintained hinges. He peered through into deeper darkness before turning and curling a finger to indicate that Cwen should follow.

She did so and crossed the threshold into the inner room.

'Ah, there you are,' a friendly voice called. A voice that nearly had them out of their skins on the spot. 'I didn't know when you'd be getting here.'

Neither of them moved as they couldn't even see who was speaking, or where they were hiding.

'The others said I should wait for you outside, but that's ridiculous; you could have come from anywhere. That's the problem with them, you see. They haven't really got a clue what they're doing. No, no. Waiting here was always going to be most sensible. This is the way you've got to come, after all.'

'Well done,' Wat congratulated their host.

'It's easy when you've some experience. Can't tell that lot upstairs anything, of course.'

'I suspect it's them we've come to see, actually,' Wat said.

'Well, of course, it is. And there's just the two of you. We were right about that as well.'

'Shall we go up then?' Wat asked as if being invited for a chat in a parlour.

'Oh, dear me, no.' The voice gave a light laugh. 'I'm going to let you stay down here, there's a lovely little room at the front with a big bar on the outside to stop anyone getting out. The animal pen, no doubt.'

'And why, exactly, would two of us do what you want?' Cwen asked fiercely.

'Because it's not just me.' The voice was amicable. 'It's me and my crossbow.' There was the sound of a crossbow being patted.

'The crossbow that did for Brother Pewlet and started all this,' Wat said.

'Oh, don't remind me.' The voice sounded very weary with the whole business. 'I told you they were all useless, didn't I?'

'And how is one crossbow bolt going to stop us both?' Cwen demanded.

'It'll stop one of you. But as it's so dark, you can't see which one I'm pointing it at. As you probably know, I'm quite good at shooting people in the dark.'

Cwen grumbled.

'And there's the knife of course. For when the crossbow bolt has done its thing. And another knife after that. Well prepared, you see.'

They didn't have much more to say to this.

'Well,' the voice said as if everything was nicely settled now. 'If you'd care to come with me I can lock you up while I pop upstairs and finally kill this monk all the trouble has been about. I tell you, I'll be glad to get this over with.'

Caput XX Animal House

'Don't turn around,' their captor ordered as he pushed them forward through a rude door made of simple split tree limbs rather than anything more sophisticated. This door barred the way into a large open space under the front of the house and they were bundled into it. The door slammed behind them before they could get a glimpse of their assailant.

The room they found themselves in at least had some light, coming in from small gaps near the roof where the frame of the building met the ground outside. They were only slits really, so there was no way either of them was going to get out that way.

This was obviously the space the animals would be brought to in bad weather, or even throughout the depths of winter. It still had scatterings of straw on the floor as well as the unmistakable odour of animals that had been kept indoors for far too long. The door was also built firmly enough to stop a small cow who wanted to get out. There was no chance of kicking the thing down.

The voice came through the door, but it was clear the man was about to leave. 'If you'd be kind enough to wait here, I'll attend to the little bit of business upstairs, then you can be on your way.'

'You're going to murder Brother Hermitage, you mean.' Cwen rattled the door with all her strength but it didn't give.

'You've had two goes so far,' Wat said. 'Are you sure you're going to get the right monk if you try again?'

'They're going to point at him this time, not give me vague descriptions that are no help at all. I'll then point at him with my crossbow and there we are.'

209

'You can't,' Cwen protested.

'I can, you know. I'm quite good.'

'I mean you can't just shoot an innocent monk in cold blood.'

'Wrong again. I've already done it once. And that turned out to be completely the wrong monk. How innocent can you get?'

'You do know Hermitage is the King's Investigator?' Wat asked.

'I have been told.'

'Quite an impetuous chap, the king. Won't take lightly to having his investigator shot. And we do know that he never needs an excuse to kill anyone, innocent or not.'

'And that's why this job is paying so well. And you don't know who I am, so you can hardly go and tell him, can you? And I don't think any of those who have paid me will be owning up.'

'But..,' Cwen began.

'It's been terribly nice having this little chat, but I must be getting on. Monks to kill and all.'

Cwen rattled the door once more at the sound of the man leaving. Soon afterwards another door could be heard closing, followed by footsteps going upstairs.

'Oh, God! He's going to shoot Hermitage.' Cwen looked all around the room for some other way of escape and even ran around it, like some mouse cornered by the farmer's broomstick.

Wat was standing in the middle of the space looking around as well. There was very little to see.

They were in a low-roofed room some twenty feet or so square, with a rough floor, covered in the muck of many winters - probably because the keeper of the animals was so bone idle he hadn't cleared the place. The ceiling was simply the timbers of the floor above and the walls seemed to be hard earth and rock, where the room had been dug out. Rotten and discarded bits of wood lay propped here and there.

Being able to reach it, he pushed his hands against the wood of the roof to see if any of the boards above were loose. He quickly found that they weren't.

He then went over to the spaces where the light came in, to see if he could make them wide enough for Cwen to get out. Between the wood above and the solid earth below, he couldn't make any impression at all.

'What do we do? What do we do?' Cwen asked in a panic.

Above their heads, they could hear the footsteps of what was probably the killer as he entered the main hall.

Wat tipped his head towards the ceiling. 'We know you're up there, Nicodemus.' He shouted his accusation. 'You and Athan and Eadgyth. All in the plot to kill the King's Investigator together.'

There was some low muttering from above, but it was hard to tell if anyone had heard them or not.

Wat looked around to see if he could find anything to stand on. The best he could come up with was to move some of the piles of muck on the floor into an even bigger pile and then climb up it. It was a measure of the urgency of his mission that he didn't even give a thought to the damage this would do to his boots.

Cwen helped as soon as she saw what he was doing and before very long he had a platform on which to stand. A platform that started gently steaming as it moved about. Perhaps it wasn't that long ago animals had been here, after all.

Putting his fine footwear onto it, he only sank in a few inches and was now able to press his head against the roof.

'The king won't take kindly to having his investigator murdered. As soon as he hears that it was you and Athan, your lives won't be worth an arrowhead. And Lady Eadgyth? William doesn't really discriminate between men and women when it comes to slaughter.'

The muttering above continued, but it did seem to be in response to the words being shouted.

'And who else is up there?' Wat called. 'I think all we'll need to do is think about the investigations Hermitage has done. We'll be able to draw up a list for William.'

'And Le Pedvin,' Cwen added.

'Oh, yes, and Le Pedvin,' Wat positively yelled. 'Dear old Le Pedvin who kills people just because they're inconvenient. At least William wants a good reason. But then, he'll have one, won't he? You murdered the King's Investigator. An excellent reason, I think.'

The voices above sounded as if they were getting quite agitated, and there were even footsteps up and down the hall.

Wat gave Cwen a look of cautious satisfaction that he had thrown some seeds of discontent into the monk murdering community.

The seeds seemed to take root quite quickly as the discussion from above became quite heated in no time at all. The muttering voices were raised, and a difference of opinion was clear.

'Ah, that is you, Athan,' Wat called up on hearing one voice above the others. 'I thought it would be, but nice to have it confirmed.'

This brought about more noise and even the stamping of some feet.

'Hermitage?' Cwen shouted. 'Are you up there?'

This brought no direct response and Cwen looked to Wat, hope in her eyes that Hermitage hadn't got to the house yet. Or had even changed his mind completely and had decided to leave Eadgyth to her fate and forget about Pewlet, who was dead, after all. 'You leave him alone,' she instructed the killers who were a whole room away.

They listened hard but couldn't make out actual words. At one point, the footsteps seemed to move away, as if those above wanted to have a discussion out of earshot of the people under the floor who were eavesdropping.

After a few moments, a single set of footsteps returned to the area above their heads. There was a bit of scrambling about and it sounded as if someone was getting down onto their knees.

'They've had a discussion and have come up with another plan.' The voice of the crossbow killer came through the floor.

'I hope it's better than the last one,' Wat replied.

'Oh, it is,' the killer assured them. 'And a lot more profitable.'

'Surprise me,' Wat invited.

'Aha, yes, exactly,' the killer replied. 'First of all, they've elected me as their spokesman because, despite what you may say, you haven't really got a clue who is up here.'

'Oh, we have,' Cwen answered. 'We've been taught all about clues by Hermitage. And we've got a lot of them.'

'Which is lovely for you. But then the surprise bit is that they've asked me to kill you as well, just to be on the safe side.'

Cwen and Wat were silent at that.

'Wouldn't do to have you spouting a lot of lies to the king, who might believe you, not being very smart. And as you're locked in down there, this would seem to be the opportune moment. So, once the monk has eventually turned up we'll do him and then I'll be down for you. And do you know what the best bit about it is?'

'No,' Wat grunted.

'I get paid again. They found they did have some more money after all. Isn't that nice?'

'Lovely.' Wat hung his head and looked at Cwen, the sorrow on his face saying that he wished he'd kept his mouth shut.

'We've got to get out of here,' Cwen hissed at him. 'Hermitage isn't even here yet, so there's still time to save him.'

Wat nodded and shrugged at the same time, indicating that he agreed with the idea, but had no thoughts about how to put it into action.

He cast his eyes around the room once again, although it was just the same as the last time he looked. Apart from the pile of muck, of course. And the newly bare floor where the muck had come from. The bare floor that was now revealed as having a low gulley running along its length.

He climbed down from his muck pile and kicked more of the filth away to expose the rest of the channel.

'Water,' he whispered, nodding to the floor.

Cwen looked and seemed happy to agree that the channel in the floor probably was to get water to the animals. How this helped in the slightest, she was not sure.

Wat followed this simple water trough along the floor until it came to a stop against the outside wall of the house. Just at this spot one of the propped pieces of wood rested and Wat grabbed it and threw it to one side. He held his hand out to draw Cwen's attention to the hole in the wall this revealed.

She peered into the darkness and then looked back, none the wiser.

'The well,' Wat said quietly.

Cwen nodded that she understood. The hole in the wall would lead to the house well, which was probably just outside the door of the hall. Outside the door was good for the people, it meant that they didn't have far to go for their water.

The hole into this cellar meant that supplies could be fetched for the animals without anyone having to brave the ice and snow of a thick winter.

And, to be practical, the hole had to be big enough for someone to get in and fetch the water out in a bucket; probably a child given the job of looking after the animals.

All of which meant the hole was big enough for Cwen to get through. Wat might even make it if he was prepared to dirty his clothes.

Wat nodded that Cwen should be the first to go. He indicated with hands and facial expressions that if he tried, and got stuck in the hole, they'd be no further forward.

Giving the hole a very cautious look, but then glancing up towards the floor above for inspiration, Cwen knelt and stuck her head right in.

'It's very dark in here,' she called back in a low voice.

'The lid is probably on the well above,' Wat replied.

'Do I get right in?'

'Of course.'

Pressing forwards, Cwen put her left arm ahead of her and easily got her shoulder into the hole. The other arm followed, and she levered herself forward on her elbows, inching into the space. It was like some miniature corridor of dirt and stone and really was only a simple channel to allow a bucket to pass.

After only two or three feet, she could tell that the space in front of her had opened up. Craning around, she could see strands of daylight slipping through the cracks in a wooden door above her; doubtless the lid of the well.

Below, she could feel rather than see the water. The cool air wafted into her face and warned her that she might be about to get wet.

She shuffled forward to the edge of the space and lowered her right hand over the side. Only a few inches down she was pleased to feel the water. At least this well wasn't one of those with a great drop. She had no idea how deep the water would be.

She twisted so that she could talk to Wat. 'Hold on to my legs and lower me down a bit. I want to see how deep the water is.'

'Right oh,' Wat said.

'And watch where you're putting your hands,' she instructed.

'All right,' Wat said. 'I won't hold on at all then. You'll find out how deep the water is much more quickly.'

'My ankles will be fine,' Cwen snarled a bit. She felt Wat take a firm and comforting grip of her feet.

Inching forward as far as she dared, she put her hand into the water to her utmost reach. Once again, the news was good. There was ground there or at least some sort of ledge. It could well be that the water stayed at this level all year round, and the well was dug only as deep as it needed to be.

'I'm going in,' she called back.

'Make it quick,' Wat instructed. 'They seem to be getting a

bit excited up there. Could be that Hermitage is on the way.'

Cwen shuffled once more, her feet free to move and immediately realised that she'd rather not go into this water headfirst, no matter how shallow it was. 'Pull me out,' she hissed.

Wat did so, and she immediately turned around and indicated that she needed to go back in, feet first this time.

Holding her under her arms. Wat helped her back into the hole.

She got to the edge of the small tunnel and just had to take her courage in her hands and let herself drop into the water. If it wasn't a ledge, and the water really was deep she could slip straight under. And if the well was narrow, she wouldn't have room to use her arms and swim back up to the surface. And she couldn't swim anyway.

Luckily, she only realised all this after she'd gone in. The water was freezing cold but not at all deep. Standing in the bottom of the well, which had loose stones and rocks for a floor, she could clearly see the opening above, and the entrance back into the animal house, through which Wat was now peering. At least he had the grace to look a bit worried.

'Right,' she said. 'I'm in.'

Wat made encouraging noises.

'What do I do now?'

'Pardon?'

'What do I do now? Now that I am in the well, up to my knees in freezing cold water, what is it that I do? What's the plan?'

'Plan?' Wat asked.

'You do have a plan?'

'Oh, yes,' Wat assured her.

Cwen sighed. 'It's to get into the well, isn't it?'

'That's about it, yes.'

'And after I've got into the well?'

'Erm,' Wat sounded thoughtful.

Cwen wished he'd done the thinking bit before she got in the well.

'Look for a way out,' Wat suggested.

'A way out?'

Even from the other side of the wall, Wat could tell she had her hands on her hips.

'Look for a way out, from a well?' Cwen said, making it quite clear that Wat was perfectly capable of answering that question himself. 'How many ways out of wells are there? Normally? How many ways in for that matter? Calling upon your wide experience of wells?'

'Climb up the rope,' Wat said excitedly.

'What rope?'

'The rope on the bucket. There's bound to be one. What good is a well without a bucket and rope?'

'What good is a well when the bucket is left at the bottom to rot? Buckets are generally kept at the top of wells, so they keep better, and you can put the lid on the well.'

'Oh, yes.'

There was a painful silence.

'Can you climb up?' Wat asked.

'Can you come here so I can hold your face under the water for a while?'

'This is not helping Hermitage,' Wat said.

'You are so right,' Cwen agreed. 'Unless he wants a drink, of course.'

'How far up is the top?'

'Too far for me.'

'What if you were standing on me?'

'Now that does sound like a good idea.'

'Right.' Wat prepared himself. 'I'll come in. If I stand in the water, you can climb on my shoulders.'

'Even better, you put your head in the water and I'll stand on your feet.'

Wat girded his strength. Climbing through the hole was going to be a challenge. Standing in the cold water while Cwen stood on his shoulder was going to require fortitude. Putting up with her after this was going to be impossible.

Caput XXI Into Harm's Way

Brother Hermitage's approach to the house of Gifard was cautious and careful. It was also full of trepidation, concern and just plain worry. This meant that it was taking an awfully long time.

His head told him that this was so that Wat and Cwen would have plenty of time to get into position; whatever position it was they were going to get into. His heart told him that he really didn't need to go anywhere near this place. There might be people in there who wished him harm.

His head argued that this was ridiculous. The whole idea that anyone would simply want to kill him, just for being King's Investigator was ludicrous. He didn't even want to be King's Investigator in the first place. If these people really didn't want him doing the job perhaps they could put in a word with King William and he could give up.

His heart and his head threw the name of Brother Athan at him and he knew he was in trouble. There was no doubt Athan wished him harm, he'd said so on many occasions. And he'd said so long before Hermitage had even become King's Investigator. Back in De'Ath's Dingle Athan had wished him harm. He'd even described quite a lot of the harm in painful detail.

And if Nicodemus was involved in this, which seemed likely, there was a strong possibility Athan was in it as well.

And they could both be in the house. More trepidation was called for.

By now, the people inside the house might be wondering why there was a monk standing outside, Hermitage's progress having come to a complete stop. He pondered his position once more, as well as the amount of time that had passed, and concluded that he really needed to get on with this. There was the question of Eadgyth, after all. And Brother Pewlet. There was nothing for it; he had to carry on. Wat and Cwen would surely be waiting for him by now, ready to spring their trap.

He added a further pause to consider whether trapping people at all was quite right and proper. Yes, they were probably wrong-doers, but even so. The only conclusion he could reach was that it was too late now. Matters had been set in hand and there was nothing to do but get on with them. Now. Immediately. Which only required that he put one foot in front of the other until he arrived at the house.

Ah, but what to do when he got there? Should he approach through the main door, or was that too presumptuous? Should he look for an alternative entrance? One more befitting a monk than some great guest of the family.

As he added yet another bit of waiting to review his options, the front door opened.

Relief flooded through him. Perhaps Wat and Cwen had entered the house and discovered there was no one there at all. The miscreants had let Lady Eadgyth go and had all decided to go home. There would probably be a note of confession about the death of Pewlet, which he could take to Abbot Abbo. That was all right then.

'Are you coming?' A voice called out, with quite obvious impatience.

Hermitage could see that this was not Wat or Cwen. Not unless they'd changed their clothes and then started wearing a hood. The figure was also considerably larger than either of his friends. Probably larger than both put together.

'We haven't got all day.' The hooded one called. 'Do you want to rescue this hostage or not?' The voice was gruff and growly, almost as if the one inside the hood was trying to disguise his voice.

'Aha,' Hermitage called, as brightly as he could manage. There was something about the size and shape of this hooded character that worried away at the back of his head. There were many large people in the world, a lot of them in the church, but this one had a ring of familiarity about it. The Bishop of Dorchester, perhaps? He thought it unlikely that the Bishop of Dorchester would be holding Eadgyth hostage to get at the King's Investigator. Hermitage had only ever seen the bishop from a distance and hadn't investigated him at all. No, it must be someone else. A different bishop altogether.

He realised that this situation was causing him no end of trouble. His feet and legs had stopped working and now his head had joined in. Being hurried into a house of harm had somehow stopped his rational thought. Without rational thought, there was really very little left. He had become fixated on bishops suddenly. He had a vision of entering the house and finding the place full of them. Even Athan had been made a bishop. He swallowed. No, that didn't help.

'Well?' the figure called again.

Hermitage managed to get his legs going again, and in the right direction, although they were still slow. He could hear the hooded one's sigh of impatience from yards away.

Eventually, he was at the foot of four simple steps that led up to the main door, a weighty slab of oak that would keep any invader at bay. (Unless the invader was in Hastings and the householder went there to be killed.)

'Put this on.' A hand was held out holding a loose cut of material. Hermitage looked at it.

'You have to take it,' the man said. 'Ye gods,' he added with a mutter.

Hermitage managed to persuade his arm to reach out and take the object. Then he got his eyes to look at it.

'It's a hood,' the figure at the door explained, shaking his head. 'It goes on your head. Like a hood.'

Hermitage nodded that he understood, and then tried to remember where his head was.

'Oh, for goodness sake.' The large man snatched the hood back, opened it up and rammed it down over Hermitage's head.

'Thank you,' Hermitage said, as it only seemed polite.

'Now, get in here.' The man stepped aside and indicated that Hermitage was expected to enter.

Hermitage knew he was expected to enter, that was the reason he'd come all this way, after all. Still, when it came to actually doing it, there seemed to be a problem. He didn't want to go in.

The man let out a massive sigh, stepped down from the door, went around behind Hermitage and pushed him forward. 'I knew this would be trouble,' he explained.

Hermitage couldn't help but climb the steps and went through the door. As he did so he recalled some tales of people rescuing hostages. They'd been knights and the like and he was sure they hadn't worn hoods or had to be forced over the threshold of the place where the fair maiden was being held. They had all gone charging in, dealing wild blows hither and thither and then been rewarded by the king. Or something like that.

Hermitage was in, but that was about it.

A further generous push from behind got him through the entrance lobby and into the hall proper. Now there was a sight you didn't see every day.

There were no bishops, which was a bit of a relief, but there was a circle of hooded people standing around the edge of the room. He couldn't really take them in, this situation being more than he could cope with, but he did notice that one of them seemed to be wearing white, and had a big beard sticking out from under his hood. Perhaps the Bishop of Dorchester was here, after all.

It was a very big room and the hoods were widely spaced, almost as if they didn't get on and wanted to keep their distance. He couldn't see them all in one glance, never mind from inside a hood with only small holes for eyes, so he had to turn for an idea of how many there were. Not many, it seemed. If this was a secret church conclave it was very select. He'd been expecting a significant gathering, a congregation, no less. It was a bit of a disappointment to find that it was only a handful of people who wanted him dead.

One of these hooded characters stood in the middle of the room, perhaps he was the one in charge, and would explain what was going on.

But there was Mistress Eadgyth, tied to a chair and not looking very happy about it. Hardly surprising, really. He recalled that she had never been a particularly cheerful person but being tied to a chair was bound to take the edge off anyone's day.

He thought that he probably ought to say something at this point, just to calm her worries. She was doubtless relieved that he had arrived and that her trial would soon be over.

He had to say that she didn't look very relieved. She looked more cross than anything. And she hadn't had a word to say to him from the moment he walked in. You might think that the hostage, upon seeing her saviour would at least say "at last" or "praise God" or something. But not a word. In fact, she seemed to be glaring at the hoods around the room, rather than paying him any attention at all.

This rather odd behaviour of a hostage on the brink of rescue did bring his mind back into focus and he was able to consider the situation in a little more detail.

Including the man behind him, there were only six hooded members of the conclave in the room. Perhaps there were more outside, or in other rooms? Or maybe this was the organising committee and the rest would come in when summoned.

He knew conclaves could be small, from his own experience of one debate that only involved him and the speaker, but five, to go to all this trouble? If Nicodemus was one of them, and Athan another, that left only four. He considered the members more closely and saw that one looked like a nun.

There was no reason to think a nun could not be a member of a conclave; he just hadn't been expecting it, that was all. If this was a conclave to root out heresy, then it was quite reasonable a nun should be involved. There must be heresy in convents; who better than a nun to deal with it.

He'd only really dealt with one nun, Sister Mildburgh, and she'd been very capable of dealing with anything. Could it be that this was her? Athan, Nicodemus and now Mildburgh? In which case, who were the other three?

He found he was confusing himself, which happened quite a lot. He had still not resolved in his head whether this was a gathering to deal with the heretical thoughts of Brother Pewlet, or whether it really was a band intent on doing harm to him as King's Investigator. One moment he thought the one thing, then the other. Perhaps he could ask? It was not an easy question to frame. What did he say? "Excuse me, but are you here to kill me?" He didn't like to ask that, in case it put ideas in their heads.

'Get in there,' the man behind called and gave yet another shove, directing Hermitage towards the middle of the room where what must be the leader stood waiting.

He tried to recall what Nicodemus looked like, what height and shape he had, and consider whether this fellow in the room could be him.

No, he told himself, he still must not leap to conclusions. Nicodemus's name on the parchment could still be a coincidence. Parchment was very precious, after all. It could have gone through many hands.

Once he stood before the central figure, there was a silence in the room. Hermitage wondered if he was supposed to say something. He also chose this moment to wonder why Wat and Cwen had not burst in. He was to rescue the hostage and they were to rescue him, that's what he'd been expecting.

It was probably that they were waiting just outside the door to hear what was going on. If this did turn out to be about heresy, then there was nothing to worry about.

No, that was wrong. If this was about heresy, then these people wanted to kill Hermitage to stop him investigating them. If it was just to kill Hermitage then the result would be the same, just without the heresy. He supposed it didn't really matter to him whether Athan and Nicodemus were involved in this at all.

Wat and Cwen could come in any time they liked. About now would do.

Hermitage almost jumped out of his own reverie when the silence was broken. 'You are the King's Investigator?' a hood off to the side of the room asked. A hood that sounded a lot like Nicodemus. The hood coughed and changed its voice to a deep drone that clearly wasn't natural. 'You are the King's Investigator?' it repeated.

'Erm, yes, I suppose so,' Hermitage replied from inside his own hood.

'The Brother Hermitage one?' the hood checked.

'Well, yes.' If they wanted to check that he was not Brother Simon, that was another bad sign.

'Excellent,' another hood spoke and this one had a definite twang of Athan to it. That unhappy, aggressive voice would be hard to disguise, even through the thickest hood.

Hermitage gulped. This really might be Nicodemus and Athan then. In which case the reason for his impending death was personal. That seemed worse than being murdered for being King's Investigator, somehow. If he was killed for doing a job he didn't want to do anyway, he wouldn't feel quite so bad about it.

Right now would really be an excellent moment for Wat and Cwen to arrive and say "aha", or something equally conclusive. He listened hard but there was no sound of doors being thrown open, or even of footsteps approaching.

'Of course, if he took his hood off we'd be able to see who it is.' The nun said this, and she delivered her words on the back of a cart-load of contempt.

Hermitage tried to recall if this sounded like Sister Mildburgh. He had tried to avoid nuns in general and was ashamed to say that they all sounded alike to him. Scary. This one was scary, so for all he knew it could indeed be Sister Mildburgh.

'All in good time,' the Athan sounding hood said. 'You may prepare,' he added.

Nobody moved to do any preparing of anything.

'You,' the hood repeated.

The hoods all turned to face the speaker.

'You.' The hood now pointed to the one in the middle of the room. 'For goodness sake, who did you think I was talking to?'

'Oh, right,' the hooded shape in the middle of the room shrugged. He turned and walked across the room to get something from behind the door.

Hermitage was very curious about what was going on. This conclave seemed remarkably poorly organised to do whatever it was they were up to. They were disagreeing with one another, didn't know who was supposed to do what and didn't even seem comfortable in their hoods.

Unfortunately, the one who had been told that he could proceed seemed to know exactly what he was doing as he returned from his journey across the room carrying a large crossbow.

Under Hermitage's horrified gaze, he put the thing on the floor and, with great difficulty, started to sit. Everyone looked on as the killer struggled with his bad leg, none of them wanting to offend by offering to help, or pass any comment at all. Eventually, he got down to a sitting position and organised the crossbow so that the crosspiece sat under his feet.

'What the devil are you playing at?' This was the Athan-hood again.

'Spanning,' the man on the floor explained.

'What?'

'Spanning the bow. I've got to span it first, haven't I? Prime it, if you like.'

'You've got to shoot someone, that's what you've got to do.'

'And I can't shoot anyone if the bow's not spanned, can I?'

Both men sounded as if they were finding it a real trial, talking to idiots like this.

'The string is not tight. It must be tight to shoot the bolt, yes? You see this?' The man held the loose crossbow string between his fingers. 'Not going to shoot anyone, is it? I have to pull the string back and hook it into the trigger.'

'Why didn't you do that before? We can't hang around here while you lie down playing with your weapon.'

'I'm hardly going to leave a spanned bow around the place, am I? Be dangerous. The slightest knock and it could go off.'

'Dangerous? You're a killer with a crossbow, for heaven's sake. You're supposed to be dangerous.'

'To everyone else, not to me.' The man said this with a pronounced tone that included the other hoods as "everyone else".

Amid much tutting and sighing, the room waited while the man got himself in position. He pulled a pair of gloves from his belt and, with the bow braced by his feet, hauled on the string until it clicked into place.

'Ready now?' the one who might be Athan asked.

'Just got to get the bolt.' He reached to a small pack now and took out a short arrow.

Hermitage was considering turning and running at this point but knew that he'd only be stopped and brought back. He also thought about shouting out "now" to encourage Wat and Cwen in their bursting in. All he could think of to delay proceedings was to talk. At least he was good at that.

'So, it was you who shot Brother Pewlet and Simon.'

'That's right,' the crossbow wielder replied.

'Why?' Hermitage tried to make it sound like an accusation.

'Well, you pull the trigger thing, here,' the man pointed to the spot, 'and the rest just happens.'

'No, I mean why did you shoot them? What had they done?'

'They were in the wrong place and said the wrong things.'

'And the killer wasn't doing his job properly.' Athan said, Hermitage now being resigned to the fact that this was him.

'Right, ready now.' The crossbowman seemed happy with his preparations and stood, hauling the weapon up with him.

'Good.' The hood that really must be Athan stepped forward. 'Hoods off everyone,' he instructed.

There was a bit of complaint at this.

'He's going to be dead in a minute, so it won't matter, will it? And I think, after recent experiences, that we really need to make sure we're getting the right man this time.'

The rest of the conclave could see the sense of this.

'And I don't see why the King's Investigator shouldn't get to see who's doing what.'

The hoods all turned to look at one another, before concluding that perhaps they could safely remove their hoods.

Athan went first, to lead the way while the others still prevaricated; and it was Athan.

'Brother Athan,' Hermitage said, hoping that the name would shame him. It didn't.

'I should stand away if I were you,' the crossbowman warned as he raised the bow. 'At this range, the bolt will probably go right through him.'

Hermitage really did not want his last moment to be spent facing a grinning Brother Athan while a stranger shot him to death.

Athan continued to smile and stepped over to Hermitage. He leaned forward and pulled the hood from the investigator's head.

'Ah,' said the crossbow killer as he considered the face of the monk before him.

Caput XXII Well Well

Wat was standing in the cold water while Cwen attempted to climb up to get on top of his shoulders. The well was narrow and not designed for this sort of thing, it was enough of a squeeze for them both just to stand side by side.

'Get down on your knees and I can sit on your shoulders.'

'If I get down on my knees, I'll never get up again. There isn't room in here.'

'Well, squat a bit then. I can't just spring up you know.'

'Here.' Wat held out his hands like a cup in front of him. Put your foot in this and I'll hoist you up. You can hold on to the wall.'

'I can't get my knee up.' Cwen had her back to the wall of the well and the only way to lift her knee would be to risk giving Wat a rather personal injury.

'Go sideways.'

'How can I go sideways? The well is a circle.'

Wat tried leaning as far back against the wall as he could, but this really was only a one-person well. Even pressed back, he could still touch the wall opposite without reaching. Well, he could if Cwen wasn't in the way.

'Just bend down a bit,' Cwen ordered. 'I'll see if I can climb on your back.'

'How can I bend down? You're in the way. And if I do bend down I'll only bang my head on the wall opposite.'

'What do you suggest then?' Cwen's temper was now joining them in the well, and there definitely wouldn't be room for the three of them.

Wat gave it some thought. 'You bend down and I'll climb on your back.'

'What?'

'You're shorter than I am, you'll have more room.'

'I can't take your great weight.'

'I do not have a great weight, I'm very lithe.'

'Lithe? Who told you that? Some very fat people?'

'It'll only be for a moment.'

'It won't even be for a moment.'

'It is Hermitage up there that we're trying to stop being murdered.'

'And we will if you'd put a bit of effort in and lift me up.'

'Right.' Wat sounded very determined.

He squatted down until his knees were touching the wall opposite, one either side of Cwen. He then put both arms out and clasped her tight around the back of her knees.

'Here, what do you think you're doing?' she demanded.

'Lifting you up to stop a murder. Now shut up.' With her legs firmly in his grasp, he slowly stood until her feet were a couple of feet off the ground.

'Now what?' Cwen asked as she was still well short of the top of the well.

'Stay there.'

'I've got nowhere to go.'

Wat adjusted his feet until he could get his knees under Cwen's feet and squatted slightly. 'Stand on my knees.' She did so. 'Now, ready for the next bit?'

'What next bit?' She sounded a bit worried at this.

Wat made a platform of his hands and pushed them up.

'Oy,' Cwen called with a squeal. 'Get your hands off my bottom.'

'Get your bottom off my hands,' Wat replied as he pushed her upwards. 'Now put your knees on my shoulders.'

Cwen squirmed around and managed to lift one knee. 'I shan't forget this, you know.'

'Wonderful. Now, put your hands on my head and push up until you can stand on my shoulders. The weight of Cwen, which was slight anyway, lifted from his hands and he felt her feet on his shoulders. 'Can you reach the top?'

'Nearly,' Cwen called down from above. 'Just a bit more. Can you stand on tiptoe?'

'Love to,' Wat gritted his teeth and stood as tall as he could on the wobbly rocks in the bottom of the well.

'Just a tiny bit more.' Cwen was straining to get as high as she could.

Wat felt one foot lift from his shoulder and thought that she must have a grip of the top of the well.

Then he felt the foot descend on the top of his head and the weight of Cwen followed. She must be balancing on his head on one leg.

'Oof. A bit of warning would help,' he said.

'Yes,' Cwen replied firmly. 'It would, wouldn't it.'

'Is my head getting you anywhere near the top of the well?'

'Yes, I can touch the lid now, but it won't move. It feels like there's something heavy on it.'

'That'll probably be the heavy thing people put on well lids to stop them blowing away. If you come down, I'll stand on your head and see if I can shift it.'

'I'm not putting my hands anywhere near your bottom.' She struggled with the wood above her head to see if there was any way she could get a purchase on it. 'Just a moment, I think I can get my fingers through a gap in the wood. Ah yes. It feels soft, must be an old lid, been there for years. I'll just give it a pull and see what happens.'

The old lid to the well, which must have been there for years, came apart in Cwen's hand and the heavy thing, that was stopping the lid from blowing away, dropped past her face and headed for the depths.

'Look...,' was the only bit of "look out" that she managed to say before the grunt from Wat indicated that the heavy thing had landed.

'Oh, bloody hell,' Wat wailed. 'That was my foot. Anything else you'd like to throw at me?'

'Quite a few bits of old wood, by the look of it,' Cwen replied as the wood of the well lid headed downwards. 'But it's all pretty rotten and horrible so it won't hurt much.'

Wat's comment on this was drowned by the clatter of descending wood, which was probably just as well.

Light was now flooding into the well with the lid gone and Wat chanced a look up, hoping that nothing else was on its way down. He could see that Cwen was very close to the top and with a just bit more height would be able to get her hands over the lip of the well. He reached up and tapped her ankle with his hand.

'What do you want?' Cwen called.

'You off my head would be nice. I'll brace myself and you stand on my hands. I'll try to lift you, so you can get over the top of the well.'

The one foot remained on his head, while the other waved around searching for his hand. Eventually, they found one another, and Wat held his arm rigid as he tried to take the weight.

In fact, it wasn't a problem at all. He found that he could easily carry Cwen on one arm. Perhaps, once they were out of this, they could go round the country as entertainers; Wat and Cwen, the Amazing Balancing Weavers. He wondered where that idea had come from. Maybe it was a desperate plea for escape from a life as companion to the King's Investigator; the life that found him stuck down a well trying to climb out and stop a murder. And him only a weaver, after all.

The weight of Cwen's other foot now left his head and he held up both arms to give her a solid platform.

When she managed to get a firm grip on the top of the well and lifted herself entirely from Wat, he suddenly felt so light that he should be able to jump out of the well in one bound. That would be another good trick to put in their act. Perhaps they could even make their own well to take along, just to show what they were capable of.

'I'll lower the bucket, so you can get up the rope,' Cwen called down, once she was completely clear of the well.

'Lower the bucket so I can get up the rope,' Wat called up, not able to hear her clearly.

'Good idea,' Cwen called down, in a rather rude manner.

'Don't shout,' Wat called up, trying not to shout. 'The house is full of killers and I'd rather the man with the crossbow didn't find me stuck down a well.'

'Yes, sir,' Cwen sneered a bit.

Wat held his hands over his head, suspecting that the bucket might be about to arrive quite quickly. He'd had enough of standing in the bottom of a well having things dropped on him.

The bucket appeared in the circle of daylight at the top of the well and began to slowly descend.

'There's no windlass or anything up here.' Cwen's face appeared over the edge. 'I'll have to tie the end of the rope to something before you climb.' She disappeared.

Wat received the bucket, which was as rotten as the rest of the well and examined the rope. It was only good for a rotten bucket in a not-very-deep well. He would have to be careful using it to get out. Putting any weight on the thing would mean a quick trip back to the bottom of the well.

'All right,' Cwen reappeared. 'It's tied to a tree.'

Wat tested the rope and felt it stretch rather alarmingly. Putting as much of his weight as he could on the walls of the well, he cautiously used the rope to lever himself up. As he did so, he found that he could brace his back against one wall of the well and use his feet on the other. That might have been the way to get out in the first place. Best not mention that to Cwen, he thought.

Using the rope sparingly, he eventually got up to the level of the top and only then realised that the air in the well had been horribly dank and damp. Hardly surprising, really.

Cwen was there and took his arm as he rolled over the side of the well onto the ground. As he knelt, recovering from his climb, he saw that the well was really no more than a hole in the ground, which used to have a lid on it. No charming stone circle with a thatched roof over it to stop things from falling in for this place. Talk about cheap.

Wat stood, looked at Cwen and could not stop himself giving a snort of laughter. 'Look at the state of you,' he said.

'Me?' Cwen asked. 'Have you seen yourself?'

Wat did look now and moaned in genuine pain. 'Oh my God. Look at my boots, they're ruined.'

Cwen walked around him as if appraising a prize cow. 'And the back of your jerkin is torn to shreds.'

'What? Oh, this is awful.' He held his hands out to his side as if trying to avoid any contact with his filthy and dishevelled clothes.

'Well.' Cwen folded her arms in some satisfaction at his condition, as if it was all he deserved. 'I don't think you've got time to change before we rescue Hermitage from the killer?'

'Oh, God, yes.' Wat quickly recalled why they'd been in the

well in the first place. He turned and faced the house. 'At least the people in there can't have been looking out of the window to see weavers climbing out of their well.'

'And there's no sign of Hermitage,' Cwen noted. 'He must be in there already.'

'It's taken us an age to get out of that thing.' He glared at the well. 'We could be too late.' He took hurried steps towards the front door of the house, ignoring the fact that he looked a complete state and wouldn't really want to be seen by anyone.

Bounding up the steps, they both pushed at the door and it swung open before them. Stepping quickly through the entrance hall, they saw there was only one way to go, through another door that must lead into the main hall itself.

Wat put both hands to this and threw it back as hard as he could.

'Ah,' he said, not sure what to say about the sight that met his eyes.

Cwen's short burst of laughter didn't help.

Hermitage was in the middle of the room, facing a man with a hood on and a crossbow in his arm. To one side stood Athan, hood in hand, while the rest of the room had a gaggle of hooded figures looking on, judging from the eye holes in the fronts of their hoods.

'Well, I never,' Wat said.

Athan quickly put his hood back on his head.

Hermitage spun on the spot and beamed his gratitude for the arrival. He did frown as he looked at the state of them. They looked like they'd fallen down a well. He started to edge his way back from the crossbow and towards his rescuers.

'It's too late putting the hood on again, Athan,' Wat

announced. 'Putting a hood on after people have seen your face isn't terribly effective.'

'Idiot,' Cwen added.

'Wat the weaver,' Athan growled.

'And Cwen the weaver,' Cwen said.

'You're too late,' Athan crowed a bit.

'I don't think so,' Wat replied. 'Hermitage being dead would be too late. Hermitage is still alive, so we're not too late at all.'

'We shall see.' Athan sounded quite confident.

'And Nicodemus is here as well, I expect.' Wat surveyed the various hooded figures, who were all now shifting rather awkwardly. 'And mistress Eadgyth the hostage.' He gave her a little bow. 'Held hostage by the very people you were plotting with, eh? Charming.'

Eadgyth bounced up and down in her chair a bit, making it quite clear that she expected someone to untie her. No one seemed inclined to do so, hostage takers or rescuers. 'Let me go this minute,' she demanded.

'You got yourself into this, mother. Now get out of it.' Cwen turned up her nose at her mother and looked away.

Eadgyth continued to complain and moan. 'My own daughter,' she said to the room. 'You see what I mean?'

'Hermitage?' Cwen asked, calmly. 'Is that your hood?' She nodded to the piece of material lying on the floor at his feet.

'Erm, it was.'

Ignoring everyone else, Cwen walked slowly over to the hood, picked it up, went across to her mother and stuck the thing over her head. She turned it so that the eye holes were at the back. 'We may have to listen to you, but we don't have to look at you as well.' She returned to Wat's side.

The language from inside the hood of mistress Eadgyth

was truly shocking.

'And who else do we have?' Wat asked. 'A nun, by the look of it. Would that be Sister Mildburgh, by any chance?' The female hooded figure, who had already been pretty stiff, stiffened further.

'Do you think so?' Hermitage asked. He was now back with Wat and Cwen, the crossbow killer having not taken the opportunity of shooting him, for which he was grateful.

'Undoubtedly. And a druid?' Wat looked and sounded very surprised. 'You've come a long way.'

The hooded druid bowed an acknowledgement to Wat.

'So,' Wat turned a circle and counted them off on his fingers. 'Athan, Nicodemus, Mildburgh, Eadgyth, a Druid, a killer with a crossbow and one more.' He folded his arms as he considered the final hood, who stood close to the door. 'There's only one man I know who's fat enough to put a hood on and still be recognisable. How are you, Briston?'

There was no reply from the hood.

'Briston?' Hermitage asked. 'The weaver?'

'That's the one. Doubtless got some very crooked scheme underway. Wants to get rid of the King's Investigator and probably get Cwen back into the bargain.'

Cwen glared at the hood. 'If we pushed very hard we could get him down the well,' she suggested.

'Won't need to.' Wat sounded indifferent. 'Once the king gets word of the people who were trying to finish off his investigator, they'll think being shoved headfirst down a well is a bit of a luxury.'

'Very clever, Wat.' Briston removed his hood and smiled a thin smile. 'But then, you always were too clever for your own good.'

Wat nodded his head to accept the criticism.

'And in this case, you're far too clever for your own good and that of your friends.' He reached a hand out and pushed the door to the hall shut. 'You're right, it would have been good to get Cwen back in the fold. Her nimble fingers do fine work. Work people are prepared to pay handsomely for. But, I shall just have to manage without, won't I? Have to struggle against the competition, which is mainly you, by the way.'

Wat shrugged that this really wasn't his problem.

'But then if the world can manage without a King's Investigator, the weaving world can manage without Wat.' He raised his hand and pointed at the man with the crossbow. He also raised his voice and shouted his command into the room 'Kill them, kill them all!'

Caput XXIII Which Investigator?

'King's Investigator!' Brother Simon cried from his sickbed.

Brother Lethry, who had been charged with looking after Simon once Hermitage and the others had left, woke from his doze and considered the man on the cot. All he had been told to do was to keep an eye on the sick monk, and he hadn't really managed even that. Watching people who didn't do anything was hardly stimulating, and it took a lot of stimulation to keep Brother Lethry awake at most times.

Regularly chastised for his laziness and general lack of action in any walk of monastic life, he had considered the task of sitting in a cell watching a sleeping brother to be a Godsend; enforced idleness, the best kind. Almost as soon as he sat, he nodded off.

Of all the monks confined to their cells after the business with Brother Nult, Lethry had been the one the abbot turned to for assistance. This was mainly because Lethry had stood by watching the carnage, and not actually got involved himself. The abbot had explained that this was still reprehensible as Lethry should have reported the fight as soon as he saw it break out.

Lethry had simply shrugged as he was shut in his cell, where he settled down for a long-overdue nap.

It was clear, even to Lethry's well-developed lack of attention, that this monk was sick, the big bloodstain on his side being the first clue. The brother was also sweating profusely and mumbling incoherently.

There had been a lively debate between the cells of locked-up monks about the appropriate treatment for Simon's condition. Some argued that being shot was just another form of sore stomach. Yes, the soreness was caused by an arrow going in, but the treatment should be the same: mugwort, pounded, boiled and mixed with oil of almond, made into a plaster.

Others said that this was nonsense. Being shot was the thing that needed attention. Obviously, that called for the root of the Ravens Leek, which was good for wounds.

As it was Simon's side that was damaged, Knotgrass juice with oil was the thing. One should always use Knotgrass for a side.

Then again, the fever needed treatment, which clearly called for Smearwort dried and then smoked over the patient. This had the double advantage that it also drove out devils, in case one had crept in.

One of the more attentive brothers had pointed out that as the monastery didn't have any of these herbs, a bandage and some water was the best the man was going to get; that and Brother Lethry to watch over him.

Several of his brothers pointed out that watching over the sick monk did not mean just sitting there while the fellow died. Lethry really needed to pay attention, for once.

Unfortunately, the abbot had not given Lethry any direct instruction about what to do if there was any change in Simon's condition or if anything untoward happened at all. And if Brother Lethry had not been given instruction, he didn't do anything. Most of the time he didn't do anything when he had been given instruction, so the outcome was the same. Brother Simon's feverish utterances grew louder and more intense, and Brother Lethry found it impossible to sleep with all the noise.

'King's Investigator,' Simon repeated. He sounded quite agitated about this, but as Brother Lethry had not the first clue what it meant, he simply sat some more and watched. He knew what a king was, obviously, perhaps investigator was some new herb or wort that cured the shouting madness. But if it was only for kings, there was no chance of this monk getting any.

'I must,' Simon started but did not finish. 'My duty,' he called. 'Ah, let me pass.' He then started writhing a bit on the bed.

This development did worry Lethry. If the sick monk threw himself out of bed, he would have to fetch help to lift him back up. And all the other monks were still locked in their cells.

Without any preliminaries, Simon sat up. He simply lifted his head from his cot and sat bolt upright, his fever clearly giving him great strength.

Lethry watched with interest.

Simon looked around without seeing. His eyes were obviously working but they seemed to be fixed on some distant vision that was off outside the walls somewhere.

Lethry tried to follow the gaze but couldn't see anything noteworthy.

Simon now swung his legs over the side of the cot and looked directly at Lethry. 'King's Investigator,' he said again.

Lethry shrugged. 'We haven't got any,' he said, in the very loud voice you had to use with sick people.

Simon now stood, which caused Lethry to raise his eyebrows. He hadn't been warned that the monk might walk about. He moved his chair back to give some space.

At the noise of the chair, Simon's focus descended on Lethry. 'Ah,' he cried, raising an arm to point at his attendant.

'Ah?' Lethry asked.

Simon now looked worried, as if some internal debate was raging. His eyes darted from side to side and his mouth opened and closed rapidly.

Eventually, he seemed to reach some conclusion and turned for the door.

'Just a moment,' Lethry said. 'I don't think you're allowed out.'

Simon turned and gave Lethry a glare that said he could do whatever he liked. He appeared to be in control of his actions, but something about that look in his eye said that he wasn't taking those actions in the same world that Lethry was sitting in.

Simon lifted the latch on the door, threw it open and strode out. Lethry followed. He had been told to watch the sick monk and clearly couldn't do that if he wasn't with him. Watch the monk was such a simple instruction, even Lethry couldn't think of a way to avoid it. Wherever this Simon went, so went he.

Where Simon did go was a bit random. He seemed to be looking for something, but at the same time didn't know where he was. He mumbled at some walls, growled at a couple of doors and at one point knelt to have a quietly intense conversation with a rock.

This rock obviously gave him some very sound advice and he stood once more, scanned his surroundings and spotted the main door to the monastery compound.

'Ah, now,' Lethry said, pretty sure that they shouldn't be leaving the monastery completely. He hadn't been told that the sick monk wasn't allowed to leave, but then he hadn't really expected him to want to. Or be capable of doing so.

His own over-arching instruction "never leave the monastery without permission" was ingrained; along with its sub-clause "You will never be given permission to leave the monastery."

Now he was torn. "Watch the monk" meant leaving the monastery, for which he did not have permission. Leaving the monastery should not be done, but that meant not watching the monk, which he had been told to do. This was the sort of question that Brother Pewlet had been good at. But then he was dead, so was not going to be able to help.

As Simon approached the main gate and began to search for the latch, Lethry resolved his dilemma. He would walk backwards to the abbot's study, all the time keeping an eye on the sick monk, then he would ask for permission to leave. If that wasn't granted he would just have to go back to his cell. He was ready for a rest after all this excitement.

Stepping as quickly backwards as he could, trying to work out when he would be within shouting distance of the abbot, he saw that Simon had found the latch and opened the gate.

Lethry turned and ran for the abbot.

Outside the gate, Simon looked along the track that led through the woods and back to the main road. 'King's Investigator,' he barked to the trees and strode off, some awful motive driving him along, despite his condition.

He seemed to have some definite objective in his mind, even if that mind was disturbed, if not deranged. Whatever this was, it was going to be on the receiving end of something quite remarkable when Simon got there.

. . .

'He just kept saying King's Investigator,' Lethry reported to Abbot Abbo.

'Why didn't you stay with him?' Abbo rose from the chair

in his study with urgency.

'I'm not allowed to leave the monastery.'

'Oh, for heaven's sake, brother,' Abbo scolded. 'Have you no sense in your head? When I give you an order that doesn't suit you, you seem quite capable of ignoring it.'

Lethry looked hurt.

'Don't sleep in chapel?' Abbo prompted.

'I had a sleeping ague.'

'Really? And a snoring ague to go with it.' Abbo gave no more time to this debate and swept from the room, beckoning that Lethry should follow.

Once outside, they could see that the monastery gate had been left open.

'At least the brothers are in their cells,' Abbo said, envisaging the entire community out there, frightening the locals. 'They are in their cells?' he asked Lethry.

'Oh, yes, Father,' Lethry assured him. 'I imagine they must be.'

'Imagine, eh?' Abbo didn't sound comforted. He quickly led the way to the gate where there was no sign of Simon. 'He must be moving quickly, for a man with an arrow wound.'

'He did seem out of sorts.'

'Out of sorts? I'll say he must be. Come.'

Abbo stepped through the open gate and out onto the path through the woods. 'He must be making for the main road. He said nothing about what he was going to do?'

'No, father.' Lethry struggled to keep up. 'Just King's Investigator and something about his duty and how we must let him pass.'

'I can't believe he's going to try and deal with Pewlet's killer, he didn't seem the type.'

'Perhaps he's gone to look for some King's Investigator in

the woods?'

'He's what?' Abbo stopped walking and turned to face Lethry.

'Gone to look for King's Investigator in the woods. You know, to treat his wound.'

Abbo sighed and shook his head. 'You idiot.' He resumed his rapid pace.

Lethry just shrugged. He'd been called worse.

As they drew towards the edge of the wood, still not having spotted Simon, a noise came through the trees to their ears.

'Sounds like a lot of activity,' Abbo puzzled. 'Who'd be moving up the road in such numbers. A caravan, maybe?' He pressed on along the path and saw what was making the commotion. It was indeed a caravan, but rather a special one. 'Oh, no,' he said, in a voice as pale as death. 'Dear God, no. Not them.'

'There's another one,' a voice from the caravan called out as a man pointed towards Abbo and Lethry. What gave the abbot and his monk concern was that the man was pointing with a large pikestaff, wore a shining helm on his head and spoke with a pronounced Norman accent.

'Why the devil is this wood full of monks?' Another Norman soldier asked as he strode over to look.

'Saxons?' the other soldier suggested as if that explained everything.

'I don't know what they're doing in there, but I don't like it. Bring them along.'

Abbo tried smiling at the soldier, but it didn't do any good. They were both grabbed by the arm and hauled into the heart of this parade of Norman strength.

At least they appeared to be towards the back of the train, where the supplies and less important people travelled. Abbo had a horrible feeling who might be at the front of this cavalcade, and he would much rather stay at the back.

'What are you doing here, monk?' the apparently more important soldier asked.

'Oh,' Abbo sounded light and disinterested. 'Our monastery is nearby, just through the woods. We were simply out and about.'

'Out and about near the king's own entourage?' The man sounded suspicious. Suspicious Normans were always best avoided.

'The king, eh?' Abbo's fake surprise could not hide the gulp in his throat.

'We were looking for mushrooms,' Lethry added, which was no help at all.

'I'll give you mushrooms,' the soldier barked.

'Oh,' Lethry said. 'Thank you very much.' For which he got a clip round the ear; a clip round the ear from a Norman wearing a mailed glove which almost knocked him senseless.

Abbot Abbo supported his brother and glared at the Norman. 'There is no call for that,' he said in his best commanding manner. It seemed to have some effect as the Norman simply scowled.

'You can go with the other one then.'

'Other one?'

'The first monk that came out of the woods looking for mushrooms. The mad one.'

'Brother Simon?' Abbo asked. 'You have him? That's wonderful. He is sick and wandered away in the depths of his fever. We are searching for him.'

'And not looking for mushrooms at all.' The Norman raised his glove towards Lethry, who was too insensible to notice.

Abbo tried his smile again, which still didn't work.

'So sick he keeps saying he's the king's something or other and demands to be let pass.'

'Aha, just so. The fever you know.'

Abbo and Lethry were grabbed once more and this time marched further up the caravan, towards the more important people, which was a worry.

In this area the soldiers were better-dressed and better-equipped, the carts were in better order and well-groomed horses with well-groomed riders patrolled the edges of the route.

One large cart, driven by two uniformed soldiers and pulled by massive carthorses, had Brother Simon walking at its side, berating a very large Norman who looked like he had had enough. This Norman noticed the approach of Abbo and Lethry.

'Is he with you?' he demanded.

'Brother Simon? Er, yes, I suppose he is. He's sick.'

'You're telling me he's sick. Looks like he's been shot as well. Did you do that?'

'Me?' Abbo was appalled. 'Certainly not. I am abbot of the monastery nearby.'

'Well, I don't know what you Saxons get up to, do I?' The Norman seemed to think being shot by an abbot was perfectly normal. Perhaps in Normandy, it was.

'Well, who did then?'

'That's what we're trying to find out.'

'He keeps saying he's the King's Investigator. What's that all about?'

'A delusion of his sickness.'

'I am the King's Investigator,' Simon cried to all and sundry.

'See,' the Norman said.

'And I am here on the king's business,' Simon wailed on.

The Norman rolled his eyes.

'I am the King's Investigator, and it is my duty, nay my calling. I am here to investigate the king.'

'You're not doing anything to the king, you loon.' The Norman poked Simon in the chest.

'His fever has disturbed his mind,' Abbo explained. 'We can take care of him.'

'You better,' the Norman warned. At least he seemed prepared to let them go.

Abbo put a hand on Simon's shoulder and just got a fevered glare in return.

'What's going on back here?' A new voice disturbed their activities, but this one had a depth of authority that everyone present felt they could drown in.

The Normans stood up straight as a rider on a fine horse appeared in front of them.

As far as Abbo and Lethry could tell, one of the four horsemen of the apocalypse was travelling with this company; and there was no doubting which one it was. The image before them was one even Famine himself would worry made him look a bit thin.

The mounted cadaver appraised them through a single, baleful eye. The other was covered by a patch and it was clear from the man's demeanour that whoever had taken that eye had come out much the worse.

It also seemed that the loss of the eye, which must have been some time ago, had taken away this man's appetite. He obviously hadn't eaten anything for years. There was no other explanation for the skeletal frame that somehow continued to support life.

'My Lord Le Pedvin.' The Norman who had been about to let them go bowed.

Le Pedvin ignored him completely. 'Why are there monks?' he asked the monks.

'Oh, you know,' Abbo managed, wanting to say that there were always monks.

'I am the King's Investigator,' Simon shouted before anyone could stop him.

'That's convenient,' Le Pedvin said. 'The king's half-brother Odo was asking about you.' He leant forward and considered Simon in some detail. He looked him up and down and then sat back in his saddle to take in the whole man. 'You're not him.' He concluded firmly.

'I demand that I be allowed to investigate the king.'

'Not likely. Anyway, the King's Investigator is a completely different monk. What's your name?'

'Brother Simon,' Simon announced, proudly.

Le Pedvin shook his head. 'The investigator is called Heritage, or something.'

'Brother Hermitage?' Abbo suggested.

'That's the one,' Le Pedvin agreed. 'Don't know why we need one at all, but the king seems to like him.' (That would be news to Hermitage.)

'He is deranged with a fever,' Abbo explained, nodding his head towards Simon.

'Hm.' Le Pedvin didn't seem completely happy with this. 'Deranged or not, we can't have odd monks going around pretending to do the king's work. I think you three have got some explaining to do.'

Lethry looked very lost as he had never been able to explain anything.

'It's nothing to worry about, really.' Abbo gave as light a

look as he could manage.

'Excellent,' Le Pedvin nodded. 'I tend not to worry when I let my soldiers stick their swords in monks and leave them by the side of the road anyway, so perhaps we'll handle it like that.' He nodded to the nearest soldier who drew his sword with an unhealthy grimace.

'But then again,' Abbot Abbo drew a deep breath. 'Always happy to go over things. It is rather a long story though.'

Caput XXIV Crossbow Corner

'Typical,' Cwen huffed at Briston. 'Kill them all? Can you hear yourself?'

'Be quiet,' Briston ordered.

'It's ridiculous.' Cwen waved a lacklustre hand in his direction, dismissing his scheme as chaff on the wind. 'You're a weaver, Briston,' she went on. 'And not a very good one at that. What are you doing going around hiring killers and telling them to kill people?'

Briston pointed a rather shaky finger at Cwen. 'Mind your own business.'

'Probably dragged into all this by Nicodemus, I shouldn't wonder,' Wat suggested. He watched Briston's eyes dart across the room. 'And Nicodemus is..,' he made his audience wait while he held out his arm and turned in the right direction. 'That one.'

The one pointed at made no movement but did it very obviously.

'He persuaded you all that quietly getting rid of the King's Investigator would make your lives a whole lot easier. Well, the parts of your lives where you were doing things you really shouldn't. Greed probably, knowing Nicodemus and Athan. Got some plan to help yourself to the church's gold, or worse, the king's. Can't do that sort of thing if the King's Investigator keeps poking his nose in.'

Athan growled from inside his hood and turned it in the direction of Nicodemus.

Wat now went slowly round the room, addressing the hoods as he went.

'And what other little sins do you lot want to get away with? Sister Mildburgh? Anger, probably. Get nice and angry about someone and do them great harm; harm in the style of death, I imagine. Then what happens? The wretched King's Investigator comes along and ruins it all. Making you take the blame when you're only to blame.

'Eadgyth? Avarice, I'd say. Want what belongs to other people and it's so inconvenient when someone comes along and tells you to put it back.

'Briston? Oh, it'll be some completely ridiculous plan to get away from all the people who wish you harm. People who wish you harm with perfectly good reason, I suspect. But you'll want to take everything you've already stolen from them with you. Can't have the King's Investigator pointing the finger and saying, "he went that way."' He turned to the last hood lining the room. 'But a druid? Why on earth would a druid wish Hermitage harm? What are you doing mixed up with this hopeless lot?'

The druid kept his peace.

'Hermitage dealt with that business in Wales, but that was hardly enough to warrant all this.'[14]

Still, the druid said nothing.

'Might be a different druid for all I know,' Wat shrugged. 'Who can tell you apart?'

'And then we have our killer.' Wat folded his arms and faced the one with the crossbow. 'Hired by the others, no doubt, but not very good at his job as he killed the wrong monk.'

'Wasn't my fault,' Bargis complained. 'They didn't tell me who to kill properly.'

Hermitage had followed Wat's exposition with interest, and by turning on the spot to face each hood. He knew which one was Eadgyth and could spot the druid, Athan had

---

[14] Hermitage, Wat and Some Druids; hence the druid.

already revealed himself but Nicodemus and Mildburgh were still not confirmed. And neither was the man who was there to do the actual killing.

He was fascinated by the reasoning though and would congratulate Wat on it later if there was a later. But there was a gaping hole. Surely Wat and these others could see it? Maybe not? Should he point it out? He thought he'd better before someone shot him.

'It won't make any difference,' he said. 'Whether I'm dead or not won't change things.'

'You'll be a bit more dead,' Briston said through gritted teeth.

'Well, yes, but then the king doesn't care for me anyway. If I was killed he'd just shrug his shoulders and appoint a new investigator.'

There was a bit of a heavy silence in the room at that.

'It's like all those nobles in battle. It's not the individual who's of any interest at all, it's the title. If the Earl of somewhere or other gets shot and stabbed and trampled to death, his son pops up and there's a new earl. No one cares who the earl is, as long as there is one. You see?'

The room clearly did see, now. They also hadn't seen before.

'You may be the most important, powerful person for miles around, but you're going to die, we all do. Then there will be another one. And the people who look up to you will just as soon look up to someone else if you're not around anymore. Look at William himself. First, there was Harold, then there wasn't. There was always a King of England.

'If you shoot me, which of course, you can, a new investigator will pop up in no time.'

'Unless the king is weary of the whole investigator business and decides not to bother.' This was obviously Nicodemus's voice, but the hood stayed in place. 'We know that Lord Le Pedvin thinks the whole thing a complete waste of time. With the current King's Investigator dead, the king might be persuaded not to bother with another one.'

Hermitage reluctantly acknowledged that this was sound reasoning as well.

'Nudging the current occupant of the role into death can only help.' The hood that was doubtless Nicodemus concluded.

'That's good enough for me,' Briston said.

'And you're really going to kill us as well,' Cwen asked, clearly not believing that Briston was up to the task.

'Not personally, but yes.'

'Your old friend Wat?' Cwen indicated Wat with a hand. Wat put a very sorrowful look on his face, like the kitten who was about to be put in the sack on the bridge over the river.

'Business is business.' Briston shrugged that there was really nothing he could do. 'Well?' he turned to the killer. 'What are you waiting for?'

There was a long pause while the killer in the hood thought about something or other. 'I won't do it,' Bargis said, reaching his conclusion.

Briston looked stunned as if the hawk had folded its wings and refused to fly from his arm, even though there was a wounded sparrow hopping around right in front of it. 'What do you mean, you won't do it?' There was also muttering from the other hoods around the room.

'This whole thing has got completely out of hand. As far as I can tell, you lot are completely mad.'

'He's right there,' Wat put in.

'You're a hired killer, of course, you can do it. You've

already killed one monk and shot another. What's the problem?'

The killer let the crossbow fall in his arms. 'First of all, I haven't actually seen the money for extra people. Knowing you lot, I wouldn't be surprised if you found you didn't have it after the deed was done. You had to scrape the money together to get me to go after the one I should have done in the first place.

'Secondly, I'd already told you I wouldn't kill Wat the Weaver.'

'Thank you very much.' Wat nodded his gratitude.

'You didn't mind doing it when they were under the floor,' Athan said.

'Under the floor is one thing. Up here now is something else.'

'You'll do as you're told,' Briston instructed. 'What sort of killer have we bought?' he asked the rest of the room.

'And I'm not shooting a woman.' At this Bargis put his crossbow down on the floor and folded his arms.

'And what exactly is wrong with me?' Cwen demanded. 'I can be shot just as well as anyone else.' She folded her arms. 'In fact, lend me your bow and I'll shoot you.'

Bargis gave this suggestion half a smile until he saw the look on Cwen's face.

Briston was looking very frustrated.

'You could always pick up the bow and do it yourself,' Wat suggested.

'He's not touching my bow,' the hood of Bargis said, not that Briston showed any interest in doing so anyway.

'At least do the monk,' Briston pleaded. 'This is the right one, we all agree on that.'

'No, I don't think so.'

'You don't think it's the right one?'

'I'm sure it's the one you want killed, but I'm not going to do it.'

Briston looked around the room for some help. 'I don't know what's happened to the modern killer, I really don't. You give them good money to kill someone, carry out the trade they say they're following, and then what happens? They decide they can't be bothered. We should have got a proper killer.'

'Oh,' Bargis said, with heavy significance, 'I am a proper killer. You know that. And I've already killed one monk for you, which was what you asked for, so that's that.'

'Bad luck,' Wat sympathised with Briston.

'Look,' Briston was pleading with his hired killer to do some actual killing. 'He's standing right in front of you. You've got the bow, it won't take a moment.'

Bargis showed no signs of action.

Briston's face contorted with thought. 'What's going on here?' he asked, slowly. 'You're a killer, here's a victim, there's your bow, why won't you just shoot him? Not going to do your reputation any good when this gets out, is it?'

'It's never a very good idea to start telling tales about killers,' Bargis advised. 'When they get annoyed they tend to, you know, kill. In fact, thinking about it, I could do you now, that would stop any stories.'

'You haven't been paid to kill me,' Briston sneered a bit

'It would be for pleasure.'

'Briston, you idiot,' Cwen said. 'He won't kill Wat or me and we're witnesses. If he kills Hermitage we go and tell the king, who does a whole lot more killing than one man on his own. In fact, he'll probably come and do the lot of you, just for having the temerity to kill his investigator in the first place, whether he appoints a new one or not.'

Hermitage liked that reasoning. But there was something else nagging at the back of his head as the killer explained why he was unable to complete his assigned task at this time. Some reminiscence from much earlier days tugged at the strings of his memory and jiggled.

First, he made an association with a place. For some reason, the image of a campfire came to mind. Why would that be? He tried to avoid travel at most times, campfires were just a necessary evil in an unpleasant situation. And he had no sense that Wat or Cwen were there; that must make it years ago. A campfire, years ago, when he was travelling alone? Ah, he had it.

He took half a step towards the hooded killer, and put his head over to one side, for no particular reason. 'Is that Master Bargis?' he asked.

'What?' Briston shouted. 'You know him?'

Bargis took several moments of thought before he slowly and reluctantly removed his hood. 'Hello, Brother.'

'Oh, this is marvellous,' Briston complained. 'Why didn't you say you knew him?' he demanded of Bargis. 'And if you knew him, why the devil did you kill a monk called Pewlet at all?'

'You just said it was the King's Investigator you wanted done. This monk and I met years ago, on the road.' He nodded towards Hermitage. 'I didn't even know his name, how was I to know it was him you wanted dead?'

'He seems to know you.'

'Well, I told him my name, he never told me his. Hermitage, eh? Funny name for a monk.'

'Surely you've killed people you know before?' Briston argued. 'Some of your own family, probably. And you only met him years ago. Water under the bridge and all that. Nothing to stop you sticking an arrow in him now. Must be nice to meet old acquaintances and then shoot them?'

'And it's as the woman says, too many witnesses, and they know the king. I'm not risking it.'

Briston looked around the room for some support. 'Come on Nicodemus,' he called. 'This was all your idea in the first place, you think of something.

There was no reply to this and when the others cast their glances around the place they saw that there was one less hood than there used to be.'

'He's gone!' Briston howled. 'He's only gone and bloody well run away.'

'Very wise,' Wat nodded. 'What's that expression about rats leaving just before the house falls down?'

Briston's teeth were gritted so hard, he could barely speak. 'How would you feel about shooting Nicodemus?' he asked Bargis. 'After all, you do know him, and you know what he looks like.'

Bargis made a face of little interest. 'Fine,' he said.

'Master Bargis!' Hermitage reprimanded. 'When we met all those years ago you shared your fire and we solved a little puzzle together.[15] Now you turn out to be a killer for hire?'

'We've all got to live.'

'Except the people you shoot.'

'Except them, yes.'

'Briston,' Wat said, and he addressed the rest of the room as well. 'I suggest that you and your merry band of hoods be on your way. Put this down to one of life's little experiences. That and a whole cart-load of bad planning, ill-thought-out

---

[15] All found in the depths of Brother Hermitage. The Shorts - probably should have mentioned that at the start...

schemes and just plain greed and stupidity.'

None of the others in the room was leaping to oppose this. Even Athan seemed content to simply growl in his hood.

When the tension in the room was such that it demanded the door suddenly burst open, the door suddenly burst open.

Nicodemus strode in, hoodless and hefting a crossbow, not very expertly.

'Where did you get that?' Bargis asked.

'Always be prepared,' Nicodemus replied, his voice full of ill-intent. 'Now then,' he said as he looked around. 'When you can't get your actual killer to do the killing, you have to take matters into your own hands.'

'I'd be careful with that if I were you,' Wat cautioned, leaning away as much as he could. 'You look like you don't know what you're doing, and you might shoot someone.'

'That is the general idea.'

'Yes, but I'm not sure you'll have any control over who you hit.'

'I'll simply get all the people I don't want to hit behind me, and the ones I do in front,' Nicodemus explained in his patronising manner. 'That means you weavers and Hermitage go in front, everyone else behind. There you are.'

'So, you shoot one of us and then we all wait while you re-load?' Cwen asked. 'Rather than say, leap forward, disarm you and batter you to death with your own crossbow?'

'I think I'll shoot Wat first. You two can be easily restrained.'

'I still don't think you're capable of hitting anything you're even aiming at.' Wat seemed more worried about being shot by accident, instead of on purpose.

'He's right,' Bargis put in. 'These are tricky things. You'll as likely shoot yourself in the hand as hit anyone else.'

A Murder For Brother Hermitage

'Oh, go on,' Cwen said. 'Do that.'

'Get over there.' Nicodemus wanted no more discussion and used the crossbow to indicate that the proposed victims should gather themselves in one corner. 'In fact, if you stand one behind the other, I might get you all with one arrow.'

He then turned and indicated to the hoods in the room that they should get behind him. He waved the crossbow towards the door suggesting that the allies be prepared to leave as soon as the deed was done.

The use of the crossbow as a tool for indicating direction is not to be recommended. It is a cumbersome and awkward piece of machinery, as well as delicate. If not handled very carefully, by someone with proper practise and experience, it can produce unexpected results.

The scream from Mistress Eadgyth as she was shot in the foot was one such result.

The howls of pain were interspersed with oaths and threats and several extremely rude names, all of them directed at Nicodemus.

The man himself simply stood looking at the crossbow, apparently trying to understand why it had taken matters into its own hands.

'Told you,' Bargis and Wat said together.

Hermitage frowned deeply, as Cwen had started laughing again.

Nicodemus recovered some of his senses and considered the chaotic scene before him. Sister Mildburgh and the druid had gone over to Eadgyth and were trying to remove the crossbow bolt, which had very firmly nailed the lady's foot to the floor.

Athan and Briston were looking on in alarm that this whole business, which had already gone very wrong, was now in complete disarray. They looked to Nicodemus and the three appeared to agree that departure was for the best.

Nicodemus simply dropped the crossbow, which caused Bargis to wince, and backed towards the exit. He raised an accusing finger at them all, clearly saying that this was not over. They may have won the battle, but the war was far from done, and they were going to lose that, see if they didn't.

Nicodemus then suddenly sat on the floor as the flat of Le Pedvin's sword descended on his head with a horrible clang.

Caput XXV Normans and Druids

'Good God, look at you lot,' Le Pedvin took in the room. Eadgyth, the druid and Mildburgh still had their hoods on, Wat, Cwen and Hermitage were standing in the corner, waiting to be shot and Athan and Briston were standing beside Nicodemus, trying to look like they didn't know him.

Bargis had decided to sit down and rest his leg and had pulled up a chair.

Abbo and Lethry appeared behind the Norman and peered into the room.

'Ah, Father,' Hermitage called. 'You brought help.' He never thought he would refer to Le Pedvin as help.

'Well,' Abbo didn't sound quite so sure either. 'I brought Lord Le Pedvin.'

'I knew you'd be in the middle of this somewhere,' Le Pedvin addressed Hermitage. 'I'd ask what's going on, but I don't think I want to know.' He raised a particularly quizzical eyebrow towards Eadgyth and her foot, which was still spreading blood on the floor.

'Some men wanted to kill the King's Investigator,' Wat spoke up.

'Ah, the weaver as well, and your servant; we have the full house.'

As usual, Cwen had to be restrained from explaining herself to Le Pedvin in a very physical manner.

'Well, men and women, as it happens,' Wat said.

'Yes,' Le Pedvin drawled. 'I recognise these two.' He indicated Nicodemus on the floor and Athan, who was sidling towards the door. 'I wouldn't bother going outside if I were you,' he said calmly. 'My men have instructions to kill anyone who tries to leave.'

265

Athan stopped sidling.

'Why's that woman been fixed to the floor?' Le Pedvin pointed to Eadgyth, who wailed in response.

'It's an old cure for bunions.' Cwen just managed to stifle a snigger.

Le Pedvin clearly didn't believe this for a moment but didn't want to be bothered with the real explanation. 'Tended by a nun and a druid in hoods,' he observed.

Cwen's frame was shaking at the effort to contain her laughter. She managed a high-pitched squeak in reply. 'All part of the cure. She'll be fine.' A snort escaped her nose. 'We'll just re-load and then do the other foot.'

Le Pedvin just looked at her as if failing to understand Saxons was perfectly normal. 'And who are you?' he directed this at Bargis.

'Killer for hire, sir.' Bargis smiled.

'Hm. Are you the one who shot this other monk, the dead one?' He looked to Abbot Abbo for confirmation.

'Sure I couldn't say, sir.'

'Yes, he did.' Abbo insisted. 'Shot him with a crossbow in the cloister, in the dark.'

'In the dark?' Le Pedvin asked.

'Exactly.'

'You shoot people in the dark?' Le Pedvin sounded horribly interested.

'Bit of a speciality, sir.'

'Really?' Le Pedvin pondered for a moment. 'I might have a job for you.'

'Only too pleased to help out.'

'But? What? He..,' Abbo protested. 'He shot a monk. An innocent monk. And he wounded Brother Simon.'

Le Pedvin looked around the room. 'There seem to be

plenty of monks about, and a lot of them don't look very innocent at all. And that Brother Simon is a monk who needs wounding if I ever I met one.'

'Brother Pewlet was doing no harm to anyone, and this man shot him, by mistake.' Abbot Abbo was outraged that this was not going to be dealt with in the proper manner.

Le Pedvin sighed. 'All right, all right. You, killer.'

'Yes, sir.'

'Pay this abbot ten shillings for killing his monk.'

'What?' Bargis protested at this outrage.

'Or we can hang you.'

Bargis appeared to think about it for a moment but soon reached for the purse at his waist, muttering about the injustice of it all.

'And as we're dispensing justice,' Le Pedvin went on. 'You and you,' he pointed at Athan and Nicodemus. 'Banished. Two days to leave the country otherwise word is sent that your heads will be worth five pounds each.'

Athan's mouth opened.

'But only if they're not joined on to your bodies.'

Athan looked ready to object but decided that trying to wake Nicodemus and give him the news would be better.

'And this one,' Le Pedvin turned to Briston.

'Briston the Weaver,' Wat did the introductions.

'Oh,' Le Pedvin sounded very knowing. 'This is Briston the Weaver, is it?'

Briston did not confirm the accusation.

'The king has quite a list of people who have been asking for you to be handed over.'

'Aha,' Briston tried to sound light and airy.

'You can come with me.'

'Bad luck, Briston,' Cwen called. She seemed to be having a

lovely time, just at the moment.

'And you lot,' Le Pedvin said, which dampened her enthusiasm. 'The king's brother's been wittering on about his investigator recently. Got some job for you, I think.'

Hermitage's face and heart fell. First, a whole conclave of people gathers just to get rid of him because he's the King's Investigator. Now, he's summoned to go and be King's Investigator again. And all the time he doesn't want to be King's Investigator at all. And this time it's for his brother? Was he going to end up passed around the whole family?'

'As for the nun, the druid and the woman with the foot problem,' Le Pedvin gave this very short thought. 'I really can't be bothered. Sort yourselves out and be gone. Preferably never to be seen again.'

Mildburgh and the druid gave short nods. Eadgyth was in no state to do anything. It was all very well being told to be gone, but it wasn't that simple when a crossbow has just nailed your foot to the floor. She certainly didn't look prepared to leave it behind.

'Good.' Le Pedvin clapped his gloved hands. 'Everyone knows what they're doing, and I can get back to business. Honestly, you can't walk the roads of this wretched country without a band of loons jumping out of the woods.' He turned to the door, giving a simple wave that those who were to go with him were expected to follow.

Hermitage, Wat and Cwen exchanged their familiar hopeless looks in the face of events that bowled them along like pebbles in the surf.

'Maybe it'll be something simple this time,' Wat suggested. 'The king's brother's lost his gloves?'

'It'll be murder.' Hermitage let his head hang. 'It always is.'

'At least they won't be trying to kill you this time.' Cwen

offered a very small crumb of comfort.

Wat and Cwen followed Le Pedvin to the door and Hermitage gave one last look around the room. It really had been a bizarre situation. And all because of him. Poor Pewlet. Dead without even knowing why, and it was all Hermitage's fault. He didn't know how he would be able to live with himself after that.

He gave a very heavy sigh and turned to go.

'You would not have come to harm,' a deep and friendly voice spoke at his side and his sleeve was touched. Twisting in surprise he saw the druid, without his hood now, standing close by. He hadn't noticed him leave Eadgyth.

'That's very kind of you to say.' Hermitage didn't recognise the druid. It didn't appear to be one that he had met in Wales but then as Wat had said, large men with big beards dressed in white did tend to look similar.

'Not kind, no. Truth.'

'Aha,' Hermitage said, hoping this conversation would end quite soon.

'That is why I am here,' the druid smiled again and laid a hand on Hermitage's shoulder. Somehow, this put Hermitage's mind at rest. He also felt a calm spread through his body and the worries of the past, the future and the present rolled away. There was only the druid and him. Normally that would be enough to fill his pot of worry to overflowing. Pagans were pagans, after all.

'You did great service to our people in Wales.'

'Ah, well,' Hermitage was too modest to claim any credit. Ever.

'And I joined this conclave simply to see if the tales of you were true.'

'Tales?' Surely there weren't any tales of Brother

Hermitage? Who on earth would want to listen to all his trials and tribulations. The very idea was ridiculous. People would have far better things to do with their time to listen to a load of nonsense about him. Chronicles of Brother Hermitage? What an idiotic idea.

'I have seen that they are,' the druid went on, nodding his head towards Eadgyth and Mildburgh. 'These fools had other plans, but they would not have come to pass.'

'The man did have a crossbow.' Hermitage pointed out.

'But he could not shoot you.' The druid sounded as if he had known this all along. 'Even killers turn away in your presence.'

'Well,' Hermitage mumbled, feeling quite keen to leave the strange druid and get back to Wat and Cwen.

The druid put both hands on Hermitage's shoulders now and looked him straight in the eye. Hermitage could not help but look back, and there seemed to be a depth to the druid that went on and on. It was as if the entire druid population was behind this man, their eyes at the back of his, and Hermitage could see all the way down to the bottom. And it was a very long way down. In fact, the further he looked, the deeper the bottom seemed to recede.

'Our time is ending,' the druid said, although it seemed to be from a long way away. 'New forces come into play, and the land bids us farewell.'

Hermitage normally thought this sort of thing to be complete nonsense, but with a druid holding on to him and staring in a most peculiar way, the words seemed quite natural.

'But we can leave with a blessing.'

A blessing sounded good.

'A blessing for you, Brother Hermitage. Your goodness,

270

your belief, your faith, your trust, all of those things will be needed in time to come.'

'Oh, I don't know about that.' Hermitage was modest.

'We do. And so we bestow this upon you, with the last of our powers.'

Hermitage found he had nothing to say.

'You will go on, Brother Hermitage. You will go on. Just as Arthur and others will arise at the moment of the land's greatest peril, so you will arise at the moment of its greatest mystery. From the very depths of time, you will emerge, unbowed, unbroken. This we command, this we plead, this we beg. Down the aeons to come you will stand ready. You will come to the people, you will investigate, and you will bring resolution.' The druid bowed his head to Hermitage and the depths of his eyes drew back.

The words of this druid were truly peculiar. There was clearly no basis in them, but something in the manner of their delivery pierced his soul. He was sure this new feeling of some unending fate would dissipate as soon as he got away. Come back to investigate at the time of the nation's greatest mystery, eh?

'Aha,' he said, as politely as he could manage. 'Erm, do I have to?'

FINIS

And, as if that wasn't enough, Brother Hermitage will return in **The Bayeux Embroidery**.

Read the first chapter of this remarkable tale below.

The Bayeux Embroidery

by

Howard of Warwick

The Umpteenth Chronicles of Brother Hermitage

Caput I Your Mission, and You're Going to Accept It.

Brother Hermitage, Wat the Weaver and Cwen stood waiting outside the tent of King William of England, Duke of Normandy. This expanse of canvas was pitched on a field just off the northern road from Derby, and the place was busy with Normans going about their business. What that business was, was none of their business, and so they just stood and did their waiting in silence.

Of all the accommodations that had sprung up when the great caravan came to a halt, they knew this was William's tent because the guard, who was standing not five feet away, had yelled the king's title at them at the top of his voice. He had screamed with pride that this was William's tent and that they were now standing outside it.

'You have been summoned to the tent of King William of England, Duke of Normandy,' the guard added at full volume for the world to hear. Being summoned was obviously a great honour and the people before him would probably be grateful that he was letting everyone know.

'Yes, thank you.' Brother Hermitage nodded his polite acknowledgement and gave a little smile.

The guard scowled back. He was clearly happy that he had imparted the necessary information but was worried that these three people did not seem to be taking their privilege seriously. A young monk, a very well-dressed looking merchant with an impudent look under his unkempt black hair, and a slip of girl who kept glaring at him. These were not the sort of people who deserved to be summoned to the king's tent. Perhaps there was a mistake and his scowl would uncover it.

He stood tall and proud, but these three were almost slouching. It was a disgrace. The greatest achievement of his life was to be shouting at people outside the tent of the king. Of course, it was his duty and he had been ordered to be here. Perhaps one day he'd be summoned, but he knew in his heart that this was a dream too far.

Still, they were Saxons, so what could you expect? As far as he had been able to tell, the whole country was full of savages. It was highly likely that the king had summoned them here so he could kill them. What a wonderful way to go.

'Can we go in?' Wat asked, nodding towards the tent flap.

'Can you what?' The guard's voice had been loud before, now it was almost shaking the ground and had risen towards a shriek.

'Go in,' Wat repeated, nonchalantly. 'You know, into the tent we've been summoned to go into. This one.' He pointed to confirm they were all talking about the same tent.

'Into the king's tent?' The guard's response was that of a man whose outrage had discovered appalling new heights.

'That's the one,' Wat confirmed.

'No, you may not.' The man almost bounced on his feet and the urge to hit someone was oozing from him. 'What you may do is wait here. Right here.'

Wat shrugged that they could do that. 'Shall we shout at the king then?'

The guard obviously couldn't comprehend this statement.

'He won't be able to hear us from here unless we shout,' Cwen said. 'Him having summoned us and all. He probably wants to speak to us. Like he usually does.'

This was simply too much for the guard who just looked repeatedly from left to right, desperately seeking some escape from this nonsense.

Relief came as the tent flap was thrown aside and the shape of William's chief doer of horrible things, Le Pedvin, emerged. There was really no need for the tent to flap much at all to let this figure through, as it had all the substance of a slight breeze that passed by last week. How the cadaverous shape managed to kill people so frequently was a mystery, but not one that any of the Saxons wanted to test.

Le Pedvin's sole, despairing eye considered the small gathering before him, the patch across his other showing no interest at all. 'What are you waiting for?' he asked the idiots who stood outside a tent when they'd been summoned to attend the king.

'Yes,' the guard barked. 'What are you waiting for? Get in the tent this minute.' He waved his pikestaff in the required direction.

Hermitage, Wat and Cwen all gave the guard their own looks. Hermitage's was of puzzlement that he'd only just been saying that they couldn't go in. He did wish people would make their minds up. Wat's was contemptuous for a fool who would bite his own ear off if he was told to. Cwen's look was the one that made the guard shiver.

'I don't know,' the guard muttered to Le Pedvin as the three entered the tent. 'Bloody Saxons, eh?'

Inside the king's tent, all was as it should be for a monarch whose chief occupation was conquering people. It was more military than regal, with weapons and armour scattered about. A large table towards the back did have a significant quantity of parchment on it, as well as a scribe who sat behind it, reading things, putting them down and making notes with a quill as the matter demanded. Every now and again the scribe looked up, as if hoping that he could have the king's attention - at last. He saw that he couldn't and went back to his work.

Hermitage was fascinated by the sheer volume of parchment, and slightly horrified by the way it was thrown hither and thither with careless abandon. He longed to read the words that flashed by but suspected they would be very mundane. He was quietly confident that King William would not have a commentary on the lexicography of the post-Exodus prophets amongst his urgent business.

The king was sitting in an ordinary camp chair, considering a map that he held in his hands. Doubtless, it showed the world split into the two bits that mattered; what he had already conquered, and the bits he hadn't done yet.

'They're here.' It was clear that Le Pedvin couldn't see why the king wanted the Saxons at all.

William looked up from his map and considered the three of them. There was nothing particular about his face, no marks or disfigurements that would warrant the trickle of fear that ran down three Saxon backs. Even Cwen, who thought that fear was what other people did, found her breathing had sharpened. The face was simply that of a conqueror. A man of middle age who went round conquering things; people, mainly. And he did his conquering by killing; a lot of killing. The face simply said that he was ready to do some more at any moment now. An enquiring glance from William was usually enquiring if you'd like to be killed now or later.

'Ah, the monk,' William said, recognition coming to him. The look of impending doom lifted from his face and the Saxons breathed again.

'Your Majesty.' Hermitage bowed.

'And the other two.'

Wat bowed while Cwen tried hard not to but found her

head had gone down against her will.

'A weaver.' William gestured towards Wat and made the word half a question, half a statement.

'Indeed, Your Majesty.' Hermitage agreed. He could feel Cwen's eyes burning into him, instructing him to point out that she was a weaver as well.

King William's eyes were right in front of him though and he felt they took priority.

The king just shook his head slightly, confused why a Saxon monk had a weaver with him. Perhaps it was just what they did around here. 'Could be useful, I suppose.' He moved on from the question.

Hermitage gave Wat and Cwen a worried look. He knew perfectly well what the reason for his summoning would be: murder. It was always murder. He was the King's Investigator, after all. It was a position he didn't want and one he suspected the king didn't even understand, but there wasn't much he could do about it. King William was the conqueror and it was generally advisable to do whatever he wanted.

Having been made Investigator under Harold, he supposed that he should be grateful that the role continued. Many of those who had served under Harold were now under the ground, so it could be worse.

But weavers? How on earth could weavers be useful in a murder? Was there a King's Weaver perhaps? Or had there been? Had he been called to investigate the murder of a weaver? The weavers' grand moot he attended with Wat had ended up with him investigating murder, but he put that down to the fact that everywhere he went someone ended up being killed.16 If it was bad enough being the King's

---

16 A Murder for Master Wat makes a whole book out of this sentence.

Investigator; being an innocent bystander while he was around was positively life threatening.

'What do you know about nuns?' the king asked.

It never took much to confuse Hermitage. People who said things that appeared to be completely disconnected usually did the trick.

'Nuns, Majesty?'

'Yes, nuns. I assume you have them here.'

Hermitage quickly understood that the king meant England. 'Oh, yes, Majesty. We do have nuns.' He knew they had nuns. Nuns scared the life out of him. In fact, they scared the life out of most people; it was probably part of their training. He'd had to deal with nuns as well as weavers in his role as investigator.17 Could it be he was working his way through the murder of every role in the kingdom? He'd be Investigator for years at this rate.

'Are you all right?'

Hermitage was brought back to his senses as he realised he had drifted off a bit.

'Of course, he isn't,' Le Pedvin coughed.

'Nuns, Majesty, and weavers,' Hermitage nodded. 'Yes, we have them both.'

'Good. There are a lot of dead ones I want you to look at.'

Hermitage didn't have any words that worked in response to that. A lot of dead nuns? Who on earth would have a lot of dead nuns that needed looking at? He knew that William did kill a lot of people, but they were generally soldiers or nobles. Nuns were hardly likely to take arms against the invader; certainly not in great numbers. He was sure he would have heard of the slaughter of an army of nuns if it had taken place.

---

17 The imaginatively titled *Hermitage, Wat and Some Nuns*

And what was he supposed to do if he did look at a lot of dead nuns? Confirm that they were dead? Surely anyone could do that. 'Dead nuns, Majesty?' It was always worth checking, perhaps he'd misheard.

'Dead weaving nuns,' the king said.

No, it wasn't worth checking at all. The king had simply gone mad. Or madder.

'I see,' Hermitage nodded cautiously. If the king wanted him to go away and investigate some dead weaving nuns, he would just smile politely and go off to do so. If he couldn't actually find any, that was hardly his fault. He didn't dare look directly at Wat and Cwen but could tell that their understanding of what was going on here was no better than his.

'I'm not mad,' the king said. Hermitage nodded at that as well.

'My brother has them.'

Hermitage took his time replying, just to make sure he was following this. 'Your brother has some dead weaving nuns.'

'Well, half brother, Odo.'

'Aha.'

'And obviously the nuns aren't weaving any more, not now that they're dead.'

'Of course.' Hermitage agreed with this. Everyone knew that weaving nuns stopped weaving when they died.

The king sighed. That was never a good sign. 'What's so difficult about this?' he grumbled. 'My half-brother, Odo, has gathered some nuns to make a great tapestry of recent events. I made him Bishop of Bayeux and he's going to hang the thing in the church there, so that everyone can see what a great success the conquest of England has been.'

That did make some sense, of a sort; at least it didn't seem completely insane. Hermitage had only heard rumours of this tapestry and it sounded most peculiar. Still, kings were laws unto themselves and so he supposed their brothers were as well. If this Odo wanted a tapestry, he could have one. If he wanted it made by nuns, why not? Hermitage felt that he didn't really want to pry into this too much. He also felt he wasn't going to get much choice.

He chanced a glance at Wat, whose face said that he too knew of this tapestry. Why it had to be made by nuns was a question that could wait until later. Preferably much later.

'A Bayeux tapestry,' Hermitage said.

The king thought about this for a moment. 'Yes, if you like. Don't think it needs a name though; it's only a tapestry.'

Hermitage could feel Wat stiffen slightly at this.

'And the nuns,' Hermitage pressed on, reluctantly. 'They're sort of, erm..,'

'Dead. Yes. The nuns are dead. Odo sent word that they were all working on the tapestry and now they're dead.'

Hermitage really didn't like the sound of them all being dead. 'How many are there, I mean were there? Nuns, that is?'

'I don't know, do I?' The king's anger started to seep out; seep out like a waterfall from a very high place. A waterfall full of fallen logs, most likely; with points on. 'You'll have to ask Odo, won't you?'

'Naturally,' Hermitage agreed, although he couldn't see that there was anything natural in any of this.

'Off you go then,' the king waved that they could leave now that they had all the information they needed. 'I told him I have just the monk for a job like this. I want this tapestry finished and up on display, so you'd better sort this dead nun business out.'

'Excellent,' Hermitage said; another word he wasn't at all happy about. There was one question remaining though. 'We'll erm, just set off to, erm, Bayeux then. Somehow.' He didn't like to ask the king to provide transport. It seemed a bit rude, somehow.

'Bayeux? What on earth are you going there for?'

Hermitage had been lost so often in such a short space of time that he really didn't have any sort of answer. 'Odo. Bishop. Bayeux. Tapestry?' It made sense to him.

'Yes, but he's the Earl of Kent, isn't he?'

'Is he?'

'Of course, he is, you idiot.'

'Told you,' Le Pedvin drawled.

'So that's where the dead nuns are.' Wat helped Hermitage out.

'Exactly.'

'Kent?' Hermitage said.

'You have heard of it?' William sounded as if he was losing confidence in his investigator.

Hermitage would be quite happy about that, but people probably died from William's lack of confidence.

'Of course, of course. Kent, yes, quite. Canterbury, the archbishop and such.'

The king was frowning at them all now. 'You did deal with the murder of Umair, the Saracen? That was you?'

'Oh, yes, Majesty.' Hermitage confirmed.[18]

'And de Turold's little accident?'

'Absolutely.'[19]

'As well as the business in Normandy?'

---

[18] *The Case of The Curious Corpse* for reference.
[19] *The Garderobe of Death* for reference as well.

'That too.'20

King William just shook his head as if he was finding this hard to believe.

'This is going to end badly,' Le Pedvin said to himself, loudly enough that everyone else could hear.

Hermitage thought that it hadn't started that well.

'Well, get off and see what you can do. But be warned.' The king raised a finger.

Hermitage didn't know what else there could be to be warned about.

'Odo is not the reasonable man I am.' William smiled.

Hermitage couldn't stop his mouth dropping open.

'When things don't go his way, he tends to take it out on people. You'd better sort out these dead nuns of his or you'll be joining them.'

For the very briefest of moments Hermitage had thought that this mission might not be too bad. It had raised the opportunity for travel to Kent and the shrine of Canterbury. He would be in the same town as the archbishop himself; what a treasure.

He had also reasoned that William, being the king of the Normans, must be the worst of the lot. Surely, Normans would make the most Norman person their leader? To hear that he was nicer than his brother was a real shock. King William terrified him; Le Pedvin wormed inside his head and worried him from the inside out. What this brother was capable of, he dreaded to think.

The glare from King William said that he was going to find out very soon.

---

[20] *Hermitage, Wat and Some Murder or Other*; what a lot of references.